Once Around the Fountain

Once Around the Fountain

ALAN BEHR

Welcome Rain Publishers
NEW YORK

Library of Congress Cataloging-in-Publication Data

Behr, Alan.

    Once around the fountain / Alah Behr.

      p. cm.

    ISBN 1-56649-224-6

      1. Europe—Description and travel. 2. Europe—Social life and

customs—20th century. I. Title.

D923 .B44 2001

940.55'8—dc21

                        2001026982

Direct any inquiries to

Welcome Rain Publishers LLC,

23 West 26th Street

New York, NY 10010.

First Edition: October 2001

1 3 5 7 9 10 8 6 4 2

To Julie

Acknowledgments

I gratefully acknowledge the support of those editors who published installments from my travel series, stories from which serve as the basis for what follows. To name a few: David Alff, Michele Babineau, Milly Ball, Laura Begley, Karyn Bilezerian, Larry Bleiberg, John Bordsen, Mary Ellen Botter, Bari Brenner, Francine Brown, Christopher Buckley, Michael Buller, Susannah Clark, Randy Curwen, Alison DaRosa, Victor Dwyer, Laurie Evans, Betsy Gratis, Linda Halsey, Ann Johnston Haas, Allen Holder, Bob Jenkins, John Macdonald, Tom McCarthey, Kathleen McKernan, Jerry Morris, Maureen Murphey, Don Nichols, Mary Lou Nolan, Tom Passavant, Marjorie Robins, Diana Scott, Howard Shapiro, Bob Sheue, Neal Santelmann, Susan Spencer, Janice Stillman, Leslie Allyson Ward and Ed Wetschler. In particular, I thank my friend Thomas Swick, who continues to set high standards as both travel writer and travel editor. I should also thank my mother, Sary Behr Fox, who first had the idea that I should go to Europe (at age sixteen) and then the idea that I should write about it (at age thirty-three). Sadly, I must offer a posthumous acknowledgment to the travel writer Jeannie Block, for encouraging and guiding me at the start and for authoring the best piece of business advice I've ever received: "Never deal with a flunky."

I extend special thanks to the literary agents Judith Hansen and Thomas Wallace, for their generous—that is, wholly gratuitous—counsel.

Finally, I must thank everyone at Welcome Rain Publishers, especially John Weber, Chuck Kim, and Karyn Slutsky, for believing in this book and making it a reality.

A final note: To respect privacy, some names and personal details of people mentioned in the text have been altered.

Lost Love's Labor

Chapter 1

I rode the airport limousine between a bearded Swede and an insurance man from Cleveland. The Swede, a bachelor in late middle age, was a buyer of films for Swedish state television. This was perhaps sufficient reason for him to maintain an effete reserve, like the prep-school dandy in the company of the soccer team. The man from Cleveland had an affinity for me because I was a lawyer for a large insurance company. When you work in insurance, you need to overcome the prejudice that you are dull, unless you actually are dull, like the amiable man from Cleveland. The Swede began tapping the door frame in time to music in his head and looked at Long Island City as if hoping to receive one last good memory of New York. I asked him about life in Sweden, and I shared chocolate with both men. Why I was carrying chocolate to Germany—coals to Newcastle, snow to the Eskimos—is a mystery to me.

"My mother-in-law is from Malmö," Cleveland said.

I'd never heard of the place, but the Swede added, "It's the third largest city in Sweden." He said it in the perfunctory manner of a weary doctor to a hypochondriac: the information had been given; questions were not welcome. He went back to tapping the door frame while Cleveland told me his life story.

After check-in at Icelandair, I met two flight attendants from a Danish airline. Paul was Danish and Marie was an attractive, graceful Swede. She was from Malmö and I impressed her terribly by saying that of course I knew of it: Malmö was the third largest city in Sweden for goodness' sake. We bought snacks at a shop near the gate and traded stories. Paul and Marie didn't like Los Angeles but loved San Francisco, which showed they had taste and naturally endeared them to me. They were flying standby. If they failed to make this flight, they would have to go back to friends on West 62nd Street—at an apartment building visible from my dining room, in fact—then take a train to Baltimore and fly from there. At least the price was right, they said. Budget travelers learn to take their chances, to accept their secondary status with a worldwide transportation business that preens itself before expense-account travelers, yet wears its old house-coat whenever a bargain hunter pays call.

At the gate, Claudia, a German anarcho-syndicalist, railed against the Nicaraguan Contras (au courant right-wing guerrillas) and Pershing II missiles (nuclear-tipped implements of politics by another means). She wore wonderfully ugly goosedown pants and an oversized black sweater knitted by her grandmother, with the result that she looked like a rag doll left too long in the wash. Claudia had dyed her fair hair black and had pale, pink features. She claimed she didn't mind traveling on her own and asked if I did. I hadn't wanted to think about it and replied that I was visiting friends and would not be alone very much. She again said she didn't mind traveling alone, adding just enough firmness to her voice to leave no doubt she hated it. As I made myself comfortable at my seat in the coach section of the antediluvian DC-8, I saw Paul and Marie settling down in business class, joking and pleased with themselves. Only when I found their happiness growing irritating did I understand how much I minded traveling alone.

Chapter 2

Dörte introduced herself to me on the Icelandair bus from Luxembourg City to Cologne. She had the quick, furtive manner of a New Yorker, despite the German accent. Green eyed, she had one of those hard German faces that, never comfortable with itself, forms around perma-nently tightened muscles. It would take time, perhaps a lifetime, for

American ease to massage itself in. I had planned to sleep, but Dörte was in that anxious, talkative mood of someone for whom the next step on a journey carries emotional weight. She was born in Cologne but lived in a colorful, incompletely gentrified part of Manhattan, having gone through considerable difficulty to get resident-alien status. She was on her way to see her divorced parents, after which she would visit the U.S. consulate in Frankfurt for an interview about her American residency. "America doesn't want Europeans anymore," she said bitterly. "The quotas favor Asians. Why is that so, I ask? America is Western, for God's sake. You can't be everything to everyone and still be a nation."

"What should America be?" I asked her.

"Something. Anything. Look at Japan. Japan is something. It's particular, you know what I mean?"

"Homogeneous?"

"Yes, definitely. I'm not saying it is wrong to have minorities. That is very good I think, but the other way is bad too. A nation can't be a random collection of people who come together just to make money. But you can't say these things to Americans. They've grown fat—I'm sorry, but to a European, it is embarrassing when they come over here with their big stomachs and fat asses—and they are complacent. Instead of debating hard questions, they'll call you a racist if you sleep on white linen."

"Yet you want to live in America, not Germany."

"Yes, because—" Here, at last, Dörte's manic energy failed her. For the first time she looked sleepy, lost. "—because America is a dishonest place. I like the dishonesty."

"In what way do you mean by dishonest?"

"You can remake yourself however you like. No one cares. In Germany, you will probably remain exactly as you started." She emphasized the point with a karate chop. "I cannot stand this sometimes."

Dörte hadn't slept on the airplane. Like a cymbal-clanging toy monkey with its battery run low, she fell into a kind of torpor, but when, at last, the city came into view, her energy returned. "Come on," she said with such renewed vigor I swore I could hear the cymbals crashing. "I'll show you Cologne." We stowed our bags at the train station and went straight to the cathedral.

When I was sixteen, I took a student-bus facsimile of the old Grand Tour. The trip had started in Amsterdam, which, though it was June, had the weather of New Orleans in December. I had to wear two long-sleeved shirts at a time—all that I'd brought. The youth hostel where we were staying had no towels, so I bought a cheap one that absorbed nothing and slopped water around chilled skin. We were fourteen in a room, which I thought odious. Except for one fascinating night in an Indonesian restaurant, I agreed with the general assessment of the sixteen-year-olds present that Europe, on first examination, offered no transcendent joy. But I had never seen the Gothic. The second place my group had reached was Cologne. When first we saw the cathedral, rising to its spires amid the banal city, exclamations of incredulity filled the bus. Statues curved up either side of the portals like birds taking wing. Flying buttresses were like abstract caryatids supporting the walls with outstretched arms. Stained glass cascaded down the spaces between them in unruly rainbows of light. Perhaps, we students speculated, Europe had a few things to teach us after all.

The Gothic cathedral was intended to reach skyward, to crest as near to heaven as allowed to the hand of man. And it was meant to impress. When you approach Chartres from the highway to its south, its cathedral appears over the fields as it would have to medieval pilgrims. It stands alone atop the rise along the horizon, seemingly floating on a wave of green, the secular town in which it rests still invisible. Cologne, a more substantial city, forces its cathedral to do battle against multistory modernity.

If Cologne and other German cities look as if they were built on the cheap and ugly in 1955, that is because they were. War had done its work all too well. Each lumbering American bomber held a crew of ten men usually of college age; they were cocooned within an aluminum tube, along with high-octane fuel, gunpowder, and explosives. Precision daylight bombing, as their mission was then called, required them to drop unguided ordnance onto military installations and factories, which they sometimes hit—along with streets, fields, lakes, houses, and churches. The Americans were sporting targets and were slaughtered in such numbers that anyone who survived twenty-five sorties was allowed to quit the business and go home, regardless of success. Flying by cover of night for self-protection, the British didn't even try for precision. Their idea of a productive attack was, essentially, to pummel a city with explosives and incendiaries. On the night of May 30–31, 1942, the Royal Air Force launched its first "thousand-bomber raid." The target was Cologne. The attackers burned out the city center—six hundred acres in all—yet the cathedral survived.

The destruction of urban Germany, though undertaken at great cost, continued for the better part of the long war it was intended to shorten. The period that followed was a dubious time in which to rebuild. When the history of Western architecture is plotted from the Romanesque through the end of the twentieth century, the period from 1945 through 1980 can only be seen as its nadir. The pared-down elegance of the Bauhaus had been degraded by buildings modeled on packing crates, with the result that, within a generation, a great city could from a distance pass for an outsized freight yard. Cologne and Tokyo—another city replanned by World War II bombers—are homely and, by pathetic irony, scrupulously maintained.

By the end of the war, twenty thousand had died in bombing raids on Cologne, and the cathedral had suffered fourteen hits. Repairs to the church were completed in 1956, and visible injury was, by this, my second visit, largely confined to geometric shapes substituting for stretches of medieval stained glass. Since then, the cathedral has withstood northern Europe's largest earthquake, taking only minor damage. It towers above a city rebuilt on the quick by the lowest bidder, a Gothic thumb in the modernist eye.

Chapter 3

Dörte had to nudge me away from the cathedral. No sooner had she succeeded than I was sitting with her at a table at Cölner Hofbräu Früh Sion, grimacing into a glass of *Kölsch*, a local style of beer. I don't care for beer and generally don't drink my breakfast, but Dörte insisted that this was the thing to do. Each of our glasses had a level marker at two-tenths of a liter; cursed be the bartender who poured to a height below the marker, and pity the customer who would dare ask *Bitte, Herr Ober,* for a little more.

Dörte said she had been living in California with an overworked surgeon just starting his residency. When she found she preferred a different man, she abruptly changed partners, an act she described with such coolness, it could just as well have been a change of clothing.

I suppose my story was written on my face, and when Dörte asked if something was troubling me, I said that my girlfriend of three years, Elena, had just moved out. "I can't explain," Elena would say when I asked why, adding only, if pressed further, "It's just you." Elena had accompanied me on my last three trips to Europe, which had been a somewhat different experience for her because she had been born in Romania. She was dark haired, poised, alluring. She was capable of quiet grace but ill at ease around strangers and suspicious even of those she knew well. Her desk drawers were always locked. On pretexts, she had opened my letters.

I had met Elena only weeks after she had abandoned her husband by removing all her possessions from their home in Brooklyn while he was at work. To finance the move, she had borrowed money from one of her lovers. On the excuse of delivering the mail, her estranged husband drove unannounced from Brooklyn to her apartment house in Connecticut in hope of seeing her. I know this because I was upstairs the day he arrived, having spent my first night with his wife; she received him in the parking lot for a few minutes, took her mail, and he drove back to Brooklyn.

Now, three years later, it was my turn. I was not unaware that, in tallying the attributes one seeks in a spouse, in the space after Elena's name several important boxes could not be checked, but with my own compendium of faults, and a gregariousness that did not complement Elena's taciturnity, I was not offering her a package of delight either. Logic never being what love is about, I wanted her back. I knew the odds in favor of that happening were small.

Dörte listened with critical detachment, and when I had finished, she said, "It happens all the time," as if commiserating over a parking ticket. "Don't call Elena under any circumstances," she ordered.

"That's hard. I keep hoping I can say something—"

"Don't call her," Dörte interrupted. "Not once. Let her come to you. Women respect strength in a man. You know these American women who say they like a man who isn't ashamed to cry?" She gave a slight upward nod of the head and added a terse frown—nonverbal German for total disbelief.

I liked talking to Dörte. She would never forget to consider all her options or to make a decision based on what was best for herself, but she made no attempt to mask it with false empathy. She was not afraid to speak her mind, and I suspected that the man she left had plenty of time to see it coming. I have always worried less about what people say, however unpleasant it may be, than what they don't.

Chapter 4

German train stations have a spot set aside as the *Treffpunkt* (meeting place), but Susanne had thought that, since I was carrying suitcases, it would be easier for me if we met near the taxi stand in the Essen *Hauptbahnhof* (main station). The problem was, there were taxi stands on either end of the long station. I lugged my baggage clear through its length, then back, before we found each other.

I had met Susanne Jäger more than two years before, in the Strand Bookstore, in Lower Manhattan. "Eight miles of books" was the slogan; surly clerks were the hallmark. We had both been searching for volumes on photography. Susanne, then still a teenager, was working for a year as an au pair in New York. She became friendly with Elena and me, went on photo trips with us, had caused some problems for herself with the authorities regarding an overstay on her visa, had gone to the University of Regensburg for a few hated months, then returned to Mülheim an der Ruhr, to live with her parents while apprenticing as a photographer. Her big news was she had just fallen in love with another apprentice.

I hadn't seen Susanne since she had returned to Germany fourteen months before. The sweetness remained, but the fleshy cheeks of waning childhood had firmed and grown lean. We loaded the car for my introduction to the Jäger family.

Now that Susanne's brother, Uwe, had left home for his tour in the Bundeswehr (the German army), the household consisted of Susanne's father, Klaus, who drove a bakery truck; her mother, Margarit, a housewife; a great aunt named Frieda whose husband had died of spotted fever on the Russian front; and Susanne. The house had been built on land owned by the family of Susanne's mother. It had three stories, with all rooms leading off a central staircase, keys protruding below the door handles. An aged boarder in the downstairs apartment had lost her wits and had been consigned to a geriatric-care facility; the one-bedroom apartment had become Susanne's and, for the duration of my stay it would become mine, Susanne graciously vacating it to room with Frieda. In the driveway was a Mercedes, fourteen years old and in sound condition. There was a small "party house" on the lawn, in a space where a swimming pool had once been planned; a hutch for a pet rabbit; and around both were shrubs with spiderwebs that sparkled each morning with dew.

Klaus supported the entire family. He spent part of each evening reading a guidebook to Jamaica, where he and Margarit were to vacation next.
This was serious business. You see German couples in New York, following
their guidebooks like treasure maps, either the man or the woman in
front—the pathfinder. The other walks behind with confident strides,
head sweeping from side to side—the spotter.

At dinner the first night, I met Peter Rüßmann, Susanne's new
boyfriend. He had a warm smile and wore his fair hair short. He had that
cheerful and sly German forwardness, evident in funny, often complex
stories that aimed true to their punch lines. He was clearly smitten with
Susanne and just as clearly trying not to show it.

We all ate *Zwiebelkuchen* (onion cake) at dinner and drank *Federweißer*,
which looked like apple cider and tasted like light champagne. It was fetal
wine, meaning it had not completed fermentation. Susanne said there
was the tiniest splash of alcohol in it. I was thirsty and helped myself lib-
erally. When I stood up, the room danced. I wanted to sit but couldn't
find a chair that would hold still; I made it to the living room, where I
snagged one by the arm, wrestled it down, and sank into it. We sat there
in a family circle around pretzels and chocolate.

Susanne would greet me each morning in my borrowed room, grabbing a strap hanging from enormous, heavy shutters, brace herself with
her feet in tandem, and, with long, vigorous yanks, bring sun into the
room. There is a naturalness to German life, a rejection of the artifice of
chic. Susanne hauled in the sunlight as German women once hauled
water from the well, as my German grandmother used to pick berries in
the woods and carry them home inside her apron: there was nothing
dainty about it and nothing indelicate either.

Breakfast would follow: boiled eggs with orange yolks, preserves, and
four kinds of bread, usually served by Frieda, who did much to look after
the household. Susanne and I would then travel by car or train, but the
car was better because Susanne had the navigation skills of a homing
pigeon on Federweißer, and I got to see a good deal of Germany while she
scrambled to set us back on course. On the first day out, we got into the
village of Kettwig only after circumnavigating it, planning to take the boat
to the Krupp estate known as Villa Hügel. The schedule showed that the
last boat of the season had already left—two weeks before. On we drove.
I was used to the industrial muck of the American Northeast, the grimy
refineries of New Jersey, the desolate redbrick woolen mills of

Philadelphia, every glass pane shattered. Along the Ruhr, farms interspersed themselves between the factories like mortar between bricks. We passed horses and cows in fields, were passed in turn by cars rally racing along highways, then we parked where families promenaded along riverside paths. We ate blueberry pancakes in whipped cream at a riverfront café and walked up the hill to the imperious Villa Hügel.

The structure was built in a convoluted style I could not place. Everything you'd expect in a grand nineteenth-century house was there: a columned portico, spreading wings of light stone, glittering windows that poked holes into a phalanx of rooms. But why did three rather neoclassical floors end at a bread-loaf setback? It was as if the building had been assembled from spare parts found in the warehouses of its contractors. The overall effect was somehow both ostentatious and austere.

The house was finished in 1873 to the specifications of Alfred Krupp, *der Kanonenkönig* (the cannon king) of German industry. He had taken control of his late father's crumbling, seven-man cast-steel works at the age of fourteen, while living in the family's main asset: a cottage where he slept on a pallet in the attic with his three siblings. In a feat of entrepreneurship that was extraordinary even by outsized American standards, Alfred turned the moribund firm into the greatest industrial empire in Europe, employing twenty thousand.

Although he had no architectural training, Alfred designed his third home, Villa Hügel. Alfred believed that architecture was a branch of engineering, not of art; his mansion would be built in accordance with his scrupulous expectations of "comfort and convenience." Although at least nine architects were connected with the project at various times, the owner was successful in assuring that neither aesthetics nor formal architectural principles would stand in the way of eccentricity. Alfred loved the smell of horse manure and feared drafts. In his plans, the windows would be permanently sealed; he would locate his study over the stables, with air shafts facilitating the circulation of the refreshing odor of dung.

Construction was delayed when the southwest corner began to subside into the former colliery over which the house was being built. A further postponement was caused by the Franco-Prussian War, sending French and German coworkers to their opposing regiments. When finally completed, the complex had, depending on who was counting, between two and three hundred rooms.

Like so many arms merchants, Alfred Krupp could prove a fair-weather patriot and an all-weather industrial privateer. The firm had orders in hand from both sides at the outbreak of the Austro-Prussian War of 1866. Since Essen was part of Prussia, the Prussian government quite sensibly asked if Alfred really intended to sell guns to the enemy. Alfred had no love for the Austrian monarchy, which, earlier in his career, had swindled him out of a nearly ruinous sum. Yet he visited Chancellor Otto von Bismarck in Berlin to say he would indeed fulfill the enemy's order and, by the way, would the Prussian State Bank loan him two million thalers? He was told to put up collateral with a bank affiliate. Alfred appealed to the king, who affirmed the judgment and chastised him for stubbornness. Alfred collapsed in an attack of nerves. A secured loan was taken out, and war ended before the Austrians could get their shipment of Krupp guns.

By the advent of the First World War, 99.9975 percent of company stock was held by Alfred's elder daughter, Bertha Krupp. She was the namesake for *die dicke Bertha* ("the fat Bertha," but commonly translated as Big Bertha), which was either the model of Krupp 420-millimeter howitzer that breached the fortresses of Belgium in the opening weeks of the war or the gun that shelled Paris near its end—or perhaps both. At his wedding to Bertha, Gustav von Bohlen und Halbach was granted, by the kaiser himself, the addition of Krupp to his name. Along with their son Alfried, Gustav ran the firm during World War II, when it relied heavily on the considerable economic advantage of slave labor from concentration camps such as Auschwitz, where the slaves, for which the company paid the government four marks a day as rent, were Jewish, Polish, Dutch, Czech, and French. At its height, the Krupp slave population numbered close to one hundred thousand—this according to a report made to the international court at Nuremberg when Alfried Krupp von Bohlen und Halbach was indicted for war crimes. He was convicted, and the company was taken from him, as was his fortune. He served three years in Landsberg Jail, Bavaria, of his sentence to twelve, before the U.S. high commissioner pardoned him. The business and fortune were then duly restored to him, and he went on to become the richest man in Europe.

The first thing Susanne and I saw in the entrance hall of Villa Hügel, now a museum, was a portrait of a good customer, Kaiser Wilhelm I (in uniform) and family by Paul Bülow. The second floor had a two-story-tall fireplace to rival the one that enveloped Orson Welles in *Citizen Kane*. In the Lower Hall were hung paintings of Bertha, Gustav, Alfried, and other bygone Krupps, and more images of kaisers, all protected by innumerable, cantankerous guards. These sentinels of art conservation had only one service to perform before they died, and that was to preserve these profoundly unimportant images from destruction by camera flashes. In principle, I could only applaud them. On my student Grand Tour, no amount of persuasion by elders could stop the fireworks of my group's Kodaks at Tintoretto oils and Giotto frescoes—each light burst potentially harming them. The Italian guards sheepishly, wearily pleaded (occasionally) with the children please to stop.

Here, it was *"Kein Blitz!"* barked by a tall, gray-haired man in crisp Krupp uniform. There are a number of ways to intone "No flash," but the way he said it, you could have sworn the follow-up was, "or I'll shoot."

I didn't have a flash on my Leica; I had merely withdrawn a filter from my camera bag. *"Das ist kein Blitz. Es ist nur ein Filter,"* I said in a tone of strained patience familiar to Germans, Jews, and New Yorkers; it reminds the listener that only begrudging propriety has kept you from adding the word *asshole.*

In the garden of Villa Hügel were chestnuts and pines, rolling hills, a Hansel and Gretel cottage. Susanne opened a nut she found on the ground. "Sometimes it is bitter, sometimes it tastes like nothing," she said. My hunk tasted like wood.

Chapter 5

In the district of the Düsseldorf train station lived a substantial cluster of the Turkish workers who fueled Germany's industrial engine, along with a surprising number of Africans. Sex shops contributed handsomely to the area's economy. Susanne and I walked past several of them to the Königsallee, an expensive shopping street that runs on either side of a duck- and swan-dotted canal of notable beauty. As with most German cities, there is also an *Altstadt* (old town)—made from the rebuilt remains of whatever charming architecture had survived the bombings, the old facades veneered over new cores. Before lunch, we stopped at a microbrewery. It was *echt* northern German down to the glasses marked at 0.2 liter, the dark wood, the kegs rolled by robust waiters, the kegs that served as tables, and the occasional but copious beer spill. I believe there were antlers on the wall. Susanne insisted we take lunch, however, at a

Lebanese stand, rather than spring for a sit-down meal. Chicken, french fries, and something unidentified were rolled into a piece of pita bread. Susanne unloaded about the pretensions of the Königsallee as her whatever-in-a-pita disappeared, leaving behind a grease-splashed wrapper.

Peter owned a Volkswagen Beetle. Its exterior was decorated with characters from American and French cartoons: Mickey Mouse, Donald Duck, Garfield, Masupilami. The ornamentation had aroused the suspicion of the police, who liked to stop Peter and Susanne in the course of daily travels and demand identification. Although Susanne said it was because the cops wanted a closer look at the cartoons, everyone knew it was because the solid order of things had been disturbed by merriment. You could almost read the minds of the police: first the Baader-Meinhof Gang of terrorists, now the Disney Conspirators. In this evening, however, Peter, Susanne, her brother Uwe, and I made it, unmolested by authority, to a dark, smoky *Wein Stube* (wine bar), the heraldic Mickey Mouse joyfully leading the way. We sat in the mezzanine at a table that, from the wrought-iron trademark, announced it had once cradled a Pfaff sewing machine. Peter ordered a light and tangy white from the Pfalz. He and Susanne gave each other goo-goo eyes.

Peter said he was slightly hard of hearing because his job as a conscript in the Bundeswehr was to drive a Leopard 2 tank, in which the interior noise registered 106 decibels. If war came, all knew Germany would be the battlefield; it made every man a soldier and gave urgency to civilian life, as the threat of a hurricane will do on a Caribbean island. It is hard to explain the slow-burning tension you felt in Germany in those years, when hostile armies occupied the eastern portion of the country and stood ready to overrun the rest of it or just lob in nuclear warheads to repay an old debt with compound interest. The checks and balances of global politics and military power were in place to prevent it, yet everyone knew it could happen. There were plenty still alive who had seen it happen before, only this time, because many of the best opposing soldiers were German, it would also be civil war. If a force the size of the one assembled to the east had invaded western Germany, even if nuclear pugilism had not resulted, and even if the West had won, much of the Fatherland would likely have been ground to rubble of the kind from which Düsseldorf had risen short decades before. And yet the country carried on, dreading the worst, planning for the best, relying on Peter Rüßmann, freezing in his winter clothes, his hatch opened for visibility, to steer his sixty-two-ton vehicle within range of the onslaught, so his gunner, who boasted a 98 percent accuracy rate, could blow to bits like-minded Saxons. Now in the reserves, Peter was a motorcycle messenger. Uwe had just completed special training with the atomic, biological, and chemical branch. Both had memorized code words that, if heard on the radio, were their signals to go.

Chapter 6

The old woman in my train compartment was chatty and nervous. Her mother was in her nineties; like every other member of the family, and every possible acquaintance, Mother was infirm, and the ailments were detailed for me with sincere and meticulous woe. Also in the compartment was Arno, a dermatologist from Kiel. He had a gentle disposition and spent much of the ride absorbed by a medical text illustrated with photographs and drawings of breasts. The woman said I didn't look thirty-three. Arno graciously complimented me on my German. I later discovered that he was competent in English, but he had been too shy to have a turn at it. He gave me his card and we would maintain a correspondence for a time. I like trains because you are forced into close, even exacting contact with people chosen entirely by circumstance. While it shows that much of human experience, once you move beyond the routine, takes on the characteristic of a lottery, it teaches you both to extend yourself and to adapt.

Dr. Heinrich Freiherr von Gronau was waiting at the track at the Hauptbahnhof in Hamburg. "You came up here just to see us?" he asked. I was in the unusual situation of having flattered my host by my company. Heinrich was lanky and fair haired; he carried himself with that confident good cheer of a man you could not believe had ever had a bad thing happen to him. I had met him at the firm where I first worked after law school. He had shared an office with a young American lawyer named Mitch. Heinrich had come over for about a year to hone his English, learn American law, and, being Heinrich, have a roaring good time. According to Mitch, Heinrich would punctually drag himself in each morning, looking rather worn, gradually revving up as the day progressed. By midday, he had made the necessary phone calls to plot his evening in what he called "the pubs," and by quitting time, he was all fire and mirth. He'd fly out of the office when the workday was done and come in the next morning exhausted, ready to start the process anew. Mitch asked him, "Heinrich, when do you sleep?" Heinrich answered, "I'll sleep when I get old."

I had left Susanne in the afternoon, boarded the train in Essen for the three-hour trip to Hamburg, and had just enough time to share dinner with Heinrich and Eveline, his wife, before making the night train south, to Munich. The von Gronaus lived in Blankenese, a gentrified former fishing village along the Elbe River. The houses are small, and some of them are thatch roofed, imparting much charm and requiring some interesting fire-insurance premiums. A fisherman has respect for the sea, but he will not likely show romance for it, whether in the Winslow Homer or J. M. W. Turner model, or pride in looking upon it. Blankenese's houses are notorious for windows facing away from the Elbe. If you have to work the thing, why gawk at it when you're eating?

A MILLER LITE sign, glowing in red neon, illuminated the front of the von Gronau living room. A clothing-store mannequin was dressed in black from shoes to wide-brimmed hat. The house came with a boarder, a maid who, I was told, legally had her room for life; she helped look after little Gabriele.

Heinrich, Eveline, and I sat down for Cointreau, then pasta, then soft ice cream. Gabriele made her appearance. Blue eyed, cute, and alert, she smiled at the new face at the dinner table. I presented her with a white Steiff mouse I'd picked up in Düsseldorf, and she showed her appreciation by chewing on the button in its ear.

I explained why I was traveling alone. Heinrich and Eveline had both met Elena when I'd brought her to Hamburg the previous year. "You must not call her," said Heinrich, unintentionally seconding Dörte's advice. "I know what it is like. You look at the telephone, and you want to pick it up." He illustrated by grabbing hold of an imaginary receiver, trying to force himself not to draw it to his ear. "You want to talk to her, but it is the wrong thing to do."

"A woman needs time to think it all over," said Eveline. "It is not necessarily a straight path she takes."

"If this one gets any more crooked," I said, "it will double back on itself."

"Yes, that happens too."

"The rest is fate," said Heinrich. He was right, of course. Fate, or perhaps luck: Germans believed in fate, in the manner of Jews, while most

Americans believed in luck. There is the soul of the gambler in the American makeup. Nearly everyone coming voluntarily to America had done it on the throw of the dice, and no one who throws dice believes in fate. Elena was enticing and clever, but she was no one upon whose constancy you might care to place a wager. There was something predestined in the way she handled herself, an inevitability to both her successes and failures. It was fate, not luck, that had set Elena in motion again, moving out of our apartment with few more civilities than she had observed when abandoning her marital home. What would be, would be; I would get the results in time.

Eveline asked if I'd yet reserved my sleeper to Munich. I said I was taking a *Liegeplatz*. A Liegeplatz is a sleeping arrangement designed to finish off the American romance with European train travel. It is what the French call a *couchette* and what we might call one of six cots in opposite triple-decker rows in a cramped compartment with five strangers of mixed company. My friends looked at me as if I'd proposed crossing the Sahara by camel.

Heinrich took me to the Altona-Hamburg station for the 10:04 P.M. to Munich. There are few welcoming train stations in the world, and I'd wager that none is welcoming by night. The busy ones are hollow and desolate, either about to shut down or undergoing a cursory scrubbing. The lightly traveled ones look like overland embarkation points for the journey across the Styx. Altona-Hamburg was dimly lit, diesel fumes hanging in the chill autumn air of the platform.

Chapter 7

The Liegeplatz car was attended by a tan-jacketed man from a cramped onboard office where he sold snacks and coffee. There were two washrooms past the office, then toilets. If your bunk was the second or third in your stack, you needed the narrow metal ladder to reach it. Dry land never so faithfully re-created the ambience of a submarine, but I was in luck: the two center bunks were empty, meaning there would be a somewhat reduced occupancy for the night. A middle-aged couple had the bottom cots. Herr Bottom had obviously enjoyed his beer that evening and was boasting about it to Frau Bottom. Opposite me on the upper level was a blond man wearing a single earring. He said he was a surfing instructor. He read Mario Puzo in translation and kept a Walkman in his ears every waking minute.

We stopped in the Hamburg Hauptbahnhof, and once we pulled out, as if on cue, my three companions changed into sweat suits. The communal decision was to shut the solitary window, sacrificing airflow for quiet during the nine-hour run. I slept from midnight until three, when I awoke to notice that our train had stopped. I had an hour to contemplate the question of close-quarters human contact in stagnant air when I again fell asleep, drifting in and out of consciousness until six, when I woke from a dream.

I'd had the dream once before, and I would have it several times more. The setting would vary but the plot was the same: I'd be in a crowded public place. I would see Elena and she would promise to tell me why she had left our home. The news that I would finally know the reason would fill me with happiness, but I would lose Elena in the crowd, sometimes after I'd gone off on an errand at her request. I would look for her but never find her, and I would never learn why she had gone. I rarely remember dreams and almost never do they wake me, but this one always did, and I woke to the rocking of the train, to the sound of the clacking wheels, and, within the cabin, the heavy breathing of undisturbed sleep.

I now understood that what had started as the front of the car had become its rear. The others soon awoke. A new attendant, this one in a red jacket, served coffee. The sweat suits were stowed.

Munich wore a pallor of gray in the lingering morning mist. At a stand by the track, men downed sausages the size of cucumbers as breakfast beer flowed from the tap. My friend Steffi was waiting for me at the platform. With her tussled brown hair, parted in the middle, and with deep-set eyes, workaday Anglo-Saxon nose, and pale skin, Steffi could have been any of another hundred women chosen at random in Bavaria. For Steffi, however, a conventional—one might say nondescript—appearance was camouflage. She was as ordinary, as predictable as a forest fire. But all was happiness now as she threw her arms around my neck. I'd expected, at best, the chaste greeting kiss of reacquaintance that has long been the international ritual of the arriving train. Steffi's kiss, however, was substantial. It had weight and texture. It was prosecuted with an ardor fired by imminent separation, a kiss for a departing train, not an arriving one. *"Wie schön dich wieder zu sehen!"* she said. "I have missed you."

Chapter 8

"This is not *Germany!*" declared Steffi. "This is *Bavaria!*" We had not yet left the station and I had committed the faux pas of forgetting where I really was. I fumbled for a comeback line, but before I could deliver it, Steffi led me to a trinket shop then just opening, bought me a pin of the white-and-blue Bavarian flag, and stuck it onto my lapel with such solemnity and pride, you would have thought I'd been awarded the Legion of Honor. "Germany is some other place," explained Steffi.

There was an information-systems conference in town, and we had trouble finding a room. After many false tries, we found a hotel in the packing-crate style situated opposite the Hauptbahnhof. Not only were there rooms available, but I had a choice: a single with a shower and no toilet or one with a toilet and no shower.

"Let's have the first breakfast," said Steffi. She meant rolls and hot chocolate with *Schlagsahne* (whipped cream) at a café. An hour later, she said, "Let's have the second breakfast." She meant some *Weißwurst* (the morning veal sausage), thick, doughy pretzels—and beer. Not some prissy glass with a scratch at 0.2 liter. We raised half-liter pitchers of amber and foam that were good only if drunk cold, meaning you had to drink them fast. I never finished; Steffi took another for the road. After we had walked a few minutes, she said it was time for lunch.

I had met Steffi in New York. Though she shared Elena's worldly intelligence, Steffi was much that my girlfriend was not. Elena was withdrawn and coolly undemonstrative. Steffi was extroverted, articulate, and excitable. Elena was guarded with her affections and distrustful of those who would show them unbidden; Steffi had barely known me before she had declared that she was in love. Elena went through life on a silent, low burn; Steffi was a firestorm of words.

In order to show me around, Steffi had graciously drawn from the few remaining vacation days of the thirty-six annually granted to her by the nuclear-waste recycling plant where she worked. She continued hauling me through Munich, seizing my arm whenever something she adored came into view and saying *Schau!* (look!). She had outbursts of irritation and would rail in German, which is what my grandfather had done. Like my grandmother, I replied calmly in English, the moment for translation acting as a buffer. Steffi was learning Italian because she loved Italy, and would speak Italian to me when we were in bed together.

Chapter 9

Bavaria was an independent kingdom when it sided with Austria in a war with Prussia, which the Prussians won in seven weeks during 1866. The nation we call Germany only began five years later, following a campaign of political and military duress exerted by Prussia against independent German-speaking kingdoms, grand duchies, duchies, principalities, free cities, and the imperial domain of Alsace-Lorraine. The unification of Germany, wars and all, went according to the plans and improvisations of its chancellor, Otto von Bismarck.

It was precipitated by the Spanish when they deposed their dissolute queen, Isabella II. A certain Prince Leopold, who was a relative of King Wilhelm I of Prussia, was proposed for the office of Spanish king, but France, eager to keep Prussia in its place, was against it. Following cordial negotiations with the French ambassador, Wilhelm decided to have Leopold resign his candidacy, which Leopold's father did for him, the son being out of reach on a Swiss vacation. Wilhelm did not agree, however, to the French demand that he never try that sort of thing again. Bismarck, who wrote the Prussian press release, colored the facts to give the impression that the French had precipitated a rupture in relations. France declared war.

Betting was on a French invasion of Prussia, but Prussian military reforms had created a formidable army, and the French muzzle-loading, bronze cannon were no match for the new Krupp steel breech loaders—built by the man whose new house, Villa Hügel, was then experiencing construction delays due in part to the war. Krupp technology was decisive: Prussian artillery ripped through French defenses and much red-pantalooned flesh at Wörth, Sedan, and Metz, then cut off Paris and laid siege. Three to four hundred Krupp shells hit the capital daily. The inhabitants sent out messages by carrier pigeon. The Germans let loose Saxon hawks to eat them. The Parisians tried manned hot-air balloons. Collaborating with a technician, Alfred Krupp invented the antiaircraft gun. Paris surrendered after 113 miserable days. With no foreign power left to stop them, the Germans could at last unite—under Prussian rule.

Munich, as the capital of independent Bavaria, had long been a city of beauty and sophistication. The Bavarian king, Ludwig II, squandered public funds on fairy-tale castles like Neuschwanstein, now a tourist attraction. Wilhelm insisted he would accept the imperial crown only if invited to take it by the other German princes. Ludwig's kingdom being the foremost among them, he was detailed to write the letter of invitation. Bismarck composed it for him. By a secret arrangement, Bismarck saw that Ludwig received three hundred thousand marks annually to finance the construction of those future tourist attractions. The ceremony proclaiming King Wilhelm I of Prussia as Kaiser Wilhelm I of Germany took place in the Hall of Mirrors at Versailles, with Paris still under siege and running short on food. In time, Ludwig grew insane, drowned himself, and was succeeded by his brother, who was also insane, but it mattered little since Bavaria was now controlled from Berlin.

As with any forced conversion, Bavarians' allegiance to their new god—greater Germany—was tinged with resentment, and the old god—independence—was revered alongside the new. Even reunified, contemporary Germany is not quite whole, and in Bavaria, regional pride rises to the level of chauvinism, as Steffi all too willingly showed.

It's the classic north-versus-south squabble, with a little schismatic Christianity (Protestant north, Catholic south) thrown in for color. The idea of southern sloth afflicts the cultural lives of some notably prosperous nations in frosty latitudes. In Germany, the United States, and, most notoriously, Italy, to be southern is to be seen as charming, slow, and grudgingly employed. I'd felt it when I'd moved to the American north from New Orleans. To the north Germans, the people of Bavaria are, at their worst, coarse, beer-drinking, lazy reactionaries with minds substantially narrower than their waistlines. To a Bavarian, a northern German is either a stiff-necked, priggish *Nordkopf* (north head) or (as Steffi preferred) a *scheiß Preussen* (shit Prussian).

Having been built as a royal city—with grand streets laid out for pomp and pretension—Munich remained completely out of scale with its role of provincial capital. It was big, impressive—a credible rival to Berlin in all but power. It had the good fortune to lie near the end of the bombing path from England during the Second World War. To reach Munich, the bombers had to pass through virtually the entire German air-defense system. They came seventy-one times to Munich, killing six thousand, wounding another sixteen thousand and heavily damaging three great churches, the Residenz (the former palace), and the Alte Pinakothek, which is one of the world's premier art museums.

On a purely ideological level, you could say that Munich deserved it and more. Unlike the north, with its whiffs of mercantile liberalism and Anglophilia, southern Germany was conservative and, when it had mattered, loyal to the Nazi ideal.

It is an appalling but all-too-human trait to be fiercely devoted to a group in which you hold tenuous membership. Germany, with its pliable borders, has been such a crossroads of invasion and transit that much German blood has been mixed over time. The fair-skinned, blue-eyed, blond "Aryan" of Nazi glorification is more common to Scandinavia than central Europe. As you head south in Germany, hair and eyes tend to darken, until you reach Austria, that Teutonic outpost facing down Slavs and Latins, where the true blonde is nearly as rare as in an ethnic soup like New York. The Danes, who hadn't developed a national neurosis over how Aryan they were, heroically rescued more than seven thousand of the approximately seventy-five hundred Danish Jews, secretly ferrying them to neutral, Aryan Sweden under the noses of German occupying forces. Some Austrians believe their ancestors also resisted Nazi invasion during the Anschluß of 1938; burghers of Vienna accomplished this by raising their right hands stiffly in protest, their faces twisted into smiles at the shock as they defiantly pitched flowers at their conquerors, while a small but fanatical band of patriots tore the buttons off the overcoat of the invading General Heinz Guderian and carried him on their shoulders to his lodgings.

Chapter 10

The Deutsche Arbeiterpartie, (German Workers' Party,) was founded in 1919 in Munich by a railroad laborer. Its core was a half-dozen clubbable men who held boring meetings in restaurants and beer halls, reading minutes and worrying how they would survive with only about five marks in the till. Adolf Hitler, working as a spy for the army, was ordered to infiltrate, then join. His speeches changed everything. Audiences grew. Hecklers among them were thrown down stairways, shoved outside, or beaten with rubber truncheons and riding whips. Within months, a Hitler speech drew a crowd of nearly two thousand to

Munich's most famous beer hall, the Hofbräuhaus. His demands that night—for the treatment of all Jews as aliens, and other crowd pleasers—consumed two and a half hours of speech making.

Transformed into a credible force by its new star of the podium, the organization was renamed the Nationalsozialistische Deutsche Arbeiterpartei (National Socialist German Workers' Party), abbreviated as NSDAP, but more commonly referred to in English texts as the Nazi Party. Hitler, the master orator, was given top billing. He soon outmaneuvered the ever-debating managing committee and had himself voted in as chairman; he assumed dictatorial powers, permanently ending party debate. Hitler organized his street brawlers as a private army of storm troopers under Captain Ernst Röhm, a tough, homosexual combat veteran he would later have killed in a purge known as *die Nacht der langen Messer* (the Night of the Long Knives). Hitler and a detachment of Röhm's storm troopers were in the audience at a Munich beer hall known as the Löwenbräukeller (home of the internationally popular Löwenbräu) during a rival organization's meeting. Before the speaker had said a word, storm troopers beat him up and pitched him into the crowd. Nazi speeches and thuggery would coexist in beer halls until, in 1923, Hitler staged his famous Beer Hall Putsch at the Bürgerbräukeller (no longer extant).

It started when Hitler led a small group into the main hall for the speech of the conservative General State Commissioner Gustav von Kahr, who, though holding executive authority for Bavaria, also wanted to see the elected national government overthrown. Hitler, who had served with valor as a corporal in the First World War, appeared wearing one of his two Iron Cross medals and a black morning coat of distressingly provincial cut. A Nazi bought three beers for the Hitler party, at the inflationary price of one billion marks each (about twenty-five contemporary American cents). Hitler then stood on a chair, shouted for quiet, fired a pistol shot into the ceiling, and declared a "national revolution." For a time that night, the Nazis had the upper hand in the beer hall and around Munich. The office and presses of a courageous socialist newspaper were smashed; political opponents were taken prisoner, as were people whose Jewish-sounding names were found through the telephone directory. The Nazi revolutionaries tried to gain the support of the governing elite, but in the end they were betrayed.

The next morning, to win over the populace to his coup d'état and so save himself, Hitler led an improvised parade into the center of town. It ended in a face-off with a heavily outnumbered detachment of state police. Gunfire was exchanged. Hitler's bodyguard jumped in front of his master, stopped some bullets that would have better served humanity if he hadn't bothered, but lived. About eighteen others, mostly Nazis, died. Hitler came out of it with a dislocated left shoulder. He earned a term in the nearby Landsberg Jail (the future home of Alfried Krupp von Bohlen und Halbach), where he was allowed much freedom, held political meetings, and dictated his manifesto and memoir, *Mein Kampf.*

On the Night of the Long Knives, in the summer of 1934, with Hitler safely in power as chancellor of Germany, Kahr was hacked to death, probably with a pickax, and his body dumped into a swamp near Dachau, a town just outside Munich and home of a recently built concentration camp.

Hitler loved Munich; it was the "city of Germany closest to my heart." In 1931, with *Mein Kampf* a best-seller, the Nazis opened their new headquarters at the Brown House, a building that one of those seventy-one air raids on Munich would succeed in flattening. Through local pride, a pugnacious disrespect for modernism, and a civic blind spot concerning wartime guilt, Munich rebuilt itself along traditional lines and so became the finest-looking large city in Germany. The twin green-copper domes of the Gothic Frauenkirche still stand like outsized knobs controlling picture and volume of the glockenspiel on the tower of the Neues Rathaus (New Town Hall) nearby. The Glockenspiel's figures reenact a joust and a dance celebrating triumph over plague.

One morning, Steffi and I watched the mechanical joust at eye level from an upstairs café. Old women sat at nearby tables, eating pastries, each wearing a traditional, mannish Bavarian green-felt hat that flicked feathers smartly into the air from the band at the base of the crown. Many of their kind in Munich had seen their freedoms taken by the Nazis, their men killed in war, their homes destroyed, their nation sundered. They watched the glockenspiel impassively, as if it were yet another rerun of a favorite television episode. They were weathered and stoic, glad to enjoy the meal and company, careful not to let down their guard, even as they ate and talked heartily. I'd seen that behavior in restaurants before, among white people in New Orleans after the American race riots of the 1960s; it's the look of someone who enjoys his life, has a few opinions he'd be more than happy to share, and yet knows enough to be careful about what he says in public, even among friends.

Like a drunk who loses an eye in a fight he's picked and so wins a light sentence, Munich has scraped itself together, grumbling, over its next round at the bar, at the unfairness of the odds during the brawl, and bragging, out of earshot of the parole officer, about how many punches it landed.

Chapter 11

W e were leaving the Alte Pinakothek when Steffi went head to head with a museum guard. He was an older fellow sliding toward a comfortable pension, a short, round, pacific counterpart to the humorless paranoids of the Krupp villa. You could imagine him turning a blind eye to a pretty girl from Lyon as she popped her flash at a Dürer. Perhaps that was why he was working the coatroom. All he asked of Steffi was that she give up the steel numbered tag he had handed her earlier, and she could have her coat back. It seemed a fair enough exchange to me, but Steffi had lost the tag. The guard wanted to accommodate, but orders were orders; would you please keep looking?

Steffi dredged the recesses of her leather bag, without success. *"Ich kann das verdammte Dingsbums nicht finden!"* (I can't find the damned thingamajig!)

"I'm sure you have it," I said, trying to be helpful. Wrong move. Steffi tugged at the bag, shoved hands into pockets, swore by God and the devil that no such thing had ever entered her possession, described her coat and implored its repatriation. "I'm sorry," I said to her in English, knowing the guard couldn't understand, "but I'm sure I saw you put it into your bag." Unable to follow the reply but afraid now that the purse would end up on his head or mine, the guard told us to wait a second, all the while making nervous, fussy gestures with his hands. He disappeared and returned quickly with the coat, guilt ridden for his breach of regulations, relieved to see the backs of us.

Outside, Steffi demanded, "What did you do that for? Why didn't you stand with me against that man?"

If this were a stationary liaison rather than one born of the ephemeral attractions of travel, I would have offered a colorful retort. But there are never quarrels in shipboard romances. Without the need to establish or maintain precedent, I replied only that I regretted my disloyalty. Quieted but depressed, Steffi soothed herself with a detour to one of the cheap but brightly lit mini department stores found on every main street in central Europe, the kind the bulges with candy, inexpensive wallets and handbags, school supplies, clothing, and, on tables outside, shoes at sale prices. Steffi bought some pantyhose, but when she came out with her purchase, she looked even sadder than before. She took hold of my arm. "You are very nice," she said. I didn't understand. "You are really very nice to me." Then it came out: while opening her wallet at the cashier, she had found the numbered steel Dingsbums from the museum. She was ashamed of herself, as anxious people who take out their anxieties on others often are; there was both gratitude in her voice and the sound of defeat. She had blown it again and, calm now, she could only accept this new failure with humility. Steffi handed the Dingsbums to me. Along with my Bavarian flag lapel pin, it was a souvenir of Munich.

My third and final souvenir I collected on my own the next morning, while Steffi was at work. It was another day with the kind of weather characteristic of central Europe in autumn: a low, enveloping gray, as if the sky ends above the clock towers and will never, within sane expectation, become sunny again. It was also the anniversary of the day my father died when I was sixteen and he only forty-eight. There was nothing to lighten my spirits, so I boarded the suburban S8 train to Dachau for a tour of the Nazi concentration camp.

Chapter 12

Want to get a Bavarian annoyed? Suggest that you would like to see Dachau. During my Grand Tour, the mere hint by three of the four Jews on the bus that the concentration camp would be that an interesting diversion sent two guides grappling for the microphone, pleading how there were so many wonderful sights in Munich, and there was so little time, and you don't possibly want to see such things. Some of the group went. I had an engagement to spend the day with a Jewish girl who lived in town. She introduced me to members of virtually every surviving Jewish family of Munich. I'd always said I'd see the camp when I next returned.

Dictatorship is hard business now. To dictate, you need a population ignorant of alternatives, and you must block potential rivals from ready avenues for dissent. Consider how that might be accomplished when people walk around with telephones in their pockets and have ready access to worldwide electronic transmission of sound, text, and image. In the Soviet Union, photocopiers were kept under lock and key. You can't run a world power that way, but you can't run a dictatorship any other way. During the middle of the twentieth century, however, the vital technologies of communication and mobility were still controllable: if you held the airports, railroads, radio stations, and newspapers, you had a country in a choke hold, maintained by the military and police. You could say nasty things that could not be contradicted. You could, for instance, point your finger at the less than 1 percent of the population that was Jewish and blame them for anything you liked.

There was a joke German Jews were telling each other during the Nazi rise, my maternal grandmother remembered. Two men are sitting on a park bench, discussing the Great War. The first says, "You know why we lost the war? It was the fault of the Jews and the bicycle riders." The second looks at his friend incredulously and asks, "Why the bicycle riders?" In 1934, on orders from her husband, Grandmother left Leipzig with her two children (my mother being the younger) and boarded the *Bremen* for America, where my grandfather was already working. Three years later, a Jewish couple my mother's family had never met gave the keys to their house in the Palatinate village of Leimersheim to a trusted friend and drove in the middle of the night to Basel, Switzerland. They were soon in Southampton, where they met their only son, then at boarding school in London, and took the *Queen Mary* to America. The ship that carried my father and his parents clear of catastrophe is now a hotel and tourist attraction in Long Beach, California. Among those who remained in Germany were many Jews, Catholics, Protestants, and dissidents who ended up in Dachau and places like it or worse. Nazi tyranny may have singled out the Jews, but no one was immune. Dachau was designed and run as a multipurpose, nonsectarian place of villainy.

Chapter 13

Dachau was gray and wet under a drizzle when I arrived; it was nearly deserted, very clean, oddly quiet. The neat rows of what looked like garden plots marked where barracks once stood, pulled down, so the authorities said, for structural unsoundness. The plots were filled not with flowers but with gravel. From one I took a single pink stone—that third and final souvenir of Germany—and put it into my carry bag. There was an Evangelical church, and a synagogue, which was locked, and I believe a Catholic chapel as well. The crematorium was shut; the bilingual sign said:

> *Das Krematorium ist wegen Erdarbeiten geschlossen. Wir bittem um Ihr Verständnis.*

> The crematorium is closed due to earthworks. We thank you for your understanding.

I remember nothing about the exhibition hall and I missed the movie. I do recall walking around a grim and desolate place, and that, in the way a familiar tune will stick with you no matter what else you think about, I kept hearing in my mind the funeral march from *Siegfried.*

A group of students came in. They were dressed in that European imitation of blue-jeaned Americans that somehow fails to get it right. The hair gave the boys away. It was both poorly cut and carefully maintained. Male brashness was muted by something foreign to American boys—caution, mixed with unease. Eight adolescents who could only have been American were walking quietly nearby with their professor and his wife. The American kids took the experience as American kids will. All were uncomfortable, most wished they hadn't come, and a few were genuinely moved and asked probing, if sometimes naive, questions. They were from a midwestern university, taking a semester abroad. This field trip was for an easy course—or so reported a pretty, bespectacled girl named Erin. She had the look of a carefree spirit pained by duty and expectation, as if her parents had just scolded her over the money she had spent on a blouse. As the others stood grimly under umbrellas, Erin blew a tiny bubble with her chewing gum.

The professor was a graying man, plainly burdened by the responsibility of delivering an education to a student body with European vacation on its mind. I got the impression that he had added Dachau to the curriculum to shock the learning into them. He now improvised, inviting me to join a discussion with the group and the wife of a local Protestant minister. We collected within a wood-paneled, contemporary meeting room, pulling skimpy armchairs into a circle. It was good to be indoors, warm, not having to look at Dachau, but the mood was funereal, and voices were kept low. The circle and the difficulty putting voice to what we had seen made the encounter more like group therapy than a seminar.

The minister's wife had spent about eighteen months in Israel, she said, aiding survivors of concentration camps and death camps. The professor asked me to tell the story of my great-grandfather, who had died here, supposedly on the night before his release. The professor said that not having been told the how and the why of the death was typical, a method of terror. The minister's wife said that some of the townspeople want to forget, would rather the memorial went away, and were opposed to turning it into an international meeting point, as had been proposed. I had some sympathy for the townies; imagine living in a place synonymous with horror, when all you want to do is take care of your family, go to work, and direct the curious to the lovely castle for which the town fathers stubbornly insist the area is famous. But the minister's wife and I sided with those who believed the preservation of this evil place as a monument and ruin was a good and necessary thing.

All the customers at the *Imbiss* (snack bar) outside the camp were American. I had sausage and bread, which I felt I could trust more than the hamburgers. I was back at the Alte Pinakothek within the hour.

Chapter 14

I went directly back to the art museum, to the froufrou joviality of the French rococo and the Boucher nude of Louise O'Murphy. Born of Irish parents, O'Murphy was the sister of three Parisian courtesans, but she was destined for better things. While with her sisters, she met Giovanni Casanova, who arranged for Boucher to paint her on a recamier, one foot on a pillow, the other half falling off. Her head is raised, and she stares beyond the picture frame with invitational curiosity. The focal point of the painting is her fine, pink backside. The linen is tussled for erotic suggestion, and the flower deposited on the floor adds an allegorical or symbolic element that gives art historians something to talk about. It is a salacious image, a pictorial invitation to carnality, and therefore pornographic, I suppose. It is also a spiritual painting because from an appreciation of this dim-looking, inviting woman you can not help but feel a kind of reverence—which is somehow made more complete by the knowledge that the sitter profited from sin: through Boucher, Louise O'Murphy caught the eye of King Louis XV, signed on as one of his mistresses, and bore two of his children.

The painting was the only thing I could look at after Dachau. I spent a long time with it until I felt myself again.

At the coat check, who should I then see off but Steffi's old nemesis, the hapless guardian of the Dingsbums. He recognized me but stood a few paces off, nervously shifted his weight back and forth, as if held in place by an invisible cord. Suddenly, he found his courage, approached, and said, "Excuse me. You were with the young woman, the one who got so upset?"

"Yes."

Cautiously, respectfully, he circled his topic. "She is not your wife?"

"No. She is a friend in Munich. Not a partner for life."

On this, we were instant chums. "She was so excited!" said the guard, eyes widening. "My God, what could I say?" He unburdened himself, man to man, relieved that he had not offended me, glad to talk, glad that, in my romantic life, I'd done nothing rash.

Steffi would have exhausted me were she my girlfriend, but she was fun to travel with, and I consider that high praise. She had a sharp mind, a good heart, and, when not anxious, a tolerant and open disposition. She was sweet and tragic and tragicomic and walking proof that among educated people, most troubles are self-inflicted.

Chapter 15

I was alone on my last evening in Munich. I thought of doing what I often did when alone on a trip—get some fast food or grab a cheap meal by the train station; but I took a walk to buoy my spirits and came upon a clean, well-lighted place called Spatenhaus An der Oper. Archways lined with dried flowers divided the restaurant into a series of white-walled dining rooms. By German tradition, sophistication is almost never a prerequisite for public gatherings, but conviviality is essential, even in large places, and you will find nooks and intimate corners in the largest beer halls. Seating is banquet style, and whatever your qualms about the lack of privacy, you need never feel the pang of exile that can come from dining alone.

An old man and a young couple shared my table. The old man had a lock of gray hair that kept falling from the side of his head. The lock would be flicked back, there to wait, like a mischievous puppy, for the chance to go once more where it was not wanted. Its owner took notice of my camera and notebook. I ordered a Wiener schnitzel, and when I was nearly through, we struck up a conversation that lasted two hours. He was a professor of medicine at Würzberg and had come to Munich to give a talk first thing the next morning. He was a substantial man: deep voiced, heavyset, with large hands. He had settled into his place at the table and seemed to conform to it, as contoured and immovable as a hill bordering a cornfield. His gray suit, white shirt, and tie had the lived-in, comfortable look of work clothes, like overalls on a farmer.

As we dined, the professor pointed out the opulently dressed after-theater crowd, which began arriving at about ten-twenty. "Fancy people," he said, hoisting a stein. He took hearty swigs, and I sipped along behind. We talked about the United States and about money and about the Russians. We discussed the German soul, international affairs, history, prices, and his view that the world will live in peace when it is united under God. He actually did most of the talking, which, given the shabby state of my intellectual German, probably saved the evening for both of us. We toasted Bismarck, whom we both admired; we toasted my study of history and who knows what else, the professor raising a last half liter of beer that he'd never finish, while I reciprocated with an empty glass of mineral water.

The young couple left and the professor said they were Austrians. A husband and wife replaced them, and the professor said the husband was a *Landsmann* of his. *Landsmann* is a great German word that denotes a person native to the same region as you but connotes a kindred spirit. The professor and the husband had been born in Jena, a city then behind an Iron Curtain grown far rustier than we knew at the time. "Only the ones like us, who have come from the East, can understand Western freedom," said the professor. "America has the freedom, but there is so much that it does not understand. Go back and let the Americans know: if it were to lose Europe, it would lose its soul." He told his Landsmann that I was an American, but also a European at heart. The professor, who was both father and grandfather, closed with paternal advice: "Maybe you will find a girl here. Marry a *European* girl." As I was already in upheaval over a Romanian, I thanked him and said no more about it.

What warmed me to him was his declaration, unsolicited and given without being told about my heritage, that "what the Nazis did to the Jews was frightful." He was sagacious and reflective, and he was plainly outraged by institutionalized evil. Like many academics nearing retirement age, if he had ever been victim to the jabbering self-indulgence of the pedagogue, he had grown out of it.

On the walk back to my hotel, a small group of Americans was making a drunken scene of the kind that commonly follows fraternity parties. One of the men had a pair of long-toed, studded white boots suitable only for the Las Vegas stage. Just beyond them, a large crowd had formed a semicircle around a man with a guitar and another with an instrument made of bottles filled to varying heights with water. Using a spoon, he played a familiar motif from *Eine Kleine Nachtmusik* with such delicacy and sensitivity that a scraggly drunk in a trench coat was moved to perform an interpretive dance. The applause of the crowd compelled the musicians to take a bow. The dance concluded without accolade. It had been a good last night in Germany.

Chapter 16

Another sleeper took me to Verona. The batteries had run down in my travel alarm clock, and though I had an entire Liegeplatz compartment to myself, I kept waking during the night to check the time. The Italian attendant was a gentle man who collected my passport for the nocturnal border crossing. We communicated in simple English and German phrases. He promised to wake me before we reached Verona, just before six, but he did not carry himself with that can-do self-assurance of German trainmen. Nocturnal Italy was passing in a steady rain, offering the backside of civilization that you see from trains: industrial compounds with spotlights silhouetting earthmoving equipment, darkened houses, a lone pair of headlights searching the blackness. I slept and lay awake intermittently through the night, feeling the train rocking, smelling the freshly washed old linen.

By five twenty-five, as we chugged toward the outskirts of Verona, I had remained undisturbed by the attendant. I knocked quietly on his compartment. A rustling ensued, a light flicked on, and there he stood, wearing only a half-buttoned shirt, underpants, and slippers. I gently addressed the watchman who had promised to wake me. "Will the train arrive in Verona at five fifty-two?"

"I hope so," he replied.

Welcome to Italy.

From Verona, through Milan, and then to Genoa, which I'd first visited five years before, on a driving tour with my brother Kenneth. Up to that point, the Italy I had known had been Florence, Venice, Rome—the Italy of Renaissance monuments and sculpture; of gelato; of leather-goods shops tended by pretty American college girls taking art degrees; of smiling men waving sheets of postcards, unfolded accordion style with the come-on, "special student discount."

Kenneth and I had also come down from Milan but by the *autostrada*, and the first thing Kenneth said when we got off the ramp was, "We're someplace where we're not supposed to be." Roped to gray wharves, ahead were ships lying fat and motionless in their moorings like a slumbering walrus herd; beyond, the city rose in irregular terraces into the mist. Genoa, benign from a distance, grew ominous as we drew nearer. Streets cut among blocks of tall, flat facades in disharmonious stages of decomposition, seemingly walling us into an enclosure bounded opposite by the harbor. The buildings were half in ruin though still in use, with layers of earthen and reddish brown surfacing exposed in odd patches and the stucco pitted where whole slabs had fallen away, exposing gray stone and chipped brickwork. The only relief offered the eye came from green and burgundy-red louvered *persiane* shutters and bright clothes within the uncountable acres of swaying laundry.

When side streets appeared, they were narrow and hilly and bred many colorful, disreputable-looking people. There were also attractive women, hawklike young boys on motor scooters, and the inevitable outsider who had lost his way and was trying to look inconspicuous. Across from the train station, the Cinema Superba announced EVERYDAY SEXY MOVIE, with an arrow aiming toward a basement screening room. Inside the station, a youthful British tourist, drugged by a tablet dropped into his beer by young men who had then robbed him of everything, begged, still dazed, for a telephone token to call his consulate.

Chapter 17

So I was back in Genoa—*la superba* by ancient reputation. In the preposterously Victorian room of my supposedly first-class hotel, the bed sagged like an overweight dachshund and the shower handle came off at the touch, landing on my bare feet. Chest-high Lucite protected the vile wallpaper of the breakfast room. I was alone for breakfast my first morning, save for a dignified, elderly *signora* sitting two tables over, growing hungry. She and I scanned the room for assistance; none was forthcoming. The signora got up and made a reconnaissance, without success. With that pantomime often required of travelers, we gestured incredulity to each other. I gave up, went to the ancient kitchen, and, finding no sign of life save a pot of boiling water, prepared two neat baskets, each with bread, packaged croissants, and whatever else looked agreeable. Signora was pleased with my gift, the waitress then arrived in a fluster, and, to preserve her self-esteem, served yet more bread with the coffee.

On Via Venti Settembre I did what a man must do: buy replacements for the things the girlfriend made off with. The woman at Pratesi was the kind of gentle middle-aged lady who populates respectable shops worldwide—the beneficent, seasoned counterpoint to the fashionable saleswoman in her twenties still brimming with unrealizable expectations. The lady was patient and eager to show me anything I wanted and spoke neither English nor German. She left me alone in the shop, costly goods coating the counter. She ran down the block and returned with a gentleman from another store. He was studying English and his vocabulary had advanced past "hello, I am studying English" to "I am sorry, but I do not understand."

To show that I wanted place mats and coordinated napkins appropriate for both day and evening, I motioned for paper, then drew a picture of the sun and another of a crescent moon, arching my pen point between them. Message comprehended: the recommendation was for off white, and the deal was done. I left a note for later translation, thanking both for their help.

Gianni and Lorenza Bacchelli, husband–and–wife lawyers, had set up practice and home in Genoa some years before. I had met them at a summer program in international law at Columbia, my attendance sponsored by the firm for which I was then employed and where I had met Heinrich von Gronau. Lorenza was a charming hostess, a brilliant cook, a loving mother, and—I mentioned the bit about practicing law. In the operation of the firm, which specialized in admiralty law, the Bacchellis shared responsibilities, save for the hour before lunch, when Lorenza slipped out to cook up something dazzling. She was in when I arrived at their spacious apartment. In the Genovese manner, a mosaic filled the foyer hallway floor. The Miró lithograph Gianni had bought when last in New York was prominently displayed. On the dining table stood tall, elegant silver candlesticks, each sprouting a thin, pink taper.

Young Enrico had been waiting by the window, watching for my taxicab. When he was born, I'd sent him two small teddy bears with bells inside. He had named them Patata (potato) and Cebolla (onion), and they were still favorites. This time I brought him toy cars from Germany and a Sigikind duck for the infant, Ferdinando. Gianni arrived late, wearing a beard that sprouted grays. Jennifer, the Scottish nanny, dined with the family. She was exposing the boys to English, and Enrico was developing a Scottish accent, tinged with a lilt. Jennifer liked the phrase *for sure*, and the whole family now used it when showing approval. The food; the wine; the fresh bread cut on the diagonal; the twin silver candlesticks holding their thin pink tapers; the antique table of thick, dark wood; the little boys; the husband and wife: there is nothing like a scene of refined domesticity to make a bachelor wonder what he is doing with his life.

Chapter 18

Another night train. No Liegeplatz this time, but a regular first-class seat. I had the compartment to myself until Milan, where a Dutchman reeking of hashish took the opposite three seats for his bed. He coughed all the way to Zurich, where I exited.

A couple of people on the train had asked me what had happened on the New York Stock Exchange. I was surprised to pass a magazine stand where the international edition of *Newsweek* sported the word CRASH on its cover. I immediately called my stockbroker, who happens to be my youngest brother, Eric. In a rare moment of foresight, on the last trading day before the disaster, in response to a suspiciously unsteady market but against Eric's strong objections, I had sold all the shares I could without taking a loss. Eric had been less lucky; he had speculated in market futures, got caught in a whipsaw effect, and lost a terrible amount of money. Like all good brokers, being wildly wrong now and then never stopped him, and whenever he was right, it only encouraged him.

With the help of the tourist office at the Hauptbahnhof, I booked a room on the north bank of the Limmat River, at a microscopic, box-shaped hotel called the Krone. Switzerland is more expensive than Italy, but—cleanliness being a national fetish—even small, cheap hotels can generally be relied upon to be tidy and habitable. While on the Bernina Express to St.-Moritz one year, I shared a compartment with a Swiss who said he had a difficult time convincing a woman in Italy to sell the antique mantelpiece from a house she owned. The woman said she would never sell it to a Swiss because she had been to that country and had actually seen men wash the streets; she simply could not do business with any people capable of such bizarre behavior. With effort, the man convinced her that he came from a part of Switzerland where no one would dream of washing a street, and so closed the sale.

I had to be careful whenever heading for the little Krone, because if I should let my mind wander as I searched for its minimal street front, I'd easily miss it. My room was so compact that I had to put my suitcase on the bed in order to open the door. The staff aimed to please, however, and the place was predictably clean—including the communal bathroom. The hotel even had a restaurant, and the food was good.

I was glad to be back in Switzerland. Three cultures of Europe converge in the Alps, forming a country that carries the signature of each on a page understandable to all. It is the land of polite Frenchmen, humble Germans, and honest Italians; it is the improbable ethnic miracle of Europe. Yet you aren't there long before you are reminded that even the most worldly and fashionable Swiss is only three or four generations off the farm. There is much of the citizen-soldier monotony that gets a man to work early and sometimes home late, with all the exactitude of the Germans but with fewer of their neuroses.

I was once walking back to my hotel in the early evening in a small Swiss metropolis that appeared to be under a nine o'clock curfew. It was after that hour, on blackened, empty streets, that two young Australian men approached me and asked where they might find some excitement.

"Like what?" I asked.

They were guarded, but the wire-haired man, a touch more assertive than his friend, came out with it. "You know, bars—strip clubs."

"Not around here, it looks like."

"Anything nearby that you know of?"

This was clearly a plea born of desperation, but a wartime blackout could have made the town no darker. "Guys, I have to be honest with you," I said, pointing west. "Take a train to Paris."

Zurich's raunchy neighborhood, the Niederdorf, was lively the night I arrived, but in a manner so tame that even the bevy of homosexuals in leather outfits looked well scrubbed and harmless. The prostitutes were discreet, and the habitués of the roughest bars looked like young bankers during off hours—which was exactly the case.

If the Niederdorf smacks of pretence, daytime Zurich is the real thing. The Swiss, like the Japanese, are always at their best during regular business hours. Everyone is buying, selling, investing, or scrubbing something, or walking the dog. The art museum holds a collection both carefully maintained and intermittently dull. The chocolate shops, however, are the envy of the civilized world. A truth that can never be gainsaid: all that is glorious in life, all that is noble and refined, all that is capable of pushing human experience into a transcendence such that the hand of God may be felt in the work of man, starts at the Sprüngli shop on the Paradeplatz in Zurich. Nice ladies mind counters aromatic with chocolate and pastries. The effect is like visiting a prosperous aunt who happens to be handy with sweets and credit-card verification. The ladies sometimes give free tastes and generally have a sense of fun about their jobs. Like the cable-car conductors of San Francisco, who clang out one-note tunes on their century-old bells, they know that they are custodians of a national treasure that can do no wrong, even if it serves little practical purpose.

It is said that the vaults of the banks extend under the orderly and nondescript main street, the Bahnhofstrasse, and that you can trod upon tons of gold in a stroll to the Bally Capital shop and back. While doing so, I saw a particularly striking young woman. I turned my head as she walked past, and I saw that she had turned her head to look at me. I thought how grateful I was to be abroad—and how flattered. I also thought that, if this small, nonverbal praise was enough to lift my spirits, those spirits must be very low indeed. A streetcar kicked up fallen leaves. Men stood before the windows of the banks, watching reports of market gyrations worldwide. I moved on.

Chapter 19

I was standing in front of the Krone, in jacket and tie, carrying a bouquet of flowers and a wrapped Steiff mouse when a car looped in an illegal, fast, and finely controlled U-turn that ended in front of me. I hadn't met Paula before, but we recognized each other at once. It gets that way when you travel enough: the people you need to know are easy to spot. Paula drove with precision and agility, complaining about the annoyances of the road and the cabby who stopped in front of us. She had tussled blond hair, newly permed, spoke good English, and was pregnant, due in February. I apologized for not being able to make her wedding, but she said she understood, given the distance and all. We were at her suburban house in minutes.

At the door stood Ursula Rossi—tall and beautiful. She is astounding that way: an ageless woman who always looks correct to the occasion. I had met Ursula and her younger daughter Katrina at the airport in Crete four years before. Ursula had gone on vacation with Katrina, who had struck up a holiday romance with a Greek named Stefanos. Along the way, Katrina had invited Zoë to join Ursula's party. Zoë was Greek but had grown up in Cologne; she spoke fluent Greek and German and some English. The better hotels were booked on Mykonos, the island where we were all heading. As soon as we left the airplane, annoying men stuck hard-backed, plastic-coated brochures of cheap hotels into our faces. From their number, Ursula selected a hotel overlooking the water and gave me the address. I had taken care to book a room at a good hotel, where, on my arrival, I was told that my reservation was lost, there were no vacancies, and, sorry, the woman who handles these things has gone to Athens to see her dentist. I ended up at an inexpensive hotel where I made friends with a man who, despite his predominantly American accent, said he was an Englishman who had declined the title of Lord Such and Such in favor of his son. We found we had common acquaintances. He talked me into trying his London tailor, Huntsman, though it would be years before I'd have the chance to act on it. He offered a provocative autobiographical comment: "My mother, whom I despise, was a du Pont." He kept a stash of chilled retsina in his room, and his favorite line was, "Wait while I get a refill." You just had to like the guy.

The hotel had been shown to me by a sweaty man with a day's growth of black beard. Because she had borne him only two children, he had thrown over his wife in favor of a younger woman, who he insisted would bear three more. The ex-wife ran the place with the tireless help of a teenage daughter while the ex-husband trolled for customers at the airport, a job requiring little skill or sobriety and thus suiting his talents to their fullest. The hotel had only a double room to offer, requiring that I pay for two, but the ex-husband, with a pimp's prurient grin, predicted that I would rake in a woman from a beach or bar soon enough.

When I walked in on Ursula and her party, chatting in a room at their hotel nearby, I was received as an old, returning friend. For the next three days, we traveled as a group, to the beaches, to the nightclubs and tavernas, to the Burnt-Out Corner, a small restaurant that the Englishman had promised served the best moussaka in Greece. Because we had three rooms in two closely situated hotels, and because Stefanos and Katrina wanted to cohabit, and because Ursula deserved a room of her own, I had Zoë for a houseguest. She took the spare bed the ex-husband had encouraged me to fill with a woman, but she refused all intimate contact due to a boyfriend named Phillip. Ursula and I became friends during walks up the long path from town. We bonded over the desecration of our footwear by the gravel: it ruined her Gucci sandals and ripped open one of my loafers.

On an island overpopulated with the young and beautiful, Katrina stood out. She had long, brown hair, high cheekbones, and clever, quick eyes. She was among the few women I have ever met who could justifiably be called sultry. Men stared at her; a chiseled, slim American lesbian with a large telephoto lens on her camera made a heartfelt try for her. On the beach, Katrina wore only a red thong and was indeed a sight to behold. She was also smart, well educated, multilingual, had fine taste in clothes—and was a heroin addict.

I did not know that pivotal fact. A cover story had been devised concerning the large bandage on Katrina's arm, which hid track marks and an infection from a contaminated needle. Every evening, Ursula secretly and carefully redressed the wound.

In the four years between our meeting on that island and this visit to Switzerland, Ursula had shared with me the story of Katrina's affliction, of treatments sought across Europe. Her addiction had begun in Florence out of, Ursula believed, curiosity for thrills. It was a paradox of Switzerland that, amid its affluence, a drug scene of unimagined depth and openness flourished; that addicts congregated openly in a designated section of the park behind the Zurich Hauptbahnhof; and that, as AIDS spread, workers dispensed clean needles and what health advice would be listened to. A nation doesn't need a legacy of war to breed within it a strain of self-destruction; many of the addicts, like Katrina, came from leading families or the merely affluent.

Chapter 20

I had not seen Katrina since Greece. She had married a man from Yugoslavia (as it was then known) and, two weeks before my arrival, had given birth to a son named Jürgen. In the foyer of her parents' house, Katrina gave me that looking-through-you stare of hers, the kind that made you understand she was sizing up the sort of man you were. She shrugged off childbirth as I had seen her do with lesser disruptions: it happened, it was over, she felt fine, her son was a blessing. I hadn't met Radomir before, and I greeted a curious-looking fellow with dark hair cut rather short on the sides but cascading down his shoulders. He wore a funky, unconstructed jacket and black patent leather shoes that came to points like lance blades. He demonstrated a command of European literature. He said that every place has its own madness, be it the United States or Yugoslavia. On the latter, he was to prove eerily prescient, as civil war and atrocity were only a few years off. Radomir was smart and odd in that eastern European way that sees life as surreal, searches for its meaning, and obligingly accepts that the search is futile.

Katrina and Radomir had met in Heidelberg, while she was in a rehabilitation program. Radomir had to extricate himself from a marriage of convenience to a German woman, solemnized to avoid repatriation to Yugoslavia. There was something about a Yugoslavian official and the timely gift of a bottle of whiskey. Radomir did not have a drug problem. He adored his two-week-old son, a little ball sprouting thin, black hair. He had not, however, done much about finding a job.

The Rossi sisters were not living on equal terms. Paula had worked and her husband, Kurt, was making a mark for himself at an international bank—a young man to watch. He was now at home, nursing the pains of a tooth extraction, but he was said to be thrilled that Paula was to bear their first child. Ursula's husband, Antonio, was a hardworking businessman who came from the Italian-speaking canton, the Ticino. He had left a conference in Baden-Baden at eight that morning on little sleep, driving through fog and past the wreckage of road accidents to get into his office and a full day of work. Now he had to host the family and me. He was a key man at a major pharmaceutical company and first in line to take over as chief executive officer.

We sat down to a table in which the common language was fluent English, enjoying quail eggs and quail, all cooked by Ursula. We adjourned to a coffee table and to chestnuts Ursula had picked herself during one of her beloved golfing excursions. I chased them with a local beverage: liquid fire known as Williams pear brandy. If you are ever stuck at the top of K2 in a blizzard, open a Williams.

Neither Katrina, Ursula, nor I could remember the name of the Greek woman from Cologne who had been with us on Mykonos, the one I've here called Zoë. Katrina said that the empty bed in my room had proven of great utility when she and the Greek man had decided to keep company. "At first the girl didn't like the idea of sharing your room," said Katrina. "She asked what she should do. I said, 'Just tell him you have a boyfriend named Phillip.'"

Chapter 21

The next day, Ursula picked me up in her small Ford. We took the scenic route along an open road tracing the villa-studded shore of Lake Zurich, then stopped at Rapperswil, which was as quaint and pristine as a Swiss castle town should be. There was a deer park on the castle grounds, and Ursula, who was born in Bremen and spoke fine German, showed her command of the incomprehensible local dialect by wooing Swiss deer. They came over to listen while Ursula lectured them on their beauty. There was a lawyers' luncheon in the castle. Because so many lawyers would ruin our appetites, we felt, we ate nearby at a place that had simplified its menu to two main courses: fish schnitzel or swine schnitzel. I went for the latter, a bowl of vegetable soup, and walnut ice cream.

I like talking to women about women. I like it more than talking to men about women. Men end up agreeing with each other about what princes we are for putting up with women. As a generality, the point of view has merits, but as a method of dealing with a problem that is solvable or accepting the consequences of one that is not, it has limitations. It takes an insightful woman to hear the feminine dialect that is incomprehensible to men, especially when it is spoken by a woman of few words, like Elena.

"I only saw her when we got together in New York last year," said Ursula, "but we had some time together, didn't we?"

"Enough time to form an opinion?"

"I'll tell you, I thought she was immature. You see this here all the time with people who come from the east of Europe. Not all of them, but with some it is like a sickness. They must have all the things—the cars, the clothes, the houses—and they can never have enough. That is the impression she made. Americans are willing to cross social lines, which is admirable. But you can't make yourself into someone else's checkbook, because then something else enters the picture that isn't entirely about love and honor."

"What is it?"

"Opportunity. In America, there is too much. With two sticks, you can make a fire; with a fire and a chicken, you can make dinner. Americans can have the whole farm, but then what do they to do with it?"

Back at the Rossi house, a single quail rested on a plate on the kitchen counter, a relic of the evening's meal. How curious to be in the kitchen from which Ursula's fine dinner had come, to see it now in daylight, its tricks revealed in its utensils and the wrapped leftovers and that last remaining quail. A great meal should be like seduction, and seeing a kitchen by day is like waking for breakfast with your lover of the night before: the black dress traded for one of your T-shirts, the mystery exchanged for honesty.

Radomir was home, dressed in floppy pantaloons and green high-laced sneakers. He held Jürgen, tenderly cradling his head. The baby wore an outfit knitted by Ursula. Katrina was somewhere on the town with friends, Radomir said nonchalantly. Ursula stirred slightly when she heard that, then recovered. For all her reform, Katrina was not yet ready to fly solo. Radomir carried his son into another room, where he kept a guitar to play for him and books to read to him. I quietly told Ursula that I thought Radomir could be a good father but that, in the end, she might end up raising her grandson herself.

I returned to Zurich in a company car loaned by Antonio. It was a Chevrolet, which the driver extolled most of the trip, saying he preferred it to any Mercedes. I was going to have dinner at the riverfront Hotel Zum Storchen, which I'd enjoyed before, but the more I pictured myself sitting along the terrace, eating an expensive, monastic meal, the more the mental image repelled me.

Instead, I had a simple dinner at the Krone for less than the price of an appetizer at the Zum Storchen. I was the only one dining alone. How moronic, I thought, to traverse Europe on my own, seeking the companionship of friends in five diverse cities. One ticket, please. Table for one. A single room without bath. A claret is fine, thank you; do you have half bottles? I wanted to telephone Elena, but I didn't. I finished my meal, took a walk, and went to bed.

Chapter 22

Courtesy of a voucher from Icelandair, I had a place in a partially filled second-class compartment on the train from Basel to Luxembourg City. It was not a bed, it was not a Liegeplatz. It was an ordinary upright seat, a *Sitzplatz*, but what did you expect for fifteen bucks? A young German came in and I answered sure, you can have the window if you're going farther than I am. As he knew, and I did not, he would have a fair chance at getting some sleep; for me it would now be a question of luck. For a night-train companion, he was quite neighborly. He said he was a hospital orderly. He had just finished vacationing in youth hostels and, with a two-day growth of wheat-colored beard and rumpled clothing, had the shabbiness to prove it. He asked what I did for a living and when I told him, he looked at me incredulously. "Excuse me," he said politely, "but, in America, a lawyer makes a lot of money, right?"

I had only to look at myself in the bathroom mirror to observe the worn face, the stubble, and the rumpled clothing to understand why the orderly had approached me with such camaraderie. I liked to boast that, if you don't at some point during a trip end up cold, tired, hungry, and wrinkled, you've done something wrong. I was traveling as a young man should; every sight and sound resonated with a newly discovered truth. The face in the mirror, no longer in its first youth, now stared back at me, pale and wan, pleading for the five-star comforts of middle age.

Another visitor in the cabin was a sweet, fretful, rather loud woman aged about fifty. She spoke in French, then broken English, then revealed that she was born in Germany, and so we found a common language. She intermittently disturbed the sleep of the orderly and fairly well kept me up much of the abbreviated night, for the ride ended at 4:33 A.M. at the *Gare Centrale*, Luxembourg City.

I invited the woman, whose name was Maria, to a predawn breakfast at the station's dreary buffet. We talked until it was time for her to catch the 5:39 to visit her mother in Germany. Maria was married to a Frenchman with a Hungarian last name who worked in Geneva, but her own family was from East Prussia. When the Russians marched through in 1945, they demanded that her grandfather surrender his watch, and when he had none, they punished him with a bullet through the head. She asked about my family history, and when I told her, she said she was sympathetic to the Jews. I helped get her luggage aboard her train, she chatting all the while about how I must make it to Beaujolais on September 15 next year for the new wine. Her conversation was a shield; she wanted to talk to anyone about anything. Had she not a train to catch, Maria would have held me with a discourse on postage stamps or turnips. Unlike Steffi, who squandered her anxiety on aggressiveness, Maria had internalized hers, and in that sacrifice had molded it into suffering.

I had a wet, early-morning walking tour of Luxembourg City, collected my bags and, at the bus stop outside the station, met a middle-aged Jewish couple from my part of the world. The husband thought it was marvelous that I'd saved all that money and time by taking an early-evening train from Zurich to Basel, then the night train here. The wife, fearing inspiration, said, "And it would have cost you a thousand dollars to put me in the hospital afterward!" It must have been a point worth emphasizing, because when I saw them again by chance at the airport, she was emphatically repeating the phrase.

I had sympathy for the wife's misgivings. In the fifteen nights I had been away from home, I had spent only ten in stationary beds. It was an amazingly stupid thing to do with a set of matching luggage filled with custom-made clothing and a fistful of unspent traveler's checks. But I'd done what I'd set out to do: I'd journeyed, seen old friends, and, since I also hoped to start a career as a travel writer, collected material for articles. On the stopover in Reykjavik, I bought a shearling jacket that cost more than what I had saved on hotels.

I shared a taxi from the airport with a couple from the Upper East Side. The cabbie said the world would soon end, so he had given up sex in favor of masturbation. He still managed to look after himself and had lost twenty-five pounds on a diet of tuna fish and carrots. His dashboard held plastic figurines and a television set, which he watched as he drove. It was good to be home again.

Chapter 23

No message from Elena on my answering machine. No reply in the mailbox to the six-thousand-word letter I had left her before departing. I called and she wasn't home. It was a long trip to take to work through the pain of an inevitable event that hadn't yet happened; I'd still have to wait for it. What did greet me was the recorded message from the travel editor of the *Oakland Tribune*, informing me that my first travel story—on Oxford and Cambridge—had been accepted.

Elena called the day after I arrived, invited me to lunch, which she consumed with her usual solemnity, saving to the end the news that we were through. It upset me terribly, despite being no surprise.

Good friends looked after me as best they could. One, a bisexual woman, took me to a strip joint one night. She showed me how to put a dollar bill into a girl's garter belt, a move that she accomplished with such dexterity and sincere respect, it was the most eye-catching event of the evening.

My travel articles from the trip appeared in newspapers around the United States. I was in business.

Wretched Excess

Chapter 1

That summer, I was back in Genoa, at the Bacchellis' mosaic-lined foyer. A scurry of feet brought Enrico, in his pajamas, crashing into my legs for a hug. This earned him a Garfield watch and a toy car I'd picked up in Lübeck the week before. The car was soon spinning into the legs of heirloom chairs. When not so imperiling his inheritance, Enrico showed great attention to his little brother, Ferdinando, who had grown big for his age. Enrico brought the playpen into the dining room to aid the parental night watch, Ferdinando standing upright, riding as if in the basket of a hot-air balloon. Big brother then hauled out little brother and presented him to their parents as if they had just adopted him.

The parents had more to do this time because Jennifer, the nanny from Scotland, had left prematurely, having fallen in love with an Italian. Lorenza said that British girls who signed on for one-year stints were routinely lost in this manner in half that time. Helping out temporarily was Lorenza's mother, Clara. We sat down to one of Lorenza's brilliant dinners, and when the conversation came to what had happened between Elena and me, I apologized to Clara for what would be a windy tale in English, which was not a language she knew. With a grandmotherly smile she said she liked a love story. I'm sure my narrative disappointed her.

The ending wasn't happy, it wasn't teary, it wasn't poignant; it was the common mud of everyday life.

I ate breakfast the next morning at one of those crowded places where Italians take their coffee and pastry while standing and the cappuccino machine perpetually clears its throat. People arrived every few seconds, hair still moist, cologne fresh, warming to the discipline of a workday morning. Language was again a problem, but I was rescued by a young woman named Daniela. She alit from heaven, spouting basic English and then excellent German. There was nothing that, from a distance, would set her apart from any of the other just-woken women offering good money for a jolt of caffeine. But I caught the quick, penetrating eyes of a serious intellect, and when Daniela talked to me, the lashes opened like a butterfly's wings, the quick eyes growing wide and inviting. Daniela helped me order, we started talking, I abandoned a planned day trip to Rapallo and invited her to lunch.

She said yes, but when the hour came, she stood me up. She telephoned and explained that her boyfriend had surprised her with lunch. I suggested we meet for breakfast "at the same place," and she agreed.

That opened time for Rapallo. At the train station, I bought a second-class ticket. Despite numerous queries and double checks about which platform to stand on, a sudden change in routing (announced in Italian) had me unintentionally boarding a train going the opposite way—to a rain-splattered town called Voghera. I waited at its dreary station for a returning train, watching a brown, rivet-studded locomotive from the Fascist era lug away a caravan of freight, water drops cascading from its flanks onto the rain-blackened crossties. Other travelers were killing time with comic books the size of paperback novels. The return train was a local, but the conductor was sympathetic and did not charge for my repatriation. A young, dark-haired man standing at my car's forward doorway winked at me and sent air kisses with sustained, unrequited affection. The car smelled foul.

We arrived in Genoa. Because of the lost time, I shifted my destination to Portofino, but my train was again shuffled like the queen in three-card monte. I was on to the trick now and made it to the proper track for the local to Santa Margherita Ligure. From there, it was a taxi ride to Portofino, a fishing village in which rustic boats had long ago been replaced in the horseshoe harbor by yachts. There was an Hermès shop for the general run of traveler and a Benneton for the budget minded. In front of a pink-walled hotel in the harbor, a small party drank iced Moët & Chandon and beckoned me to join in.

The only man among them was a Swiss named Kaspar; in his late thirties, he had an oval face, soft chin, receding hair, and, at least during our conversation, no paramount sign of intelligence. Another of the group was British; I don't think I got her name. The remaining three were Scandinavians. Astrid was middle aged and gregarious. Hilda was very chic in white, black, and gray, topping it with a clever, wide-brimmed hat. She was already drunk and had lipstick on the end of her nose for a very long time until someone rubbed it away for her. Liv was a twenty-four-year-old blond medical student. I got the idea that she wasn't nearly as rich as the others; she was certainly nowhere near as drunk and very much more beautiful. The British woman and the Scandinavians spoke with faintly Oxford accents. They invited me to dinner at an outdoor table, and I joined them for an expensive, undercooked veal cutlet.

Evening descended, the few harbor lights glowed for no one, and dinner lingered on. I hadn't before seen Portofino so desolate in summer. It was disquieting. Nobody was around; the masts of the ships stood upright, untroubled by even a trace of wind. At this, the only active table in town, conversation was frenetic, opinionated, and insipid until I said that my next destination was Monte Carlo. "Excellent," said Astrid. "We are going there too." I said it would be fun to hook up in Monte Carlo. Agreed, said Astrid, "but you must first pass the night here." She made it sound like a test for admission. She said that, on the same day I was to leave for Monte Carlo, the four women were migrating there in a rented BMW. The car, she noted, had room for one more. The idea was intriguing, but there was something desperate and flippant about this sudden generosity; I said only that I would get back to Astrid the next morning. I exchanged hotel telephone numbers with her, and she said, "I get up at six every day. Call me as soon as you wake in the morning." I agreed, but I had missed a signal and, in frustration, Astrid raised the flag higher. She now insisted that I stay in Portofino. I declined, adding that my clothes were in a hotel in Genoa. Astrid tried again, had no greater success, grew irritable, then angry. I missed the first part of what she said but caught, "I don't like liars."

The table fell quiet; the next move was entirely mine. I said I had no place to stay in Portofino. Astrid said I could share her room. She could take the mattress off her bed, and I could have the box spring. She acted as if this were as common an invitation as the one that brought me to dinner, and that I would be offending her not to accept. I asked if the ride to Monte Carlo was still on if I declined. "Maybe we'll find someone else before then," said Astrid. "Leave if you don't mind having other men along." I said, if I was going to call her in the morning, what was her last name? "Who needs last names?" she replied. "I'm Astrid."

The curse and the blessing of places like Portofino is that they get to be chic and they stay chic because they are difficult to reach. There was no train service; the last bus to Santa Margherita's railroad station was the 10:10, and I hadn't seen any taxis. If I didn't make the last bus, I would likely miss my 7:30 A.M. rendezvous with Daniela, yet I would be unable to reach her with an explanation. She had missed our last appointment, and she had been sorry. Perhaps she would imagine I was getting back at her.

I hadn't had a woman since landing in Germany the week before—intolerable abstinence for me in those days—but I felt stirring within me a quality new and strange. I think now that it goes by the name of maturity. I placed money on the table to cover my dinner, bade my farewells, and headed for the last bus, by now stationed, silent and illuminated, somewhere atop the hill. From behind, a voice called out. I turned, and the entire table was frozen as if in tableau, looking at me as might children at the departure of a dog they'd found, only to see him taken away by his master. "Good-bye, friends," I shouted, and then I ran. I went the wrong way, lost in a desolate alley. One minute to go. Back and around. I had to find that bus. I wanted that bus. There it was: little more than a jitney, in bright orange, its interior lights yellow and harsh. The driver and passengers were seated, waiting as if for a performance to start. I jumped on board, and, as I fell into a bench, the engine sputtered to life.

I awoke in the night, wondering if I'd made a mistake in not taking advantage of such an easy situation. If I hadn't promised to see Daniela, I probably would have stayed and—then what? Satisfying Astrid was a job requirement. She was older than I, she was a heavy drinker, and she was unlikable, but when had that ever stopped me? Hilda wasn't looking like a lady eager to sleep alone either. Hadn't no less a light than Benjamin Franklin expostulated on the delights of older women? Good sense said I should not call Astrid, but my curiosity was boundless.

It's like that with me. Even in my worst despair I want the next day to dawn, just to see what will happen. I want to grab the world and shake it. I want the world to know who I am and that I am a part of it. We each get a fixed number of days, and if there is no heaven, every day matters in the extreme. You can look back on your days as might a diarist, and for any day that drifts by without a worthy event to mark it, you might just as well rip out the page and number it among the uncountable years you will spend in death. The reason that I want to live and the reason I want to travel are one and the same. Deeply private Elena used to chastise me for "never refusing a party," which, though not accurate, I'd have thought to be a compliment. I wanted to spend my life with a woman who enjoyed the act of living as much as I did, and while there were enough women to keep me entertained until that time, I had to start tightening my standards. Which meant I should let it go and get some sleep.

Early in the morning, however, my curiosity, predictably, woke me again. At just after six, I rang Astrid's hotel, as instructed. I had trouble getting a desk clerk, and the one I found didn't speak English. I went downstairs and enlisted my hotel's night clerk. He called, and after some conversation over the line, told me to pick up the extension in the phone booth. When I did, it went dead. We tried calling twice more, finally to be told that the clerk on the other end had been instructed to take no calls before noon. I left a message and was at the breakfast place at seven-thirty.

By seven-fifty, Daniela hadn't arrived. When it looked as if she would stand me up again, I realized she had misinterpreted my request to meet "at the same place." I found her at a newsstand we had visited the morning before. She had arranged to start work late in order to be with me. I was very glad I had kept the appointment.

We sat on a park bench, having our breakfast, talking about Judaism, because Daniela had pegged me for an American Jew by my German last name. She had long found the religion intriguing, but there were so few Jews in Italy to ask questions about it, would I mind clarifying a few points? For instance, she had Jewish friends who said you can "feel" Jewish without being religious. Did I think this was possible? I said that, with Judaism, nearly all contradictions are sustainable. I had to believe that Italian girls weren't given courses in Jewish history; Daniela's intellectual and social inquisitiveness was self-generated. In the end, we agreed that Daniela would write to me in German and I to her in English. She would translate for me one of the poems she had written in Italian. I took her picture.

Chapter 2

The lovesick man on the malodorous train from Voghera was enough to swear me off economy travel in Italy. With a first-class ticket in my camera bag, I boarded a train for Monte Carlo. I lost track of the Colombian couple I had been speaking to on the platform and shared a compartment with a very proper, gray-haired signora, who had taken the opposite window seat, reading a large hardcover. Next to her was a Canadian couple, and next to me was a pair of Americans; they were all in shorts and running shoes. The standard Eurailpass was valid for first-class travel, so it was not uncommon for young North American backpackers to cohabit compartments with finely dressed, middle-aged Europeans like the signora.

The Canadian woman had removed her running shoes and hoisted her bare feet onto her seat, all but sticking them into the signora's immaculately pressed cotton skirt. The signora squeezed so close to the window that if it were the slightest bit malleable, she'd have left her impression in it. I suggested to the Canadian that her bare feet may be causing offense. "What does she expect me to do with them?" she replied with such bewilderment, you would have thought that the floor could not have been an option. A compromise was obtained: she shifted her feet to the other side of her seat, pressing them against her lover. As the train jostled along the Mediterranean coast, I picked a bag of German chocolates from my bag and offered them around. When I came to the signora, she was as if transformed. Forty years fell from her face; she was a young woman again, coyly accepting a man's gift.

Then the Colombians appeared, saying they'd found me at last and had saved me a seat. I greeted them as rescuers and repaired to their compartment, receiving a smile and a good-bye from the signora. Sharing my new digs was a Frenchwoman of about my age. Having lived for seven years in Los Angeles, she spoke English with little accent. We all looked out upon beaches filled with umbrellas, lounge chairs, and children splashing in the glistening Mediterranean. Small towns slid by; pedestrians and adolescents on scooters were stopped at the white railroad-crossing barriers, staring back at us with the mixture of fascination and dull acceptance that the temporary blockade of a passing train will induce. It's like watching the Zamboni machine clear an ice rink; you can't help yourself, and you feel an inexplicable sense of accomplishment when it is done.

Isabelle, the Frenchwoman, talked me out of Monte Carlo. Too expensive, she said. I should stay on for Nice, and she'd come over and show me around.

Chapter 3

I flirted with the idea of booking a room at the Negresco, the signature facade of the Côte d'Azur, but fine restaurants and luxury hotels depressed me whenever I was on my own. It was as if, were I to shell out for the Negresco, I would be obliged to enjoy myself, and that, should I instead have a bad time in good surroundings, I would thereby have failed utterly. If I were to take a modest room, however, enjoyment, solicited but not demanded, might yet come my way.

I got myself only as far as a self-guided tour of the Negresco lobby, where I asked a tall black man dressed in a comical getup, like that of a circus ringmaster, where I might find a bathroom. He directed me to a men's room fantastically decorated like the quarters of a Napoleonic officer. When I returned to use it one evening, the ringmaster barred me from entry; a curfew was in place for nonguests. I promised myself that if I should ever travel here again with someone I loved, this hotel and that bathroom would be mine to enjoy.

A knowledgeable couple I'd met earlier had recommended I take the other extreme, naming a lowly one-star hotel. It turned out to be the fourth floor of a commercial building. The outsized vases at the entrance revealed themselves, at close range, to be trash barrels. A dingy old woman at the desk showed me to a dingy old room. An Arab with pockmarked skin and shaggy hair eyed me as if I were lunch meat.

I decided that this was rejecting one problem only to skip into the arms of its evil twin. An American couple visibly shaken by what they too had seen suggested a two-star place nearby. Its lobby looked pleasant enough, and as I waited in line, I noticed a stand-up card at the desk:

Hôtel des Flandres
Madame Schwartzberg
Propriétaire

Translation: Mrs. Schwartzberg's place. How bad could it be? The Schwartzberg family consisted of Madame, her husband, and their teenage son. They had fled from Lorraine when the xenophobic National Front of Jean-Marie Le Pen had gained political strength there. You forget, living in New York, that a native-born Jew can yet be considered a foreigner.

The Schwartzbergs were curious about my German name. I gave the facts: father fleeing Nazis in 1937, mother doing same in 1934. It took a day or two for the son to venture, "My mother wants you to say you're Jewish."

"Okay," I said. "I'm Jewish." I'd thought it had been obvious, but at once character of the relationship changed. The Schwartzbergs confessed—secret of secrets—that they too were Jewish and granted me perquisites of the international Zionist conspiracy: warm conversation (mostly in German, our best common language), some raspberry liquor to help nurse a head cold, a pair of beach towels. They said that one-quarter of Nice had voted for Le Pen, mostly in reaction to the Arabs in Marseilles, but a Jew could never be too careful. It was like that sometimes in France. What could you do?

With the hotel as home, surrogate family and all, I added the comforts of fruit, bread, and bottled water, and set out one morning to get the washing done. The man at the laundry said he spoke "a little English." His fluency increased as I talked to him, there being nothing else for either of us to do while his wife finished ironing my shirt. It turned out he was from Montreal and spoke very good English indeed. I said that his wife was in luck; those British shirts were easy to iron.

"How do you know?" he asked.

"I iron them," I said.

"You have no wife?"

"No."

He considered this and nodded. "Good. You're better off." He translated other portions of the conversation for the lady's enjoyment while she labored.

Isabelle, my companion from the train, came around as promised. She worked at the Hotel Loews Monte-Carlo. She was plainly good at her job, being skilled at making pleasant conversation but careful to hold back details. Yet she had a melancholy air. It was not the sourness endemic to Parisian women, especially the affluent ones; it was the pain of loss. Isabelle kept me guessing about her story until we shared lunch one afternoon at a restaurant on the too-precious hilltop village of Eze. There she told how she had been engaged to a California restaurateur killed three years before in the helicopter he was piloting. His death had sent her back to France in despair. She said she would never feel love so intensely again.

Isabelle now had a lover in Brussels who split his affections between her and his wife. She knew a number of other men throughout Europe; they appeared to have no common trait except wealth. She did not care much for the company of women, especially the married ones, who had everything and yet managed to complain constantly. "I never want to be that kind of pest," she explained. She was only thirty and rather attractive in a stocky, almost earthy way, and I told her that everything would be all right in time. "You think so?" she asked with genuine curiosity. She concluded with the Californian's gesture of palming car keys as if they were her rosary.

All the cars in Villefranche-sur-Mer were mottled with mud from squalls. The mud was thick and brown on the windshields, which were clear only where the wipers had done their work. Another squall came, and Isabelle and I waited at a café while the rain fell as thick as splattering paint. Isabelle said that thunder scared her. She drove to work, and when the sun returned I walked the beach.

Chapter 4

In the backward world of nineteenth-century Europe, people went to the Alps in the summer for their health. The hotels in St.-Moritz and Zermatt closed for the winter because their customers were at the seashore. Hotels in Nice and Antibes closed for the summer when their customers returned to the Alps. If the sun should be braved, it was with hat and, for women of breeding, parasol, the better to preserve a fashionable alabaster complexion. Skin cancer was not a scourge of the leisure class, and beach volleyball was not an Olympic sport. In 1864, however, a Swiss hotelier named Johannes Badrutt convinced his English guests—one version of the story includes Americans—to take a money-back guarantee to stay for the winter. His guests returned to snowy St.-Moritz, and resort history was made. Skiing was soon brought down from Scandinavia—a lucky move for vacationers, because there wasn't much doing in the Alps in those years if you weren't a dairy farmer or a tuberculosis patient.

In time, the Mediterranean became fashionable in the hot months. Swimming it is not overly fun for Americans, with their fondness for sand the color and consistency of confectioner's sugar. Much of the sea's northern coast is lined with water-rounded gravel, requiring sunbathers to lie on straw mats rolled out like prayer rugs and walk gingerly into the surf, as if climbing over rubble.

Beaches bore me as a rule. I rate them not by sand, sun, or water but by the number of beautiful women in the highest degree of undress. On the perfect beach, the world's top fashion models have gained weight and swim nude. On my scale, therefore, the crowded, rocky, narrow beachfront of Nice rated very highly. Here I could contentedly observe bare breasts and barely covered backsides the way that a scientist on the shore of Antarctica might study emperor penguins.

Above the wide, horseshoe beach of Villefranche-sur-Mer ran a walkway quietly garrisoned by big, shy men in cheap clothes. One braved a chat with an American girl who wore a green bikini bottom, but the others held to their communal silence. Their gray ship, anchored off shore, was U.S. Navy and womanless. Anyone worried that our servicemen are hell-raisers on shore, tearing apart brothels and throwing up in alleys, would have been proud to have seen those quiet young men, gawking, not knowing what to do, one nervously whispering to a colleague, "Whooee! I've died and gone to heaven."

I don't have anything else to say about the beaches of the Riviera; they were all sand, water, and tits. Nine years later, however, a copy of *Der Spiegel* I had been reading fell open to a picture I recognized as one I had taken on that trip: a bare-breasted sunbather. The photograph illustrated a story on melanoma. It had been a slow news week in Germany.

Chapter 5

I finally saw Monaco, though only for an evening and only the casino. I dressed as if for work: gray suit, white shirt, tie. Like Gaul, the casino was divided into three parts. The large front room was vastly out of human scale, choked with zinging and clanging machines of all shapes and descriptions, flickering, colored lights, coins falling into slots. I was nearly thrown out then and there, because I took a Leica rigged for low-light work from under my suit jacket and got off two shots at maximum aperture before the cops were on me. Much effort is made to help you forget that Monaco is an absolute monarchy—until you break the rules. The gambling patrol let me off with a bilingual warning; in a nation of tax exiles and wealthy visitors, one does not lightly arrest the correctly dressed.

That first room was for the gambling proletariat, who spent their earnings in one-franc coins. The second room was for the middle class. It was quieter and featured American roulette and, I believe, blackjack. The croupiers wore black pants and midblue vests, giving a sentimental, Wild West music-hall air to their work. An entrance fee of fifty francs got me into the third room. The croupiers here wore midblue shawl-collared evening jackets. Guards were posted, their tan uniforms fitted with dark green cuffs and epaulets. Across the baccarat tables, sallow-faced men and women pitched around five-hundred-franc notes like so many paper napkins. Unlike other rooms, where everyone went casual, the male gamblers here were as scrupulously overdressed for the heat as was I. A few were doing passable James Bond imitations, down to the attractive, faintly worn woman appended to one shoulder. A middle-aged woman with jet-black hair studied her hand through half glasses as if all hope would be lost if she should fail, yet she bore herself with such resignation, you understood that failure of some kind was inevitable. I went to the cashier and exchanged twenty francs in coins for a single chip—the minimum for a play at roulette. I placed my chip on my age (thirty-three), the croupier spun the wheel, and it came up zero. It was the largest single wager I had ever made on a game of chance and remains so to this day. There is no escaping the tawdry nature of gambling, the sucking reflex it induces in those who win and the desperation it induces in those who cannot. It's like prostitution, that other victimless crime: however respectable it is made, however tarted up the tart shall be, an air of seediness pervades, because the method is to exploit weakness and desire.

As curious as the evening's conclusion seemed to me, it was nothing compared to what had happened at the hot and humid railroad station in Nice while I'd waited for the train to Monaco. The solstice sun was still low in the evening sky. Standing against a pillar, looking familiar but not quite himself, was a shabby man with a two-day stubble and his shirttails hanging loose. He was chatting up two girls; while I ate ice cream, I watched his losing combat with their good sense. He recognized me and approached. It was Kaspar, the Swiss from the night in Portofino. He knew he looked in need of a bath and a rest and explained it away as the effects of seasickness. He, his father, and brother had just turned in the boat they had rented and were soon bound for home.

"I have to tell you what happened after you left that evening," he said, widening his eyes and obviously revving up for the kind of story you hear in locker rooms. "That Astrid. I tell you. She would have been a nice girl if she wasn't crazy." He laughed at his own wit. "Astrid was very angry because you had rejected her. She said to me, 'Kaspar, you must get me another man.' I said, 'How, please, am I to do this?' She said, 'That is for you to figure out.' What could I do? I went to get my brother and said this woman wanted a man, how about you, maybe? By the time I brought him back, there was much more drinking, and Astrid was very unpleasant, saying some bad things. My brother, he liked to get to know the young one, Liv. They were in a bar, and the other men were wanting to meet Liv too, and this got Astrid so angry, she hit with her hand across Liv's face. She said she was paying for Liv to be here and she said, 'Don't come back to the hotel. I want nothing more with you.' The girl was crying. It was terrible."

"Did anyone try to help her?"

"Who could? Hilda was so drunk, I had to hold her up and carry her like laundry to the hotel."

Somehow, they all made it back—just before I'd telephoned at about 6 A.M. There were no phones in the rooms, and Astrid, either hung over or still drunk and by now in a fury over getting shot down twice in the same evening, was roused from her bed to take the call at the front desk. She was heard from above, screaming her rage at the desk clerk.

Chapter 6

Word had gotten out in Germany that I was a soft touch, and large men with backpacks would appear on short notice at my apartment in New York. There was the time, while a nice young couple from the Pfalz was spending their final evening with me, that I was handed a letter by the concierge. The envelope was labeled EILZUSTELLUNG (special delivery). I recognized Susanne's diligent scrawl: ". . . boyfriend Peter is coming to New York City with his sister Biggi . . . need a place to stay, so if you have any ideas . . . sorry I can't come. Tschüß!" The time of arrival was the following evening.

The next day, the young couple left, and Peter appeared with Biggi, who spoke superb English. Brother and sister then went cross-country, through canyons and deserts and past all those natural wonders I still aim to see one day. It was in Washington Square Park, however, that they entered the history books, if rather anonymously, by participating in the biggest Hokey Pokey danced in all the world.

As London had been for me in the previous decade, Hamburg was becoming a second home, in large measure because of my friends there. I went back in October 1989, having flown in from Berlin. The Berlin Wall was a scar slashed through the city, causing many who came to it for the first time to stand in silence and causing residents who knew it well to hush their voices as they drew near. East German guards on the towers stared coldly at the tourists gawking back at them. I came away thinking the wall would be there for generations. Two weeks later, people would be dancing on it and drinking champagne.

I told my dead-wrong prediction about the wall to Heinrich von Gronau, who, with little Gabriele, picked me up at my hotel. Gabriele had grown from a cooing five-month-old into a toddler, her place in the crib being superseded by a baby sister. From her child's seat in the Range Rover, Gabriele occasionally interrupted adult conversation with queries concerning Mommy, playthings, and other facts of present importance. When her father did not attend to her in quite the way she liked, she called out softly, "Papa?" No reply being made, she raised her voice to say, "Papi?" And when that drew no response, she yelled, "Heinrich!"

I sat on the floor of the house in Blankenese, catching up with Heinrich and Eveline, Gabriele crawling over and through my legs. Eveline was dressed in the mode, three earrings running in a row down her left ear. Heinrich changed into the universal after-hours dress of northern Germany, applicable to both sexes: jeans, cotton shirt, sweater (optional), and waist-length brown (never black) leather jacket. Then the baby-sitter came.

Back into the Range Rover I went with Heinrich and Eveline, and on to the restaurant, which wore the sign GESCHLOSSENES GESELLSCHAFT, meaning the place was given over to a private party. We tried a second venue, and the same thing happened, and then a third, where the frustration repeated itself. "Heinrich is very particular," Eveline explained. "He must go to the newest and best restaurants," which was apparently what everyone else in Hamburg intended, but "for me is it not so important." We found one on the fourth try.

I was sharing stories about Berlin when Eveline asked about my love life. There is a smug yet pathetic quality to the dating anecdotes of a bachelor sliding toward his middle years. You can't help but look at a man who is of the age when most men are settled in life and not wonder, with at least a tinge of disrespect, why he follows a pattern grounded in adolescence. If I had been honest with Eveline, I would have told her how lonely I was. We switched, instead, to questions of European politics.

We ended the night at a bar on the Reeperbahn, carefully and expertly chosen by Heinrich for its being of the moment—and open. It was a lively place, crammed and smoky and filled with the rough laughter of Nordic libation.

The Reeperbahn is the great thoroughfare of St. Pauli, which was and, despite the labors of other claimants, remains the preeminent red-light district of Europe. I could appreciate it more for having lived in New Orleans, another city where tawdry entertainment is integrated into the social fabric, and where, as in Hamburg, a fine restaurant may be located convenient steps away from a brothel. St. Pauli also incorporates elements familiar from Las Vegas (modern architecture, expansive proportions) and Amsterdam's red-light district (women openly available for rent).

It has been this way because Hamburg is a liberal city. I use the word *liberal* carefully. For Americans, it conjures up the image of the earnest college student determined to make the world a better place, of the academic who scorns the wealth generated by simpler minds, of the man born rich enough to immunize himself from social experiments made on the middle classes in hope of benefiting the poor. By *liberal*, in a German context, I mean tolerant and free.

As a political idea, however, freedom is a radical one; relative to other, more durable notions such as absolute monarchy and its merit-based cousin, dictatorship, it has had a comparatively short run under the marquee. Believing in the right to speak your mind, to worship as you choose, and to trade freely for personal advantage (all without a lord or cleric with his hand sewn into the lining of your pocket) is an altogether subversive notion, as anyone in Europe until the Enlightenment knew and as much of the rest of the world knows to this day. In Germany, where various notions of liberalism haven't had good historical play, Hamburg has been something of an exception.

A European trading city without noble fealty, one in which the tempered avarice of merchants coexists with the morality of sailors, must cultivate tolerance if it is to thrive. You can suppose that, had it been a coastal city in South America, Hamburg would have grown worldly and corrupt, but as a German port and a Protestant one, it never let that happen, developing instead a certain worldliness, much sophistication, and a schizoid sense of rectitude. Which was how I came to spend the following evening at the theater, watching an orgy.

Chapter 7

I t was my idea. These things usually are whenever I get a group together. I'd assembled three Americans: a man and a woman of about my age and a slightly stout gentleman nearing retirement. I took them to the street known as Große Freitheit, meaning "great freedom," which was too apt for elaboration. Several theater clubs were on the street, giving it the communally festive appearance of Shubert Alley, which houses a cluster of those New York theaters so theatrically called "legitimate." I chose the club known as Salambo; I think I selected it because of the clever cartoon of a happy man with an erect phallus worthy of Priapus. The place is gone now, possibly the result of repeated shutdowns for illegal prostitution, which is very much to be distinguished from legal prostitution, though in what way I have not consulted the German authorities: some sort of permit, I suppose, or is there an entrance exam?

The leering, salacious, and devoutly repugnant doorman carefully reviewed the financial terms with me. I translated to my company: the minimum cost was thirty-six dollars a head, that being the price of the least expensive drink. Okay, we agreed, count us in. You could have mistaken the interior for that of an ordinary dinner club. The menus were on plastic-coated cards, left facedown on the tables. When the show was about to begin, a burly waiter came by and flipped them over to reveal the most absurd prices outside Monte Carlo.

We ordered the minimum one drink each, but eager businessmen from many nations sat in expense-account clusters, enjoying champagne from bottles that cost more than the women who filtered through the room. These women wore high heels and long dresses that closed with zippers, and on the tabs of the zippers were metal rings. Each would infiltrate among the men until she found one interested in her and, following a short discussion, would pull down her zipper, step out of her skirt, and sit in his lap, naked except for the high heels.

The main event soon followed. I now provide a critique of this lost venue of the musical stage:

The lights are dimmed. Music rises. A set of a Wild West town is unveiled—a painted backdrop, really, as you might find in a high-school production. A young Indian man steps on stage, and by Indian mean not Cheyenne, but Punjabi. He is wearing a cowboy outfit, and by the fact that it is white, we may discern our hero. He mouths along to recorded singing. The hero does not stay clothed in white for long. He has a knockwurst penis the color of a worn penny. This draws the unstopping admiration of a young, fair-skinned lady who removes her own clothes and fellates him mightily, first taking the precaution of rolling a condom onto him. I take this to be the educational portion of the evening: under all circumstances, practice safe sex with your fellow thespian. So delightful is that experience, and so useful the lesson, that the lady spreads her legs and takes in the hero where nature intended.

The youth may not ejaculate. Indeed, because there is another performance that night, he can't come at any time during the show. More men appear and so do more women. The cowboy theme gets rather lost in the shuffle of disrobing bodies. A solo spot is given to a lady with a large glass bottle. Safe sex is important even when your partner is vitreous, and she busies herself trying to pull a condom down the neck. Three tries have it flopping off or flapping skyward. Success at last, and she squats on the bottle. In it goes, as deep as Texas is wide, to universal acclaim.

The audience-participation segment, however, provides disappointing improvisational theater. Though the entire female contingent of the company is on stage and in the front rows, trying to haul one willing member of the paying crowd onto the boards to get laid for nothing—this in a place that thinks a Coca-Cola is worth thirty-six dollars in 1989—there are no takers. Disrespect for a bargain of this magnitude does no honor to the reputations of the assembled businessmen. In such poor financial judgment you could find the seeds of the recession that was to strike two years later.

The finale, needless to say, exceeds expectations. A lazy Susan stage appears—rather a miniature of that used by the Metropolitan Opera in its contemporaneous productions of *The Barber of Seville* and *Die Fledermaus.* The carousel is large enough for six players in three compartments. In the first, a man enters a woman in the missionary position. In the second, the woman works on a penis rather as I've seen a glassblower in Murano attend to a nascent vase. In the third, the woman bends over, presenting her buttocks, which her partner holds as he pumps her from behind.

I don't believe I would again experience such an enjoyable evening at the theater until I would see Ralph Fiennes in *Hamlet*. The lights rise, and I feel that fresh, invigorating delight one experiences in the presence of art.

As we walk toward the street, a naked African woman passes by the senior member of our group, smiles, and expertly rubs his groin. He turns to me, curious and confused, and asks, "Were they having sex on that stage?"

Chapter 8

Here it was, my fourth visit to Hamburg in as many years, and I hadn't done the one thing unanimously recommended to me as the highlight: get up before dawn on Sunday and buy fish. The open-air fish market follows the northern bank of the Elbe. Inevitably, many who go there have been out all night, honing their dissipation skills in St. Pauli, and the rest have risen early, some even for church.

This was a familiar concept for me. In New Orleans, it had long been a similar tradition to take coffee and beignets at Café Du Monde, in the French Quarter. People sobering up from an all-night debauch would have the chance to rub shoulders with those on their way to morning mass at St. Louis Cathedral.

I arrived at the fish market while darkness yet lingered, but a festive atmosphere prevailed. Though seafood predominated, vendors sold apparel, fruit, plants—whatever suited the tastes of shoppers in this country where, by law, stores shut for the weekend early on Saturday afternoon. A novelty dealer held up a huge dildo, posing smugly with it while I photographed him. The star, however, was Aal (eel) Dieter.

I have a theory that the very best of every profession are artists of a kind, and whatever the median income of the trade, these artists will prosper. I had not considered whether genius could reign among fishmongers, but that was before I'd seen Eel Dieter at work.

A heavyset man with slicked black hair, Eel Dieter had everything that the prerecorded performers of the previous evening lacked: a good script, skilled delivery, seamless improvisation, an understanding of his audience, and, most of all, timing. From his stage—the open sales window of a vendor's truck—Dieter pondered aloud about life's vicissitudes. He would query women in the crowd as to how they were doing and pitch jokes, not all of them intended for family listening. If the crowd needed further encouragement, he might section an eel and fling out the bits. In his left hand, Dieter would hold up, say, a sturgeon, lounging in newsprint draping it like a palm frond. Once the first fish was so presented, and its virtues briefly particularized, it all happened with the speed that fire, in flashover, envelops a room: "And I'll add this, and this and this," Dieter would say, slapping eel atop sturgeon, and flounder atop eel, until a pile of seafood swelled from his palm and he yelled, "Fifty marks!" Someone would raise his hand and shout back, and the deal would be done. Paper would envelop fish and the fifty-mark note take its place. There was never any dickering; there was even sometimes competition for the prize.

Dieter showed neither gratitude nor exaltation over a sale. He would retire the banknote to a private place, gaze contemplatively over the audience, tell self-deprecating jokes, and before you knew it fish were flying and money was gladly propelled his way.

If Dieter offered as much entertainment as could be given a crowd without benefit of a microphone, the cavernous fish-auction hall was the scene of liveliness on an altogether different scale. Here it was, daybreak, and you would think you were in the Hofbräuhaus just after dinner. Drinkers sat at long rows of beer-sloshed blond-wood tables, hoisting amber and froth, singing along with a band glowing in polychrome under colored lights. There is something about a typical German stage band that wants to be a 1970s disco sensation, and this one, in the multicolored lighting, was no exception. It roused drinkers to stand on benches, holding hands, singing, and swaying. A few exercised the all-night guzzler's constitutional right to dance wherever he feels. One group collectively tried to rescue a drunken friend from what they thought were my efforts to snap incriminating photographs of him. They were grateful to learn I was not on the payroll of his wife. After the sun had been up an hour, heads were slowly but inexorably descending into amber puddles on blond wood. Outside, bacchants and churchgoers contentedly carried away swaddled fish and tubs filled with houseplants rumored to be Dutch and disease ridden. The sun, peaking over derricks and containerships, shimmered from the feathers of the white seagulls that all but hovered overhead.

Chapter 9

During the next few months, Europe changed more than it had during all my lifetime until then. Germany all but reunited; Communist governments collapsed like so many rotten pickets along a fence too long left unpainted. People of German extraction were pouring back into the country. I found that I, too, could apply for German citizenship. The State Department assured me that my status as an American would not be compromised; indeed, the man I spoke to informed me that, as far as the U.S. government was concerned, I'd been German from birth. He gave me the news with the offhand tone of the doctor who had told me that, not only did I have asthma, I'd had it for years. One dark question held me back, and I needed the answer of a German lawyer. I called Heinrich von Gronau at his office. "Technically, yes," he said. "You could be drafted into the Bundeswehr, but this cannot possibly happen unless there is a world war. I didn't serve in the army myself."

I decided not to ask how he had avoided what I had been assured was universal male conscription; I knew that if anyone could, it was Heinrich. "Then I'm clear," I said.

"Yes, but I think you should volunteer and write a book about it."

By the start of the following summer, therefore, I had two completely separate identities. One business card and one passport, read in combination, listed me as an American lawyer. Another business card and another passport described me as a freelance German travel writer and photojournalist. I was nearing my thirty-sixth birthday and bragging to friends that I'd made it through the 1980s single. (There had been a brief, desultory marriage during law school, in the '70s.) As will happen with men given free and open access to many women, bachelorhood was becoming a habit, with all the negatives concerning character development that bachelorhood invites. But New York has a way of flushing out bad habits and felling them on the wing.

Every June, the plaza of Lincoln Center is converted into an open-air ballroom. An elevated wooden dance floor is built and bands play tango, salsa, waltz—whatever it is that people will dance to, though swing music predominates. The floor fills quickly, and those who don't have tickets stand outside to watch or simply dance on the pavement. It's one of those fun yet sophisticated events that makes New York such an agreeable place, the band playing "Begin the Beguine," the lights shining on the fox-trotting dancers, many of them quite expert, the outdoor café vending potions of fruit and spirits, the concert and ballet crowds lining the terraces of Avery Fisher Hall and the Metropolitan Opera at intermissions.

The festival started its second season on the first Saturday of that summer, a humid but temperate evening. The Peter Duschin Orchestra took the bandstand. I was standing outside the dance floor, looking for a friend I was supposed to meet.

I wish I knew what was playing at the moment when I saw a woman standing a few paces ahead and to the left. She looked and carried herself like an Italian actress, which, by heritage and training, proved nearly correct. Elegantly dressed in black, she was also scanning the capacity crowd. She had clever hazel eyes and full lips over a small, curved chin. Lustrous brown hair was swept back from a high forehead, swaying under white lights as she glanced from side to side. I said, "So you're looking for someone too." I'll admit that, as a pickup line, it lacked finesse, though it had a touch of irony. She said she was trying to find friends who had gone dancing. She gave me her name: Julie Hackett.

Behind us, the fountain sent up concentric sprouts, misting the black marble base and those sitting on it. Little girls in billowing dresses twirled to the music. I asked Julie Hackett to dance with me. The invitation surprised her and she gently, tentatively, put her arm across my shoulder. I remember standing there, holding her for the first time: the music playing, the couples of all ages dancing, stumbling, or just swaying in place on a night in virgin summer. We weren't on the dance floor but we danced just the same, I in the lead, taking a stranger nowhere to the sound of music. Then Julie's friends came and took her away, and I was alone in the night in the crowd.

Chapter 10

The weekend I met Julie Hackett, the U.S. Navy and Coast Guard sent fifteen ships into the harbor, from a three-masted barque to an aircraft carrier. Sailors in crisp white uniforms cruised the city in pairs and clusters. You could visit the ships if you liked. The *Matisse in Morocco* exhibition had just opened at The Museum of Modern Art. A group show called *Bodies* was on at the T'ai Chi Gallery. The contribution by an artist named Joni Mabe was the series Ten Men I've Slept With; abridged for the show, it consisted of body-print nudes of the artist and five male friends. At town hall on the night Julie and I met, the bassist Milt Hinton celebrated his eightieth birthday with a jazz concert featuring guest musicians. On Broadway, you could see *Grand Hotel, Cat on a Hot Tin Roof,* and *Gypsy.*

In short, along with the usual run of movies available anywhere in America that weekend, New York presented any number of activities that Julie and I, separately, could have elected to pursue. She came to the plaza of Lincoln Center only because two friends, more interested in the proceedings than she, had invited her. When I'd met her, the friends were already on the dance floor and Julie, typically late in arriving, was looking for them. I was on the plaza because a friend named Meredith had asked me to join her and the man she was dating once they came out of the ballet. Meredith was dating him because, at a black-tie wedding at the Central Park Boathouse to which she had invited me as her escort, she had picked the man out of the crowd and prevailed upon me to introduce her. I only knew Meredith because I had gone alone to a Vienna Philharmonic concert at Carnegie Hall a few years before and found my legs cramped by a metal balustrade; Meredith, seeing my discomfort, had moved one seat over and given me hers. I bought her champagne at intermission, and we became friends. I had gone alone to that concert because Elena had been working late on one of a succession of abortive career changes; this time it was mechanical drawing, as I recall. Julie and I had lived on Manhattan, rarely more than three miles away from each other, for thirteen years, yet we had not met (even though, it turned out, we had actually attended the same party two years before), and had any of these things not happened, we probably would never have met. Almost everybody blessed with a romance destined to alter his life can point to a solitary, inauspicious moment when destiny so unceremoniously left its calling card. Ours came while the music played and we, still strangers, danced.

At 7:30 P.M. the Friday after we met, Julie was to join me at the Metropolitan Museum of Art. She showed up at eight. There was no time for the planned drinks on the mezzanine. We saw a show of French paintings in Russian collections, then ate Japanese food. Thereafter, we saw each other regularly, but we made no commitments, offering each other the grace of time.

Chapter 11

I was alone again on a railroad a few weeks later, traveling from Vienna to Budapest at dinnertime. My train was called the Orient Express, but it was nothing like the once and future luxury trains of the same name. There were two first-class cars, both Romanian, both populated by disheveled Magyars. The first luxury car I tried had two stinking bathrooms with wooden-seated thrones, and only one of those was operational. Newspapers randomly carpeted the floor.

I chose the second car for its bounty of two functioning toilets. I shared a compartment with Béla, a chubby Californian, formerly of Hungary. Like Dörte, the German returning home to Cologne, Béla's journey was fired by personal history. There is no more emotionally charged travel than a homecoming; after burying my paternal grandmother in a New Orleans plot, it was nearly two decades before I could bring myself back to the city of my adolescence, and only then with a high-school chum who likewise wanted me there to help make his return easier. Béla, a touch on edge, resented having others in the first-class car, but he grew courteous and finally sociable once stroked with conversation. Also in the compartment was Jack, a nervous English teacher from San Francisco. His luggage, swelling with gifts for friends in hard-up Hungary, was a commodious obstruction. Jack had trouble sleeping, and Béla and I spent much of the evening calming him with talk. Jack was so grateful that he summoned an American couple from the compartment next door to photograph him with Béla and me.

In the dining car, on crossing the frontier, a uniformed woman gave my German passport the first (and only) stamp it would receive in Europe. Borders were coming down within the European Union, and the passport that had required much legal artistry to procure was becoming a glorified identification card.

A permamist of exhaust fumes filled East Station in Budapest. Blue-uniformed men on yellow mail trolleys blew their horns and kept on coming if you leapt to safety or if you did not. In the half hour remaining before the exchange booth would open, carnivorous men in shabby, zippered jackets wooed newcomers to trade Western money for Hungarian forint.

Around the bend was a long, bleak hall where whole families lived, sitting atop blankets and flattened cardboard boxes and rolled into blankets beside cooking pots, children's toys, empty beer cans, and the uncollected debris of meals. The blankets touched walls against which the most fatigued among those not sleeping could prop themselves and stare listlessly over the encampment. The squatters' territory lay opposite the barred ticket windows, giving the effect of a prison. A single uniformed man stood guard. Wearing a conductor's suit with his collar splayed open, his pants too short, and his peaked hat rising in the manner of a tiara, he watched with pathos and bewilderment from behind a drooping mustache.

A New York photographic stock house had requested images of this kind. I raised the smallest camera I owned and got off four shots before I received a slam to my right eye. I saw no one, then looked down to find a crone in miniature; she was aged maybe eighty, with missing teeth and more facial hair than I. She gave me a stern look that said, "How dare you!" and I felt chastened for my impertinence in midst of others' misfortunes. Then she tried bumming a cigarette with a puffing gesture. I informed her in English and German that I couldn't help. For the only time in my life, it wasn't true; I was carrying a carton of Marlboros. As she had just forced a hunk of Japanese metal into my eye, I figured it was high time this smoker cut back. She repaired to a grubby blanket and sat down, staring into the near distance, as motionless as Buddha.

Chapter 12

WE ARE VERY SORRY FOR THE ELEVATOR IS BEING OUT OF ORDER, read the sign on the only lift in the Budapest hotel.

I'd booked my room through the Hungarian government agency in Vienna. The taxi that had taken me to the hotel had shown sixty-nine forint on the meter, which was about one dollar, and the cabbie had gladly taken two dollars in Austrian schilling. In Hungary that year, any money was good as long as it was Western.

Four flights later my laden bags and I arrived at my room. Double doors worthy of a bank vault opened to a large chamber with two beds and a wardrobe that could have been part of the original 1911 decor. Not so bad, I thought as I stepped inside. The parquet separated like cracking ice and my heel disappeared into the flooring. The bathroom was in the hall, about a half day's hike away.

"There is much money but it is little," explained the concierge as he handed me thousands of forint in exchange for a single traveler's check. A smile appeared under eyes touched with a melancholy that would become familiar in Hungary.

I generally travel to prosperous nations because I abhor that imperial quality of so much contemporary travel: the white body bronzing by an azure pool, sipping a cold drink served by a black attendant who lives in a hovel. I've always been partial to Switzerland, in no small measure because I can be reasonably confident the waiters are richer than I am. Perhaps it is due to the ubiquitous poverty of America, something unique among civilized nations. The American government can spend uncountable trillions on eradicating it, but the cause is lost, as everybody but the most starry eyed intuitively grasps; poverty is as much a part of American life as optimism. I became something of a colonialist in Budapest: the natives were poor; it was a shame, it was unsightly, but it was not my problem, and it didn't depress me, as the poverty of the Caribbean never depresses the tanning insensitives of North America. I set out for a stroll among the disadvantaged, hardly aware of, or disquieted by, my good fortune. The voyeur rarely thinks of himself; he is not reflective, and he is unaware of how he looks to others.

The sooty buildings that led from the hotel to the night-blackened Danube wore their years of Communist grime like indigent dowagers in faded ball gowns. Rákóczi ut, a main avenue, looked as if under curfew. A few young couples finally appeared. Lamps glowed in the next hotel; photos of the floor show promised bare breasts. If Germany had been rebuilt in too great a haste, it was the penance of Budapest barely to have been rebuilt at all. The city looked like the Vienna of *The Third Man.*

White bulbs turned the cables of the Chain Bridge into waves of light across the Danube. On the opposite shore, the Castle Palace commanded the night under the glow of floodlights until, suddenly, all was darkness. The Castle Palace was transformed into a black hulk. The bridge must have submerged. It was eleven o'clock on a Saturday night in a European capital of two million. Lights out.

Along the river, Pest worked up a bit of Saturday-night street life. Couples strolled the pedestrian walkway behind deluxe hotels. Entrepreneurs sold Russian miliary equipment, hats, and insignia from sheets illuminated by flashlights. Leggy prostitutes patrolled just beyond, calling softly in English, "Business? Business?"

At the Vigadó, a theater with an extravagantly romantic facade, a group of American neurologists and their spouses ascended a tour coach. Dressed in black tie and evening gowns, they called to each other with New World gusto. They had come from a show staged to tell tourists about life in Hungary, and they looked like actors in inappropriate costume— the cast of a Noël Coward comedy stepping onto a Eugene O'Neill stage. I took a cab to my hotel.

Chapter 13

Canvases at the Museum of Fine Arts shared the walls with peeling paint and patches of white plaster. From a room filled with large paintings came a Vivaldi concerto, the gift of a chamber orchestra visiting from Perugia. The Italians played Bach and Vivaldi beautifully, but the triumph belonged to the Hungarians for showing how to make the best of limited resources.

Across from the curved, bookend colonnades of Heroes' Square, a stout woman was selling sheet music of the Italians' concert pieces. Russian soldiers strolled by with their families. Their smart uniforms were decorated with the unit patches I had seen on sale the night before. They refused to pose for photographs; it is hard to go from conqueror to curiosity in the blink of fortune's eye.

In the hot, antique mezzanine of my hotel that night, two barmaids left their post to sit for drinks and cigarettes with the only other patron. One girl read a magazine, the other measured the man's advances, offered in both English and German between cigar puffs.

The ground-floor restaurant was somnolent. My veal arrived over a bed of potatoes and tomatoes served cold from the refrigerator. The manager, fidgety and earnest, apologized in German. An Austrian group had just bought the hotel. He was aware of my arrival from Vienna and feared the worst. "*Nicht schlimm,*" (Not important), I assured him.

The restaurant was self-service in the morning, for eggs, meat, and matzo, while the radio broadcast a Christian religious service for our edification. At the desk, I asked for the key to the shower and was told the chambermaid would deliver it. She appeared outside my room with the key, two towels, and a packet of shampoo. Predictably, there wasn't a door between the shower and the toilet, but the maid told me not to worry; no one would come in. She was barely out of her teens. She wore a black shirt with pirated interlocking Chanel Cs across the front, had straight black hair and the stern, solid look of early maturity. Hers was a chiseled face, unused to comfort, squared to adversity. I had seen her earlier and thought she was a guest. That she was not could now be confirmed by the white socks and slippers protruding from under her jeans and from an expression of servile dispassion. In halting English, she asked if I was alone. I said yes. She asked where I was from, and I explained what "Big Apple" meant. She had taught herself English from a textbook and appreciated this arcane addition to her vocabulary.

After my shower, I saw the maid beside her cart, stealing the inevitable cigarette break. I'd brought along the carton of Marlboros because they were then something of a second currency in the former Communist countries. I detest cigarettes, and it had taken effort to debase myself to buy them. But what did I have them for if not to offer to those who did me service? I asked the young woman her name. She said it was Virág. I gave her a pack and thanked her. My generosity startled her; she smiled shyly, dipping her head, softly thanking me.

I pushed on, rounded the corner, and got as far as the stairs when I heard little feet scamper after me. It was Virág. With stiffened jaw, she asked, "When are you leaving?"

"Tuesday," I replied.

"I'm free tomorrow." Her small, hard eyes grew wide and imploring. They filled in with what, in her struggle for English words, Virág couldn't yet voice.

She came to my room when she went off duty, just after lunch. Her hair was wet from a hasty shower and she sat on my bed, fumbling with the many keys on her ring. I gave her a *Mozart Kugel* from a chocolate stash I'd picked up in Salzburg the week before. She said that she didn't wish to leave just yet, giving the excuse of wet hair. She removed the mock Chanel, and we threw back the bedcovers she had so carefully made up that morning.

We lay together afterward, daylight filtering through the curtains. Virág took one of my hands into both of hers, working through the fingers. My hand was like that of a giant enveloping hers. "Are you married?" she asked.

"No. Divorced."

"What means *divorced?*"

"Married once, but not now."

"Ah, yes." She was distracted by the motions of her own hands. "You have—" Words again were unavailable to her. I guessed she was to ask about a girlfriend, but she produced from somewhere an English-Hungarian dictionary made of long, stiff sheets fastened at the ends so it could be spread out like a railroad timetable. She pointed to a word: *wonderful.*

"Wonderful? What is wonderful?"

"Your hands are wonderful," she said. "I feel like I know you—" A little more effort and, "many time."

"A long time?"

"Yes." She was pleased and so repeated, "I feel like I know you for long time."

Chapter 14

Virág was raised in Transylvania, a Balkan shuttlecock that, in the twentieth century alone, had passed from Hungary to Romania to Hungary and back again. The Hungarian minority suffered along with the rest of Romania under the dictatorship of Nicolae Ceaucescu, enduring ethnic resentment and, Virág attested, rank persecution. Her father was a truck driver, and her mother worked at the telephone exchange, were Virág learned to use a switchboard. Virág and a friend named Judit fled Romania after the revolution that brought down Ceaucescu. Virág and Judit had gone as far as Hungary by car, then walked into Austria while the driver passed with due propriety through customs. They reconnected with the car farther inside Austria and were driven as far as Linz, there to surrender themselves at a police station, asking for asylum. They spent three weeks in jail while the Austrians examined their case. The verdict from Vienna was for the cops to drive two crying women back to Hungary.

The Hungarians said they could stay six months. When I arrived, that time was just about up. The women could have an extension, but for only six months more. Virág said that the desperate souls sleeping in the train station were in the same situation as she; the difference was that she had found work: the hotel had need of a switchboard operator. Virág let Judit take that job and asked to be a maid instead because, at $115 per month, the pay was better.

Virág showed me her Romanian passport, still bearing the socialist emblem that had been cut from flags flown on tanks during the revolution. The passport was practically useless to her; she couldn't even go to Czechoslovakia with it, only to Hungary or, if she had two hundred dollars, Yugoslavia. (It is an indication of the pace of change at this time that neither of the two alternative havens would long remain intact.) Virág stared at my twin Western passports with the envy of a poor child for a well-kept house. Then she showed me the picture of her boyfriend in Romania. He was quite young, his face all but camouflaged by expansive sunglasses and a dark beard. Her parents didn't like him and he hadn't written in months. She claimed she had met no men in Budapest because they weren't friendly.

Virág read my palm, showing me the life, heart, and head lines, as she called them. As best we could, we shared ideas about rationalism, morality and good and evil. I respected Virág. Although we barely had a common language, she managed to convey warmth, strength, and generosity. She shared with me what must have been an expensive bar of German chocolate and left me the rest. I gave her all the *Mozart Kugeln* she wanted, but there was a problem with the cigarettes. I was already in the role of protective male. Virág had given exactly half the pack I'd handed her—ten cigarettes in all—to Judit. I didn't feel right in giving her more of something dangerous, but I felt uncomfortable depriving her of a luxury. She got a few packs more.

Hotel management was unconcerned that one of its maids was drinking with a guest at its champagne bar and dining with him at the restaurant. Perhaps it was expected, or perhaps it was because thirty or so insufferably rowdy Danes held down the attention of all then on duty. Our mimosas were terrible, not because of the local sparkling wine, which was passable, but the orange juice, which was all but water. There followed an adequate goulash soup and a chocolate dessert that proved a combination of something like Miracle Whip and Bosco. The nervous manager was still at it, helping to clean and serve, in despair at his staff for their lethargic service to the Danes. Everything was accomplished in whatever language was handiest, and everything—eventually—got done.

Chapter 15

My wake-up call the next morning was by Virág, at just after seven, when she let herself into my room with her passkey. She had the day off, but a toothache had sent her crying the night before to the dentist, who refused to extract the culprit. She had to go back and would see me at three.

As Virág did not know how to swim, this seemed the right moment to try one of the 123 spas in Budapest. I went to the spa at the Gellért Hotel, another of the graying ladies of the city's past. The changing room smelled of sweat but was clean. The requirement was that you first go for a swim in the pool, where bathing suits were worn and the sexes mingled. It was mandatory to buy and wear a plastic bathing cap that had the odor of stale breakfast meat. The pool was in a cavernous, echoing hall lined in marble. Fanciful columns sported fish, sea serpents, and the god Poseidon. They crested at an arching mechanical roof that was left open a crack despite the dreariness of the day and the morning rain. Cool water cascaded from eight shut-eyed lion heads. The older guests swam as my maternal grandmother had, head out of the water, with froglike motions. They formed a sort of aquatic conga line, moving counterclockwise. A woman without a bathing cap was reprimanded by a lifeguard whistle.

A statue of a nude nymph who may have been Minerva, slightly stooped, presided over the front of the men's thermal bath. I got my ticket to the sauna and pressed the buzzer to be admitted. I entered a great room swelling in blue tile under a curving roof with cracked and stained glass blocks and arches decorated with arabesques. Here men exchanged their bathing suits for loincloths: Magyar Tarzans, in to take the cure. In grand fountains topped by nymphs, hot water flowed from taps shaped like heads. The next room had four columns, the capitals supporting kissing cherubs. Two baths were set at different temperatures. Though the sexes were separated, the aroma of eroticism permeated the decor, down to the water-nymph encore. You could imagine the husband and wife or, better still, young lovers, relaxed from their respective baths, their skin smoothed by treatments, their joints eased by massage, rushing up to their hotel room to conclude the process in bed. You'd have to stretch your imagination, however, since the sight presented at the medicine bath was of middle-aged and older men of less-than-athletic proportions, stretched out on the water, their elbows resting on the steps into the pool, their chins resting on their hands, and the sunken cheeks of their bare behinds barely submerged. Only after I'd tried every bath did I find the sauna. It looked like a public shower, with a tiled floor and a pair of chairs.

The tab for the day came to less than four dollars, including the rental of, literally, a dishtowel I'd have kept for a souvenir if I hadn't found the stains so disagreeable. Outside, three earnest but scruffy Americans asked me if you needed to wear a bathing suit in order to swim. They were disappointed by my answer, but I told the woman in the group it was possible to rent a bikini, and they entered. I dined on goulash at the Gellért's restaurant, which was really quite good.

Chapter 16

Virág called me at the room to say that her face was badly swollen from oral surgery. Her landlord didn't like men to come around, so I couldn't stop by for a sympathy call. That's what she told me. I suspected she was embarrassed. I told her I'd extend my stay just to see her again. We were both happier for it.

I walked the rainy streets as the sky darkened into night. A woman tended a sidewalk stand offering sodas at twenty cents each. She was as pale and defeated looking as anyone else in Budapest and obviously cold. She wearily raised an empty to show she would need the bottle returned. I motioned her to blow on her fingers and rub, and she smiled in response to my recognition of her discomfort. Whenever you showed anyone in gray Budapest a little brightness, the color would return to his face.

I was feeling both expended and refreshed, which meant that the spa had done its work. In the crowded underground walkway at an intersection of what was then the Lenin Ring, one of several booksellers who gave the place the feel of a covered bazaar displayed a three-volume dictionary and a book of Tom and Jerry cartoons. On a rack behind him was a sex manual showing a couple side by side, his fingers up her glory, and hers wrapped around his. The video playing into the street from a store above was *Goldfinger*. At a pharmacy around the corner, I finally saw those consumer lines that the stock house had asked after, but I took no pictures. Enough of misfortune already. In a supermarket, I bought a bottle of

Tokáji Borpárlat, the brand of Tokay brandy that Béla, on the train ride in, had recommended.

A cold rain fell that night, and the hotel lobby was crowded with Danes, a few standing with arms crossed in front of them, wet hair molded to their foreheads in streaks. A band entertained in the restaurant; the clarinetist was tall, gray, and too thin. He wore a comical gold-lamé vest, but he played Strauss waltzes passably well. The waiters managed to place themselves more often in the lobby than in the restaurant, and the fattest of them was all over a somewhat pretty, somewhat tubby girl. Hotel guests were trying with mixed success to place telephone calls abroad. The sad, stoic desk clerk who seemed to work all shifts heroically pacified them in fragments of their languages—all save the inevitable, hopelessly irritated Frenchman, whose indignation was unappeasable. The Danes thundered into the rain in squads.

Virág didn't let herself in at seven the next morning. I found her in the maid's room, disconsolate, holding a cold cloth to her face, one cheek horribly swollen, as if she had been punched in the face. She was smoking, and when she saw me, she turned away in embarrassment. I told her it was all right, that it didn't matter to me that the swelling was "ugly," as she put it, that I was there for her and that she looked lovely to me all the same. She was so much younger than I was that the male protectiveness I'd shown earlier quickly grew paternal: I gave her a hug and kissed her forehead. She tried to explain the condition, and I made out that it was an abscess and that she thought I would be happier without her. I told her that nothing could tear me away from Budapest until I saw her again.

Chapter 17

"The soldiers shot from the roof," said László Lukacs of Dearborn, Michigan. He pointed to Parliament, a romance in neo-Gothic along the Pest side of the Danube. We were standing on the castle parapets on the Buda shore of the river that divided the two parts of Budapest. "They fired machine guns into the crowds, and the bodies were cleared away in busloads."

Mr. Lukacs was in the assembly that October night in 1956 when demonstrators pulled down a statue of Stalin and launched the Hungarian Uprising. He saw the Russian tanks roll in, ultimately to crush the rebellion and destroy chunks of low, broad Pest, sending Mr. Lukacs and 190,000 others into exile. He was not allowed to return for a visit until 1965, when he was made to understand the importance of keeping his mouth shut.

Now Mr. Lukacs was a prosperous American, on a visit with his family. His son bought embroidery from one of the old women who guarded the crenellated walls, selling handicrafts to Western tourists. I departed for Fisherman's Bastion, a fortification completed in 1902 in the general style, and with all the defensive capabilities, of Cinderella's castle.

The castle district was clean and restored, a display by Budapest of how it wished to be regarded. There were streets of fine, old houses. Buskers entertained and merchants sold trinkets. From youthful entrepreneurs, I bought a T-shirt with a picture of Stalin over a legend exactly reading: EAST EUROPEAN TOURS, 1924–1989.

The government tourist office had set up a mobile exchange booth to satisfy any urge to convert hard currency into forint. Behind the money-changer was the church known as Matthias. The dark interior was a neo-Gothic caprice in okra, burgundy, gray, and pale yellow, with earth-toned arabesques climbing the pillars to the vaults. The guards, all middle-aged women, futilely scolded the tourists to show a respectful silence.

At the nearby Hilton, a dapper Russian amiably charmed Western businessmen with stories of Moscow taxi drivers while, just outside, you could buy an entire Soviet army uniform for the price of a business shirt.

I found a long consumer line suitable to photograph. It was filled with women waiting to get into Estée Lauder.

I rendezvoused with Virág at last, outside West Station, where I was to buy my ticket to Prague. I found her holding a lace-bordered handkerchief to her swollen cheek, turning her bad side away from me at every opportunity. I conscripted her as my translator, but we had to wait one hour in a line of disheveled Romanians who grimaced habitually and puffed American cigarettes. The girls behind the ticket windows had nothing resembling a computer, just rubber stamps and carbon paper, each transaction concluded by rapid-fire stomps of the bureaucratic hand. For all that, I earned a green ticket smaller than a saltine cracker and a little booklet signifying my right to a berth in the sleeper. At eleven dollars, it was cheaper to move around central and eastern Europe than to stand still in New York City.

Everything about the trains in this part of the world reminded me of the Second World War. Even the ticket sellers' cages were correct to the period. I half suspected that I would look into my German passport and find that a J for *Jude* ("Jew") had been stamped into it and that I, like my father when he was a boy, would come face to face with the Gestapo while on board. The only difference I could tell between what I had seen and photographs of the middle twentieth century was that the exiles in my company were grimier.

The long wait for my ticket was useful because it gave Virág time to relax with me about her swollen cheek. The Thermál, a hotel on Margaret Island, was one of the city's best, and I took Virág to its Espresso Kamilla for a vanilla-laced torte and Earl Grey tea. The lace-bordered handkerchief was at last pocketed in favor of utensils. Virág could not believe my generosity. Her treat set me back one dollar.

She asked that we go back to our hotel because she wanted to have what she called "knowledge." She insisted that we take the bus, tickets for which were twelve cents.

Virág was a giving and gracious lover, despite her pain. She had started to menstruate and I gave her a pair of my underpants to replace her own. Then I gave her a Jaeger sweater and anything else I could find that was of use to her and surplus to my needs. I gave her some Tokay brandy, which she sipped out of courtesy, not interest. I offered her the rest of the nearly full bottle, but ended leaving it in the room, next to a neatly folded English suit, long past its prime, that had seen its last use at the opera in Vienna the week before. "Will you see if someone can use these?" I asked.

"Yes, okay," she said heavily.

"Are you all right?"

"I am Sade." It took me a moment to realize she meant "sad."

"Why are you sad?"

She pointed to her face.

"Virág, I've lived fifteen more years than you. It does no good to be sad about things that will change. You will heal."

"But you are leaving," she said. "That will not change."

I've had to leave women behind before in my travels. This time was just the hardest. I had shaved my visit to Prague to a single night, and I could delay no longer if I was to see any of it.

On our way out, Virág introduced me to Judit, her fellow exile. She was on the antique switchboard, wearing jeans and a pink sweater. She had the knowing eyes of a woman twice her age. Judit had obviously heard about me, and this was obviously arranged to let her have a look at the American.

I knew that the restaurant Virág had chosen for our final meal together was not for tourists: it was cheap, the food was good, and the menu wasn't in German. A woman came by selling flowers in bunches of three. I bought Virág roses. In that resigned way of hers, she protested that I was being taken.

West Station had no refugees, but it had a McDonald's, in a restored nineteenth-century interior, almost gaudy in context for being swabbed and buffed. My night train to Prague was waiting. The Czech attendant spoke English, and for that alone he won a pack of cigarettes. Virág said good-bye. Her small, hard eyes were furtive and melancholy. I suppose mine looked about the same. As delicately as I could, I gave her real money and told her to save it for an emergency. She'd clearly been hoping for cash but had resolved to say nothing, trying to force back a smile when I suggested it, registering surprise at the sum when it fell into her palm. I told her to save it for an emergency. It could make the difference.

There were a few tears, but she was stoic to the end. "I am thanking you for these days," she said. "I remember them."

I took out the rest of the Marlboros and handed them over. "They're not good for you," I said. "Use them for trade."

"Two years I smoke, and my mother says to stop." A twinkling little grin at last emerged, and it gratified me. She was still a kid, but she could handle herself.

Chapter 18

I arrived in Prague on a day when rumor flowed that the Communists would attempt to regain power. Prague was still the capital of a united Czechoslovakia, and it was not yet swelling with young American expatriates eager to live cheaply or to try on adulthood at a convenient distance from home. I had heard that, by layered acts of providence, Prague had been built beautiful and had missed the wars and the wreckers' blows that had pulverized beauty across Europe. Having last seen Salzburg only the previous week, I had a point of comparison. In Salzburg, the Baroque came in whole city blocks; in Prague, it filled vast acreage. Buildings the shape and color of marzipan confections lined the streets, their gables and roofs puffing and curling into the near distance. Prague was the final European capital on my must-see list. I had therefore been anticipating it with the expectation of someone who, having read nearly all the works by a favorite author, picks up the last uninspected volume in his oeuvre. More, really: I had spent years in search of that mythical central European city, the one with the prim and harmonious architecture, the one with a Protestant sense of rectitude not taken so far as to stifle the love of physical beauty, the one with an honest and literate population proud of its heritage but accepting of a traveler. I found that place in Prague— though I had to enjoy it from my base in a guest workers' dormitory on the edge of town, the only practicable lodgings available. (I'd started at the best hotel and worked my way down, the dormitory being about as far down as down could go and still provide you with a clean private room and bath. When I paid on exiting the next morning, the rough-looking men queued up to get out gave the place the look of a work-release institution.)

I changed seventy dollars in twenties and tens into heaps of krone. "Where are you going to spend all that?" wondered the clerk who did the deal. If Budapest had made me a robber baron, in Prague I was Croesus. Apples were three cents. Orange soda was a nickel. A soft-core pornographic magazine was a dime. Suede gloves of the best quality I could find were five dollars. I bought heavy-metal compact discs; I hate heavy-metal rock, and it was all the more useless when sung in Czech, but there were exactly six compact discs to choose from in the shop. The only guidebook I could buy that was of use to me was in German, but change had been so sudden that it was obsolete.

The old signs in the city were Rosetta stones in Czech, German, and Russian; new signs were in Czech, German, and English. Czech women were very fond of mini skirts that year; in Budapest, only the hookers had dared them. The Czech government had been more repressive, so perhaps revealing clothing was yet another form of protest, part of a Velvet Revolution in which the citizenry had practiced no violence, relying on symbols and collective defiance to win freedom. I like to think they (the women) wore mini skirts in the same spirit with which they (first an artist, then members of Parliament) would soon paint and repaint a Russian T-34 tank—left in Prague as a war memorial—a vivid, inglorious pink, until it was taken from its roost in a public square and shoved into a museum.

But this could all just be a romantic American view. Maybe the women were just proud of their legs.

Wenceslas Square is not a square, but a boulevard that comes to a perfunctory halt at either end; it can look, from certain angles, as if it were an enclosed space. Along one side stands an outsized equestrian statue of St. Wenceslas—grand in bronze on his pedestal, as any official portrayal in metal would have it. On approaching the pedestal, however, I discovered the wholly ad hoc and unofficial Memorial to the Victims of Communism. Photographs were planted like pickets in sand, flowers backing and flanking the pictures—red and white roses and daisies predominating. The wax from candles left by a succession of mourners—no other word is fitting—had overflowed their holders and hardened into thick mounds. There were several images of Jan Palach, a philosophy student who, in January 1969, immolated himself at about this spot in protest against the Soviet-led invasion five months before. He died three days later, at the age of twenty. The pathos in the faces of the townsfolk who stopped at this handmade shrine was familiar to me from the Vietnam Veterans Memorial in Washington. These were the people who had lived through the tragedy it recalled, people for whom the monument was not just a tribute to a long-dead hero frozen into the saddle of his petrified horse.

I had lunch at a restaurant in a Baroque building on the square. Half of what was on the menu wasn't available, but potato soup and beef would do well enough. There was a man with an enormous tray weighted with beer steins. His sole employment was to drop one in front of every diner, the cost of beer having scant impact on the price of lunch. I spent the entire meal waving away foaming steins that alit on the table like so many houseflies. Outside, I had four-cent ice cream and took pictures for a time. I asked a guard in front of a lavender palace whom he was protecting. "Our president," he said with a pride an American would find startling. There was an older couple, corpulent and sweet, running a butcher shop I entered. When the woman saw that she was obscuring a photograph behind her, she stepped aside and pointed to make sure it was in my camera viewfinder: a portrait of Václev Havel, the playwright president. I wondered if perhaps the last time such an event had happened in Washington, it was for Franklin Roosevelt, and before that for Abraham Lincoln. I liked the robust smile on the butcher's face as she gestured to President Havel's portrait, something I hadn't seen once in

Budapest; not only was Prague so much more beautiful, but it had none of that kicked-in-the-teeth Magyar despair.

Near the art museum, I talked to a group of college students, instinctively directing my attention to the prettiest of the women, a tall blonde who said she had been as far abroad as Canada, with her parents. She was pink skinned with rounded limbs, the kind that, if toned, would have made her look athletic. She carried herself with the self-assurance recognizable anywhere among children of privilege. She asked me where I'd been in Europe and I gave her the short list. "Is this your first time in my country?" she asked.

"Yes."

"Why did you not come here before?"

I knew what she was driving at and gave her the answer she feared. "I had trouble with the idea of it—that I'd have supported, in a way, such an oppressive government. It's all different now. I'm happy to be here."

"Yes," said the student warily, forcing a smile that lasted only as long as necessary to register. There could be no doubt now: the freedom to travel, denied to nearly all, had been granted to the Communist elite of which either or both of this woman's parents had been members. But times had changed; you had to adapt. The blonde's cool disregard was that of the losing side; you could imagine the same from the French aristocrat who had survived the revolution by joining it, addressing the coarse peasant as *citoyen* even as he secretly pined for the *ancien régime*.

The encounter somehow made me miss underprivileged Virág even more. It had been good to have a woman at my side, one to care for and who cared for me. Which is all another way of saying that I'd been on my own for less than a day and already I was lonely. All men reach a point in their lives when they must evolve from hunters into farmers. I'd seen men who failed to make the change grow trivial and dull, even as they imagined that, unshackled to wife or family, they had held the secret to an exciting, eternal youth. I found that, as I grew older, my eyes welled with tears during sentimental movies I didn't even like. Bratty children were beginning to look adorable to me. When I'd see an attractive woman not much older than Virág, finely dressed and heading off to work, I'd find myself thinking not how I could get into her pants but that her parents must be very proud.

So what was Virág then? A dress rehearsal for something larger, I supposed. However much Virág had touched me, in the cold air of reflection,

perhaps a runaway chambermaid barely out of her teens was not precisely a suitable match. She had, however, reacquainted me with my own,
long-denied wish for domesticity.

Julie Hackett wasn't ready to settle down with me; too many options
were yet available to her. I didn't mind standing in line for a desirable
woman, but only if the line was moving. You never know in New York: if
you are as attractive and clever as Julie, around the next corner there may
be waiting a kind, giving, fun-loving investment banker. I'd already decided
to follow her from a watchful distance, ready to move up should the
opportunity arrive. And yet, while there was no single moment when I'd
decided it, in my mind, Julie was already the one. She didn't know it yet,
and when she did hear the news that we were right for each other, it
would have to come from within her if there was any chance it would be
believed.

Chapter 19

When I first entered Prague, only by toil of the imagination could I
have believed that ordinary Czechs and Slovaks had fought and
won a nonviolent revolution just eleven months before. Not long after
lunch, however, I passed the restaurant where I had taken it and saw a
crowd of about one hundred gathered around the entrance. On the
second-floor balcony, sound equipment was being set up, and citizens were
converging from all corners of the square, carrying placards and Czech
flags. A man tested the system with Bruce Springsteen's "Tunnel of Love,"
to the obvious amusement of the middle-aged woman standing next to me.

People of all kinds came in great numbers until thousands were assembled, filling Wenceslas Square as far as I could see. When the men controlling the soundboard saw that I was a Western photographer, they
motioned for me to stand on it for a better view. I asked what was going
on and was told in German that a rumor was afoot that the Communists
were trying for a comeback. The rally was to support democracy. Speakers
exhorted the crowd, which responded at appropriate moments with
cheers, applause, jeers, chanting, and flag waving. I hadn't a clue what was
going on except that the good guys were winning. I wished I could chant
along. A man sang ditties, accompanying himself on the guitar, and the
rough laughter at the end of his couplets disclosed he was a satirist.

Throughout the rally, which lasted half an hour, the crowd was so orderly—despite, from my vantage point, the lack of uniformed police—that a pathway had been left at the front through which women pushed baby strollers without the slightest concern.

The student protesters of my youth had been loud and angry; their cause was not without merit, but they had been brought up in comfort and had been unwilling to pledge life, fortune, or sacred honor in the prosecution of their beliefs. In contrast, this assembly of teachers, doctors, store clerks, and students had brought down tyranny. You could see it in their eyes and in their conviction: no histrionics, no grand gestures, just the solid, resolute business of defending freedoms only just won at no small risk and with no retribution exacted upon the losing side.

It is one thing to watch a mass action on television, to see a crowd behind the frosted-blond news bunny in her heavy lipstick and Republican cloth coat, a silk scarf around her neck, intoning platitudes into her microphone. It is quite another thing to be there, to witness the means by which the collective will overpowers individual will until the crowd shouts, cheers, and boos as if with a single voice. No one speaks to the neighbor whose shoulder almost touches his, but all are of one mind. By this process are the righteous defended, protests waged, wars launched, and the innocent hanged. It is the most dangerous form of human interaction because, although it can effectuate so much that is good, as it did here, it has served and spawned so much that is evil. It was active the night in 1923 when Hitler nicked the ceiling of a Munich beer hall with his pistol shot and when he ultimately swayed the electorate in his favor. It was also at work in the Nuremberg rallies, when Hitler had his way with the crowd, and in Hitler's war, when Germany marched collectively into barbarism. Mass devotion is one of the reasons I find spectator sports so odious. It's not the athletics, which bore me. What is worrisome is the spectators, with their fanaticism over prosperous young men in quest of a ball. The instinct shows itself harmlessly, but its very presence is a warning. The good that was in it found voice that afternoon in Wenceslas Square.

Whenever I'm on a long trip, involuntarily, but inevitably, I mark that point where I find myself at the farthest reach of journey. From there, every new step is homeward bound. Arrival may yet be distant in time, and the possibility may yet exist for new adventures, for fresh places and people, but the gravitational pull of home begins to overpower the ballistic thrust of travel. You tire quicker. You are sad for it, yet however much you enjoy travel, you are a touch relieved. During the rally, I realized that no one who cared for me knew precisely where I was; only Virág was even aware what city I was in, and no one else I knew had ever heard of her. I had reached the outer limit in Prague, and by my second day there, I could hear the call of home.

As I walked to the opera house only one other person, a gray-haired man, was heading there. He saw me and his pace quickened. I did as well, and he walked faster still. We were race-walking by the time he got there ahead of me, but the performance that night was sold out. I asked the speedster where he was from. New York City, of course. Home was at last in sight, its spires poking from under the horizon.

Chapter 20

The rally was in the newspaper the next morning. A copy set me back a penny and a half. I was indeed having trouble getting rid of my Czech money despite another day of trying. I only succeeded after dinner, which I shared with a pleasant, young couple from Berlin. I was on the stone Charles Bridge, which was full of good cheer. A pair of teenagers kissed interminably. A little blond girl danced, coached by her older sister, who kept the lesson roughly in time to a man strumming a washboard. Buskers dotted the length of the span, outstanding among them being the polka band with its idiosyncratic rendition of "Roll Out the Barrel"— washboard percussion and all. I gave up almost the last of my Czech money to a tall, dark-haired man in exchange for a hand-cut silhouette of my face. He drew applause for each profile his scissors mimicked, the greatest appreciation coming from off-duty Russian soldiers, once feared, now merely abhorred, an occupying army preparing to ride its pink tanks into history's sunset.

I had no idea at the time, but I arrived at the railroad station by walking alone through a park so dangerous it had been nicknamed Sherwood Forest. Someone played guitar, singing "Take Me Home, Country Roads" in Czech. Africans, Asians, and young, spotty-faced soldiers in red berets dozed on benches at the train station. A hirsute blond man and a bald-headed comrade with a big nose and a goatee shouted at each other and nearly came to blows. They were part of a group from which the blonde shortly retreated. One of the others ran after him. The blonde turned on him and, with a single punch, sent him to the floor, blood pouring from his nostrils. The rest of the pack advanced after the retreating victor, followed by six policemen. The soldiers looked on dispassionately; it was late, they were tired, and this was not their fight.

My train was the 1:15 A.M. express to Vienna. The sleeper car was an East German leftover. The chattering conductor, from the former East Berlin, wanted to know what kind of work I did that required a brace of Leicas, and what my apartment cost in New York and please, what did I earn each year? I had the compartment to myself, and the conductor let in an Austrian border guard in the dead of night. The guard was all official suspicion until he saw the German passport. We exchanged amiable greetings; in my sleep-heavy voice, my accent passed for authentic. I was not, like Virág, a foreigner on the run; my reentry into Austria ended with, "Thank you, sir. Good night."

There are only two places in Europe where, if you show up as a German, you are greeted with the hospitality customarily shown an American. One is Germany, and the other is Austria. Historic memories die hard.

I slept well throughout the remainder of the night.

So Love Me Already

Chapter 1

I magine that you are in the market for a place to store books and knick-knacks, and have decided that something practical and modern will do—say, a wall unit: well constructed, with good capacity and a pleasing walnut veneer over three-quarter-inch plywood. One day, while you're minding your own business—say, while going to meet a friend at Lincoln Center—you pass by an antiques shop, and there, in the window, stands a Hepplewhite breakfront bookcase of incomparable elegance. The carving is handled with dexterity and finesse, the lines are classical, the effect enchanting. The glazed sections are impractical for books, there is no place for your silver service, and the cost is unimaginable.

Every molecule of the good sense you have accumulated since infancy urges that you walk on. Perhaps you do, but you come back, and then again, and in the end, good sense loses out and you rearrange the house around your folly. What has taken hold is something known by many names, the truest of which is Romance.

When people are involved, the matter becomes infinitely more complex, of course—so complex that poets, novelists, and the like more readily find their muse in cases where people fall in love with people than when the question regards home decoration. The romance in my courtship of Julie lay in its seeming futility: that Julie exceeded Elena in every category that would make a woman desirable only served to increase competition. After just over one year of trying to maintain my hard-won standing in the lead, I formally relinquished my place in line.

This was not intended as a ploy to make Julie reconsider her intentions, but it had that effect. We had already jointly accepted an invitation to a wedding and, though Julie was my ex-girlfriend, we both attended— arriving separately.

The ceremony and reception were held on a sunny autumnal day at the Boathouse in Central Park. The park was a handsome backdrop, its unscrubbed, Anglophilic forests and fields primed for pastimes both earthy (in-line skating, music blaring, ball playing, drug taking) and genteel (rowing, birding, sunbathing, dining, marrying). The bride was my friend Meredith. It was Meredith who, only the year before, had invited me out to have drinks with her and the man she had earlier asked me to introduce to her at a wedding here, at the Boathouse. On my way to meet Meredith on that June night at Lincoln Center, while passing beside an open-air dance floor, I had first laid eyes on Julie. Meredith was now getting married to a different man than the one she had me introduce her to at the Boathouse.

After the interval of separation, Julie was so near to me, love seemingly so attainable, it was as if our bond had been unbroken. It was as if, by extending my hand and letting it fall upon her shoulder, we would be reunited. I had only to reach out that hand and, by mutual benediction, it might all be so; but I could not do it.

Meredith had conscripted a baritone and soprano to sing "Bei Männern, welche Liebe fühlen" (from *The Magic Flute*) for the processional. The rabbi intoned the blessing while sunbathers watched from a nearby boulder and a gondola swayed in its mooring. The service gave way to celebration. Julie and I, though seated next to each other, remained yet an arm's length apart.

Chapter 2

Three weeks later, I flew alone to Paris from Madrid. The Frenchman seated next to me was in good spirits until we landed at Orly, when he realized he'd told his girlfriend to pick him up at Charles de Gaulle. The guard at passport control didn't even open my German passport. Just one happy multinational family, we Europeans. I immediately called the friend of a friend from New York who was supposed to meet me in Paris. My friend's Parisian friend, who carried a long name punctuated by feudal title, said my friend had canceled on short notice.

I took a room in a small hotel in the Latin Quarter, its interior pleasantly remodeled in contemporary taste. The hotel seemed chiseled from the walls of an alley and was immune to the racket that progressed weekend evenings on streets just steps away. In exchange, I would have to endure the Sunday bells of St.-Séverin, which had the acoustic effect, on the morning of the Christian Sabbath, of an ecclesiastic jackhammer.

I came down to the lobby that first night to find a young woman sitting on a sofa, one leg resting awkwardly on the cushions. She had too-bright red nails and lipstick, was overfed, and wore a simpering scowl, like a chubby doll in vivid paint, left half forgotten on a shelf. She was disconsolately reading an English-language potboiler buttressed behind the stop-sign fingernails. Her name was Debbie Perlstein. She was a social worker living on Long Island, near her parents; she was traveling with the senior Perlsteins and her brother. This was her second time in Paris at parental expense, she explained.

"Like it even more the second time?" I asked.

"I hate it," said Debbie in a Long Island accent, its cadence like a handsaw cleaving a two-by-four. She added, "I'm not coming back," in the manner of a diner furious over bad service at an overrated restaurant. "We were in Stuttgart, and everything was fine," she continued. "You could go to a bar, they spoke English, they had the World Series playing. My brother is upstairs right now, calling every bar in the area, trying to find just one that has the World Series on. It's *important*. He's starting work as a sports lawyer. In New York, you get everything handed to you in a bar, but here you have to ask for it. We were in this bar last night. There was this college kid. He fell off his stool and was lying on the ground a half an hour. His friends were like, 'So what?' They just slapped his face a little. The guy was dead."

"Dead? You're sure?"

"We left before any help arrived. I live alone with my puppy, and I wanted to bring him, but my parents said I couldn't, and everyone here, I mean everyone takes along their dog, even in restaurants."

"Where would you rather travel?" I asked.

"Cancún," said Debbie with the certainty of the convert. "They don't let you use one brain cell." She held her thumb almost to her forefinger, admitting the barest hint of space between them. "Everything is taken care of, and you just relax. My mother cut her leg on a post outside, and now she says we aren't going to this big wedding we have next week because the skirt she's wearing is short and the cut will show. My father is going crazy, running all over town to find a drugstore that's open, just to get a Band-Aid." And with that, the father walked in. He did not look happy.

"Do you need a Band-Aid, Mr. Perlstein?" I asked.

"*Dr.* Perlstein," his daughter corrected.

"You have one?" the physician asked me.

I took a Band-Aid from my wallet and gave it to him. He accepted it with a grunt that may have been a thank-you, then left.

"Debbie, does your brother speak French?"

"No."

I was going to ask her to imagine working in a bar on Columbus Avenue, only to have a stranger telephone and, in French, ask if the bar is showing the World Cup soccer match. Before I could say anything, however, Debbie thoughtfully suggested that, if her brother did have any luck, she would call or come around and see if I wanted to go bar-hopping with them. I was tired, but, realizing that Debbie might thus extend her hospitality, I hurriedly changed in my room, casting random, suspicious glances at the telephone, then bolted.

There were many restaurants on the rue de la Harpe, the majority of which appeared to be Greek. Swarthy, smiling men stood sentinel before each, holding out cold meat dishes affixed with price tags, enticing pedestrians with songs of gastronomic seduction that would have made the sirens proud. Every one of the dishes looked vile. It was Saturday and the avenue was as crowded as the Bourbon Street of my New Orleans adolescence, albeit a shade less raucous. Young couples; interracial couples; teenagers in American-style clothes, hanging out and smoking; restaurants run by Egyptians, Moroccans, and the ubiquitous Greeks: the show went on through the night.

By accident, I found the Shakespeare & Co. bookstore, which was tended by a young Englishman wearing jodhpurs, reading Fielding. In an Oxford accent, he said he couldn't yet afford the coordinated boots, but he hoped to have the money soon. He was as calm and restrained as the English country gentleman his costume so theatrically referenced. He was already French enough to know that a proper bohemian sacrifices for his wardrobe.

Chapter 3

Yvonne, an ex-girlfriend, arrived from New York the next day. Meanwhile, a high-school friend who lived in Paris gave me a call, and I was thus agreeably companioned for the remainder of my stay. I'd broken off with Julie, and that was that. We'd initially planned that she would come with me to Paris—a romantic first time together in Europe—but things hadn't worked out. Time to move on. Bringing a woman to Paris is like packing food for the voyage, right? True, I'd bought Julie a couple of little things in Madrid, and—what harm was there in another token of spent affection? The idea got into my head and, like a song heard by chance one morning, it stuck with me on my first morning walk to the Right Bank.

On the Boulevard St.-Germain, a driver nearly hit me, and I gave him an irritable New York "fuck you!" My commentary so distracted a man in an open raincoat that he walked into one of the low, round-topped poles planted around Paris in a futile effort to keep motorists from driving on the sidewalks. The man rammed his testicles into the knob of the pole and was impaled there. He stood motionless for a second, coming to terms with the accident and trying to show that insouciance so integral to French poise. He rose slightly on his toes to release his scrotum from the pole, then walked on.

I'd never seen so many tour buses in front of the Louvre. A number bore license plates from Poland and what was still Czechoslovakia. I'd just been to Poland, and for a joke, had bought from a bank a fistful of zlotys (fifties and hundreds) for $1.50. One of the first freedoms exercised by the newly freed populations was the freedom to travel. If your standard of living is tied to three-cent apples and banknotes worth less than blank notepaper, you can't afford much in Paris. The bus from Prague was a communal camper, with food, bed linen—nearly every essential for the trip; it could just as well have driven into the Sahara.

Blake and Virginia Reston were also in from New York. Yvonne and I met them in the lobby of the Ritz, where they were staying. They came in with bags swelling from a Giorgio Armani detour. I'd not met Blake before, but I was old friends with Virginia, a Modigliani beauty in a Chanel suit. Blake was a renowned outdoorsman whose idea of fun was to hang by his fingertips from cliffs. He and I had each dressed in the leather jacket, tie, and loafers ensemble that says, "I'm a guy, so the hell with fashion, but then again, maybe not." The concierge found us a table at Carré des Feuillants, which, judging by the clientele, could have been a French restaurant in Tokyo. Cream soup with pheasant and chestnut bits, partridge with fois gras: Paris, at its best, never fails.

We said good-bye to the Restons, then I told Yvonne, "I've made up my mind. I'm buying a scarf for my ex-girlfriend."

"I thought I'm your ex-girlfriend."

"I mean Julie," I said sheepishly.

"You're in love with her, you know."

"She's my ex-girlfriend."

"Yeah, right. So I get a scarf too?"

A high-keyed New York businesswoman stood alone before a counter at Hermès when Yvonne and I arrived, served by a diminutive blonde wearing the shop's uniform for that season, which was built around a striking red jacket. The New Yorker was having trouble deciding, and scarf after scarf was unfolded for her with a flourish, each landing on the countertop like a sail cascading down a square-rigged mast.

I joined in, and I was just as helpless. Julie was a fashion stylist for a major department store. She could watch a movie and tell you what designer had made an actress's dress and how many seasons old it was. Her sense of color, line, and texture was uncanny. And here I was, her ex-boyfriend, trying to choose a scarf for her with little to guide me—certainly not Yvonne, who quickly tired of the process and disappeared.

It was still in progress when she returned, ten minutes later. "Nothing yet for either of you?" she asked the businesswoman.

"I know his entire story already," she said. "It's for his ex-girlfriend, right? For an ex-girlfriend you don't buy a scarf, you buy a croissant. He's in love with her." She had the same earthy accent as the young woman I'd met at the hotel, but on her it sounded almost melodic, *croissant* coming out as "cwaw-saaawnt."

"Oh, please, I know," said Yvonne, her waving in dismissal.

"I'm a sap," I said.

"Pick a scarf already." Yvonne stood with her arms crossed, her brows knitted with skepticism.

The saleswoman turned to a colleague and whispered in French, "Americans are so exasperating when they can't make up their minds."

Indeed. I hoisted a scarf in black, red, and gold. At the center, a knight rode a high-stepping horse above the words LES MUSEROLLES. There were images of shields and saddle belts and great tassels. It was bold but refined, grand but sparingly ornamented. It was Julie. So I hoped. "I'll take this one," I said, as if announcing the winning city among bidders for the Olympics. Of course, at that moment, the businesswoman said, "You know, I really like that one too," and so bought an identical scarf.

I asked the saleswoman about getting the value-added tax back—a benefit if you were taking goods out of the country. "Which passport do I need?" I produced both German and American versions.

"You have two?" she asked incredulously.

I looked at her calmly. "I couldn't make up my mind." The service she now provided was unusually attentive.

I spent much of the rest of the trip fretting about whether the gift would be correct. Like many men, I hated shopping for anything that lacked moving parts, and the unease about this acquisition was multilayered. Why had I done it? I was brooding over it one afternoon while sitting at a café on the Place de la Contrescarpe, scrawling in my journal, when a man of about thirty approached me and said something in French while pointing toward the square. I stared back dumbly because I was having one of those embarrassing moments with a foreign language when you think you've heard something ridiculous and know that the fault is in your poor comprehension. What he said had sounded like, "Will you help us catch that duck?"

"I'm sorry, would you repeat, please," I said. The man was already in motion, bounding across the gray flagstones in the center of the square. Two other young men were there, both clean cut and dressed as if going out for the evening, each futilely trying to surround and imprison a mallard. He was a steady bird. He'd let the hunters close in, then flap and quack his way through the opposition with the expertise of a running back. Like any good athlete, he knew to conserve his strength, and when he had won the round, he'd slow to a waddle. This he repeated three more times, evading four of us, as I'd now joined in the chase. Another attempt brought the duck to full flight, knee high, down a side street where, perhaps because it was so narrow, he took to his feet again, giving one of our party the chance to sneak up and nab him. He passed the bird to one of the other men, who inspected his prize for whatever it is one seeks in waterfowl and, thanking all, opened the door of a car parked on the square. He placed the duck on the passenger seat and rolled the duck's window higher. They pulled away, each looking as if prepared for an argument on the drive home.

I was standing next to the captor. He wore an oversized shirt that crested at a thin neck, long face, and the tuft of dark hair that, on a young Frenchman, is charming, but which makes an American man look like a mushroom. He had the rough, disdainful manner of an intellectual contemplating whether to steal your bicycle. "What was that all about?" I asked him.

He shrugged. "Dinner?"

Chapter 4

You can choose your partner by how clever, educated, or attractive she is or by how much property she owns or income she brings in. You can choose her by how skilled she is with children and how competently she can manage household affairs. That's all well and good. Julie had filled the fun spaces in my life; if I were to choose her, it would be for beauty, intelligence, wit, and, over it all, the chance for joy. It would be an impractical choice, which is another way of saying it was romantic. I had missed that joy and that romance. My hand, withheld from Julie's shoulder at Meredith's wedding, now reached out to her. She took it into her own.

Without proclamation or fanfare, therefore, we retired the prefix *ex* and got on with our lives together. The Hermès scarf was a hit I would later struggle to replicate.

Months later, the subject of travel came up. We had reached that point where it was becoming indelicate of me to slip off for a couple of weeks alone. No matter: I wanted her to come along. The solitary caveat, I informed her, was that she would have to pass the Fountain Test.

"You want me to say 'What's that, dear?'" she said. "Try me."

I pointed out my living-room window, to the fountain at Lincoln Center, where we had met. "You have to take the suitcase you pack, carry it yourself to there, walk once around the fountain, and back to the apartment, without assistance. If you can pack like a traveler, then we should get along just fine."

"You just watch."

There was such bravado in her reply that I said, "I'm asking too much of you, huh?"

"All men want too much," Julie replied. "Anyway, all the interesting ones."

I had a nasty secret: my kit of photographic equipment had grown more expansive on each trip, until it consumed the interior of my carry-on. It was like the puppy that, in its first car ride, snoozes adorably in your lap, quickly to grow into the slobbering hound that takes up the entire back-seat, his snout protruding from every window. I couldn't, in short, pass the Fountain Test on a dare.

My other problem was that I was unlikely to convince Julie that a night or two in a guest workers' dormitory is just the thing to spice up a vacation. Nor would a quick lunch at the old sausage stand comport with her expectations. That meant I needed to pack virtually a second wardrobe's worth of clothes fit for fine hotels and restaurants. The night before I left, I looked at my bags—one laden with cameras, the other with clothing—wondering why I just didn't give up the pretence and hire a valet named Chumley.

Julie and I flew out on separate airplanes.

Chapter 5

The flyer read—

AMSTERDAM
YOU HAVE BEEN
BUM RUSHED
BY THE BROTHERS
FROM N.Y.C.
HOME BOYZ—
HOME GIRLS
WE HAVE THE GEAR
YOU WANNA WEAR

AT: STRAIT OUTA HARLEM
HAIR-CUTS AVAILABLE BY APPOINTMENT

Hugh Gray sat on the interior stairs of his Amsterdam store, acting very un-Dutch with his easy American smile, pudgy build, two-day stubble, floppy black hat trimmed in shocking pink, and a vertically striped sweater that managed to contain every color indigenous to a Caribbean marketplace. Strait Outa Harlem did not yet have a shop sign, the flyer was Hugh's only business card, but he said the Dutch were buying his clothes: baseball and Malcolm X hats, sweatpants and T-shirts. "They watch rap on MTV, and everything they'd like to wear, I bring here," said Hugh over funky music on the stereo. "Holland in no way caters to rap culture, and I saw a niche I could fill." And so enter Hugh: black, hip, and, being American, a raging entrepreneur.

After a short courtship, Hugh had married a blond-haired, blue-eyed Dutch fashion model, settled in Amsterdam, and opened the store in partnership with a German and a Korean American, who both stopped by and, in contrast to the loquacious Hugh, told me only what they thought I needed to know, each of their abbreviated sentences fragrant with distrust.

Hugh said that the marriage between a New York black man and a local beauty had caused no problems in Amsterdam, which was contrary to his American experience: "Every day the police had me up against a wall. I literally got pulled off the Chicago El three times. The police would look at my wife and smile at her and would say, 'Who is he?'"

Then there was the time Hugh, while wearing a business suit, was trying to hail a cab at O'Hare Airport, only to end the day in a lineup because a black man had shot a policeman. Somehow—Hugh's heretofore detailed account grew vague at this point—a charge of resisting arrest ensued. It had all greatly upset his wife, and the moral of the story was that it was more restful to be a shopkeeper in Amsterdam, selling basketball jerseys, than to seek transportation in Chicago.

Chapter 6

Amsterdam was quiet that weekday morning, even at what should have been rush hour. A hazy sun gave the low, brick city a muted sheen. Rusty old bicycles were propped in rows, their front tires pressed within vertical steel poles like cows in a barn, their necks imprisoned between steel supports. A candy vendor sold fresh chocolates, and I bought a small box of liqueur-filled truffles.

There was a shop window with magazines the covers of which included a cigarette girl with her basket held by clips to her bare nipples, several of nude children, another of a nude woman making inappropriate advances toward a sheep, and another of a woman penetrated by a closed fist. I report this seemingly unforgettable display not for its shock value but because I have no recollection of it. I cataloged the store window in my journal of the trip. Also in the journal is the news that I went to the Rijksmuseum Vincent van Gogh, but I have no recollection of that either. The penance for taking meticulous notes about your travels is to realize how fragile memory can be, of seeing how many remarkable experiences are processed and retained as generalities, if retained at all.

When I'd arrived, early in the morning, I'd checked into the Amsterdam Hilton, a prosaic choice—if you aren't a John Lennon fan (c.f. "The Ballad of John and Yoko"). Julie was flying Icelandair, scheduled to arrive a few hours later. I'd sent a car to pick her up at Schiphol Airport, but her plane never landed. Throughout the day, as I called in for news, the desk clerk would read from dispatches typed on obsolete telegram forms: MS JULIE HACKETT MISSED FLIGHT IN ICELAND. SHE WILL ARRIVE TO-DAY VIA COPENHAGEN . . . MISS HACKETT AIRBORNE KLM . . . The third driver I sent for Julie missed her.

In late afternoon, I was resting in the room, the telegraph forms decorating the nightstand, when Julie blew in. Still in the Donna Karan suit she'd worn to work the day before, she raced toward me with hugs and kisses, saying, at machine-gun pace, "There is this huge guy who comes to the store every day to watch the Michael Kors video. We think he's homeless. When I'm leaving for JFK, there he is, watching. But then I see him again, in the A train. It makes hundreds of stops but he stays on, and I think, what's this about? He switches with me to the airport bus, and now I'm really wondering if he's following me, but he gets off to catch an Alitalia flight. I board my plane, and now it's raining and storming. I'm sitting by the window alone, and it's raining and raining and raining. They say we're going to be an hour and a half late because there is smoke streaming from the left engine. We see guys coming out and throwing all the suitcases out onto the runway in the rain while they fix the engine. We leave two hours late for Reykjavik, but there's no connecting flight by now to Amsterdam, so we're going to Copenhagen. But we're delayed by hours again. Don't ask why. I end up in the smoking section, along with a dozen blond soccer players who drink whiskey for breakfast, smoke their lungs black, and spend the flight trying to talk to me, like the thirteen of us can be a couple. We land in Copenhagen—a really nice, Scandinavian airport, looks like an Ikea store. I have no Danish money and I have to cash a traveler's check to buy an apple and other stuff. They finally tell us Icelandair has given up, so they put us on KLM and it's like being on a real plane for once—you get a 'hello,' you get a newspaper. In the meantime, they're faxing you wherever I go. I get out in Amsterdam—no luggage for me or a lot of the other people I started the trip with in New York. Another train, then I'm strolling around, then I'm in a cab, and I go through the winding streets in the afternoon light, the people hurrying home with their shopping, the buildings lovely in beautiful red brick. The canal houses lean toward the water, like they'll dive in. There is this church, the steeple is white and the road seems to rise and then it's a canal and we're on a bridge, and I say, 'Wow, it's Europe.' The cab jumps onto the tracks and outraces a tram. So here I am."

Julie took a quick shower, then washed her underwear, put it on wet as if that were the most natural thing in the world, added a dash of makeup, and said, "I'm starving." When we returned from dinner, it was to find Julie's suitcase in our room, delivered by one airline or another from somewhere in northern Europe. The bag was half the weight of my own. In it, perfectly folded, were enough designer outfits for both day and evening to assure that Julie would never be seen in the same thing more than twelve hours running, though she could have passed the Fountain Test one-handed.

Chapter 7

B order towns are uneasy places. Languages and cultures mix, sometimes respectfully, sometimes not. Border towns are the first points of unwelcome compromise when the neighbors go on the march, the last to be liberated after the armistice. A train took us to Maastricht, in the appendix that, dipping from the country's southeast corner, squeezes in a few extra square miles of space between Belgium and Germany. A low city of brick and stucco houses, Maastricht is two miles from Belgium and fifteen miles from Germany. Until the nineteenth century, it was one of the most fortified cities in Europe.

There used to be fifty-two churches in Maastricht, but the Dutch are not deeply reverent: statues of four bishops surrounding Mary on the Column of the Virgin are collectively known as the Bridge Club. Churches had shut down over the years, but the Catholic Sint Servaasbasiliek, or Basilica of St. Servatius, had been recently restored. The Romanesque arches wore fresh coats of gray and yellow. The Gothic vaults were festively painted with decorations accurate to their period, yet we could hear American and Canadian visitors complain that it all looked too bright, too new. There is a North American romantic need for Europe to live under a patina. We want Europe to play the wise, old father to our impudent adolescent. Europeans, if they bother to pray at all, would rather do it in clean churches.

There were more than four hundred pubs in town, and none of them appeared to suffer for patronage. Supposedly the smallest bar in the country, In Demoriaan, was too tiny to support a two-man brawl. In Den Ouden Vogelstruys was the oldest, but Café Sjiek had a pleasant look, and you could get lunch there. Julie was skeptical about Dutch cuisine, but a local man, seeing her perplexity over the choices, offered assistance. I was to grow used to kindly men who would take an interest in helping us, approaching Julie with cautious yet smooth generosity, usually while I was not present. They would keep talking once I made my presence known, if only to prove innocent intent. This gentleman was mature, his hair gray, his sweater vivid yellow. He was comfortable around women. He was, if a bit old for the role, most certainly Julie's type.

"This is a regional specialty," said the man of the soup he helped Julie order.

"What's it called?" she asked.

"Vermicelli."

The main course arrived. "Is there a local name for this?" Julie asked.

"Veal croquette." The waiter served us a Dutch wine, Sint Pieters-berger Slavante, grown near the northern limit of Continental soil that can support grapes. It was a white, tangy and dry. Next he brought a kind of pie made with rice. Confectioner's sugar was dusted across the top. "What do you call it?" Julie asked her translator.

"I don't know. Rice pie, I guess." He said he had to eat it at his mother-in-law's place every Sunday. The waiter, however, called the pie *vlaai*.

Our evening tavern was Knypke, where a troupe of singers marched into the crowd and made pretty, pale women join their act. The percussionist thumped an enormous drum slung across his chest. The pale women drank dark beer and laughed. We left late, while the party raged on.

Chapter 8

Manhattanite's driver's license is like his Tiffany credit card: little used, it signifies that he possesses higher powers than he customarily displays. Neither Julie nor I had ever owned an automobile. She had last driven in Tampa two months earlier, and then only briefly, under nervous parental supervision. I had not touched a steering wheel since a Fort Lauderdale Christmas, but Budget Rent-a-Car had a trusting nature; it handed over the keys to an Opel with automatic transmission. We'd agreed that it was best for me to do most of the driving and for Julie to assume the position of chief navigator. I took out the five road maps I'd brought and handed them to Julie, who inspected the pictures on the covers. I placed a compass between us, familiarized myself with the controls, and skimmed the English-language portion of the owner's manual.

I'd once thought Susanne's arcane sense of direction had been charming. My current navigator's idea of map reading was to point to a spot on the paper that seemed to represent where we should go and then to stick it into my face while we were in moving traffic. Whenever I'd have words with Julie about that, she would give a direction at the first of several needed turns, then throw the map into the backseat so as to clear her lap of all obstruction. By our second drive, I'd caught on that Julie wasn't really consulting the map. Her method was to rely on instincts, which consistently failed her. I came to recognize the danger signs: the peering out of all windows, the tilting back of the head as she searched within her for spiritual communion with our destination, the twittering flush that brought forth the answer, giving birth to the hesitant response, growing firmer with each syllable: "I—think—it's—*that* street."

When I tried to convey that I found the technique wanting—expressing myself with perhaps more frustration than prudence would have suggested—Julie dismissed my methodical nature as recidivist Germanism. A crossroads was approaching.

"Where do I go?" I asked.

"Go that way," Julie said firmly, pointing left.

"Why?"

"I have a feeling."

We tried several variations before ending up right where we started.

Julie had a revelation: "I'm not very good at navigation." Our morning exit from town took a half hour.

At Vaals, a village on the border, we dropped our bags at a hotel and crossed into Germany. European unification had recently ended border checks within member countries. The old customs house was shut, the barrier gates removed. Only a sign with the word DEUTSCHLAND inside the EU flag told us we were approaching Aachen, Germany. We walked to a brook with a footbridge, ducks of all colors swimming below. Two boys kicked a rubber ball to the roof of a church, once scoring a hit on the roof and once on me. The brook was the national boundary.

Chapter 9

There are two documented examples of perpetual motion: the screaming child on a long airplane flight and the lamb shank rotating on the skewer at a souvlaki stand. We had no German money, and to get change for the parking meter, I asked a souvlaki maker I found in Aachen if I could buy a single German mark from him for two Dutch guilders.

"What would I want with Dutch money?" he asked in Greek-accented German. He was a young man, but you could hear in his weathered voice and see in his deli-man demeanor the frustrations of dead-end employment.

"It's good business," I insisted. "You nearly double your money, and you can use the guilders when you go to the Netherlands."

"*If* I go to the Netherlands," he said, as if we were talking about Turkey. He gave me a mark to get rid of me, but I insisted on handing over my share of the bargain. He pushed the Dutch coins behind the counter with the disregard given worthless lottery tickets. He had come all the way from Greece to within walking distance of the Netherlands and could not conceive of why he should go there. We disliked each other with mutual, passive disregard.

Aachen had a handsome old town with stores finer than those we had seen in Maastricht. Because German shops closed on Saturday afternoons, Julie was left to despair over handbags and blouses sealed behind plate glass.

Great doors, however, admitted us to a Byzantine octagon surrounded by a sixteen-sided ambulatory. This core, the Pfalzkapelle (or Palatine

Chapel, was designed late in the eighth century by Odo of Metz for Emperor Charlemagne, who, favoring Aachen for its warm springs, held court there.

It is easy to look upon our own age as troubled, but consider the eighth century: In Constantinople, Empress Irene at last broke through the glass ceiling: she became the first female monarch of the Byzantine Empire by blinding and deposing Emperor Constantine VI, who happened to be her son. (There are sound reasons why *Byzantine* is not applied in approbation.) Nor was the West overly genteel in matters of succession. A couple of decades earlier, Charlemagne, the king of the Germanic Franks, had become king of the Lombards by besieging and taking Pavia, where his nephews, who had claim to a share of the Frankish kingdom, had fled with their widowed mother; the nephews then disappeared.

It was not merely politics but also religion that famously stirred the medieval imagination. Charlemagne did his good deed for Christianity by conquering, but also converting, the pagan Saxons. Resistance was perceived as apostasy, requiring the mass execution of forty-five hundred. As the century drew to a close, Pope Leo III was forced from Rome by political opponents. He went to Charlemagne for assistance. The Frankish king was instrumental in restoring the pope to Rome. On Christmas Day of the year 800, in St. Peter's, Leo stuck a crown onto Charlemagne's head and, to the surprise of the king, the Romans in assembly declared him their emperor. Thus concluded the eighth century, and thus began the Holy Roman Empire—the Germans' First Reich. Bismarck established the Second, and the Third, of course, was Hitler's doing.

It was in its fight with Reich Mark III that the American army took Aachen 1,144 years later—the first prewar German city captured by the West. True to form, the Americans roundly smashed up the municipality before subduing it. In one of those happy miracles of conflict, and in a reprise of the good fortune visited upon the cathedral of Cologne, Charlemagne's octagon, and the cathedral into which it was incorporated, escaped with minor damage. Its Gothic choir now held a gilded, house-shaped reliquary said to contain the bones of the emperor; a superstitious observer might call them lucky charms.

Along the perimeter walls of the Carolingian octagon, four layers of Roman arches ascend to the dome. Although the octagon admits little light, it has an enveloping feel unusual in churches—indeed, something I'd been more accustomed to finding in mosques. Western Christianity is a hierarchical faith, favoring auditorium seating in its places of worship. There were neat lines of pews in the cathedral of Aachen. The motherly octagon, however, conspired against the miliary bearing of the pews.

At the town square, parents held up children to play with the movable limbs of a bronze statue. A prayer meeting was held in a circle of song. "I can see why you like it here," said Julie. She meant Germany. I felt I had accomplished one of the most difficult tasks in travel: sharing with some-one not merely the sight of a favorite area, but its feeling.

At our hotel's restaurant, we had drinks with a couple from Vancouver. They drank heavily and told lusty stories, which Julie matched, then bettered. She came away with the nickname Tiger Lily.

By the next morning, we had another go at driving and navigating. Julie unfolded two maps, and off we went for our motor tour of the Netherlands. Julie called out the turns and we sped down open highways, covering a distance that grew unaccountably long.

Chapter 10

"We're in Belgium?" I said.

The abandoned customs house and EU sign with the word BELGIE told us we had blundered across another border. I made a U-turn legal only in war and set us back north. We would later find the correct map in the glove compartment, where Julie had thrown it as an afterthought.

We arrived at the Sint Pietersberg—Mount St. Peter—caves as the nearby church tolled "Oh! Susannah" on its noontime bells. Mount St. Peter towers about 360 feet over the Dutch countryside. Two hundred miles of limestone caves run underneath. The Romans quarried limestone inside the mountain, using the stones for fortifications. Pliny described the caves in A.D. 50. The French and the Dutch fought, in 1794, at a cave fort (later reorganized as a restaurant). World War II saw the caves used as an air-raid shelter, and later years brought mushroom cultivation. There were fossils and twelve varieties of bat, and here I exhaust my knowledge of the caves of Mount St. Peter.

We learned all this because we joined a tour led by a dour young man. He had short, neat hair and large, dark-rimmed glasses, wore a white shirt, floral-print tie, and, except for the blue jeans, could have passed for a revenue agent. His name was Louis Vandenbosch. He spent much of his time inside tunnels of solid limestone and had, somewhere in the past, determined that he was going to be the best limestone guide in all creation. He accomplished that, but not without a certain level of pedantry. He pointed with his big flashlight at a monochrome mural of the crowned Virgin and Child, and Julie asked, "Did people seek shelter in here during the last war?"

"I haven't got to that yet," he said.

"But this was a chapel, right?"

"Wrong, wrong, wrong."

Louis said that French combat engineers once tried to blow up the fortress that had stood atop the mountain. They used about thirteen hundred pounds of black powder but were off by about five hundred feet; they succeeded only in blowing down some side tunnels and several of their own men.

Louis's delivery of that fact was expectedly somber, so I tried a note of witless levity: "Well, that's French army engineering for you."

"I'm sorry," said Louis, "I was born in France."

I begged his forgiveness, hurriedly making up a French mother for myself. He said he was used to it, that he heard it all the time. There were no new jokes or insults in the limestone caves of Holland. Louis waved his great flashlight and continued onward, resolute and stern, a touch of melancholy in his eyes, wondering if his words, so carefully chosen, could even touch these tourists' souls with the mysteries of one of the world's great limestone caves.

Another mural was of a man with a pipe who appeared to be filing a handsaw used in cutting the limestone blocks.

"I'd heard you need diamond-tipped saw teeth for that work," I said.

"Wrong, wrong, wrong."

Chapter 11

I was growing comfortable with the driving, but Julie, who is quite athletic, found the car confining. *Sie hat kein Sitzfleisch* (she can't sit still) goes the German. I'd soon learn that for Julie to enjoy an opera or concert, we'd need box seats—of the kind not bolted down—so that she could fidget. When traveling by automobile, it was always best to let her get out now and then and run around. So it was when we came to a solemn place, the Netherlands American Cemetery at Margraten.

"I said a place to jog, not mourn," said Julie as we read names on headstones.

"There are plenty of paths."

"It seems so disrespectful. I should be planting poppies."

"Maybe just a brisk walk—"

Julie looked around, as if readying to steal the flowers from beneath a headstone. "No one's watching, I guess."

"I always wanted to do it in a cemetery," I said.

Julie looked at me with glowering suspicion. "You're strange, you know that?" I must have drawn a long face, because she added, diplomatically, "It's one of your charms."

So Julie went jogging, her hands inside the sleeves of her oversized sweater, circling the car. When she had grown comfortable with that, she ventured past the American oaks of the central mall and into the pathways leading to rows of white, skeletal headstones, running until she had tuckered out enough to settle back into the navigator's seat.

Genocide against my coreligionists had brought my parents separately to America, where they met and produced me. Yet I was a citizen in good standing of the nation that, in my parents' lifetime, had gone out of its way to eliminate people like me. Borders once fought so hard over were nothing but signs on the highways or rivulets patrolled by ducks and schoolboys. Here, in what was once farmland, pickets of crosses, broken only by the occasional Star of David, rose over the remains of 8,302 soldiers who grew up a hemisphere away. Most of them never lived as long as Julie or I, and nearly all died violently at the hands of men they did not know. The walkways between their bodies now gave stout service as a jogging path; the grass grown over them formed grounds through which I strolled, ate an apple, and studied a road map with borders between old enemies marked more vividly in ink than in reality.

Chapter 12

We were following a meandering route that would require two days to travel from Maastricht to Amsterdam, though a highway drive could have put us there before lunch. We missed some turns, and Julie, trying her best with the map, advised a few dicey maneuvers. After I had executed one of them, she wondered aloud, "Where would we be without U-turns?"

"Belgium," I reminded her.

The entire country was laid out for comfort, every street and bicycle path carefully marked, not a trace of litter on them. The vvv sign marked the tourist office of every hamlet large enough to support a village idiot. Triangular signs warned of crossings by whatever creature was illustrated within; we saw separate signs for cows, frogs, and schoolchildren. The first sprouts of the spring crop rose in yellow and green along the open countryside. A farmer drove his grandchildren by horse cart through a redbrick village. The nuclear-power plant outside Roermond was suitable for framing.

Under clear skies, the hills sparkled like sand dunes, but it was when clouds appeared that the landscape was at its best. The clouds closed and opened capriciously to expose a vivid blue swath through which a hard shaft of sunlight would strike fields and houses. It was the light of Dutch seventeenth-century landscape painting, the shadows deep and austere, the highlights glistening and sumptuous.

Then the scenery flattened along a broad horizon, every tuft of arable land put to work. Houses rose from nests of flowers toward orange-tiled roofs. Roads were canopied by the branches of thick trees planted in single file on either side.

The thick trees of the south then gave way to white birch and evergreen, and the ground became wet and marshy. On the road to Heusden were canal barges moored behind dikes that were not mere levees but redoubts fortified against nature.

Heusden looked like a movie set between takes. Inert windmills loomed over the empty harbor, a quaint pedestrian drawbridge, a city gate with a tower and cannon. One of the many pristine, redbrick houses, listing ever so charmingly with age, was having its wooden trim repainted by hands currently absent, the unfinished work just perceptibly an improvement over the seemingly immaculate predecessor. I had been told that the town had been run down until the 1960s; that all this perfection had been heaped upon it since. Undoubtedly, the populace was too imperfect to be allowed further habitation, as we saw virtually no one except within a couple of houses where shades were parted, revealing cozy interiors, a housewife with her kettle, a man and his newspaper.

We spent the night in a small duplex apartment in a convivially petit hotel called In den Verdwaalde Koogel, which means "in the stray bullet." The building, extant since the seventeenth century, had suffered through a number of the frequent sieges that the once fortified town had endured, taking a stray shot; in one version of the story, it had been a cannonball. The only comfort to be gathered was that, as no human being could possibly have been present in Heusden to receive hostile fire, a direct hit of any caliber would have caused no injury.

Chapter 13

Our return flight from Amsterdam, about sixty miles away, was scheduled for just after one the next afternoon. Because of the delay in her arrival, Julie had missed the Rijksmuseum and had been disappointed by what was an unspeakable omission on a first trip to the Netherlands. Over dinner, I said, "I know I'm a little overenthusiastic about planning."

"Like Attila the Hun was a little overenthusiastic about plunder."

Self-deprecation is not a clever way to start a conversation with Julie. I pressed onward. "If you let me plan this out, I can get you to the Rijksmuseum before the flight leaves."

"Okay, you've got my attention. What do I have to do?"

"Get up early."

"How early?"

"Maybe seven."

"Wait, you promised I could drive."

Oh, damn. She'd remembered. "Right."

"I'm a very good driver."

"We're getting up at six."

"You're on."

We awoke at six the next morning and were in the car by seven. No parent handing keys to a teenager for the first time could have done so with greater trepidation. In her own family, Julie's flubs with automobiles were legendary. While she had never had an accident with one, people riding with her were known to experience religious conversions after only three stop signs. A support group had been formed of fellow passengers. Car dealerships closed early on her birthday. What Julie brought to the driving experience was a lack of experience—as do nearly all Manhattanites—and a timidity bred from that inexperience. Most of us, men especially, are too stupid to realize how bad we are at driving; Julie, a sensitive and intuitive woman, was all too cognizant of her own weaknesses with machinery. Until now.

"We're about to start up!" said Julie. The engine was quickly purring.

"Yea, though I walk through the valley of the shadow of death—" I said.

"Thy rod and thy staff they comfort me," Julie interrupted.

"For I am buckled up."

"I'm the driver. I get to talk too now." We lurched forward. "This is simple."

"Sure. Just aim the car and pray."

The windmill flew by. We were headed out of town. "Okay, where are we going?" Julie waited with false piety for directions. "This is so much easier. I love being the driver! I hate being the navigator!"

With one of the maps, I got us to a main road. "We're heading—"

"In the wrong direction."

I checked the compass. "We're heading east." I had been trying for north.

Julie spun the wheel around. "This is what's been wrong the whole trip: I didn't get to drive!"

"All right, Julie, try to keep the car in *our* lane."

"I am in our lane. I drive better than you."

We were soon on the highway, and Julie, in that end-of-the-trip mood that inspires reflection, said, "Heusden was a pretty town, but it gave me the creeps. It was almost too clean, as if people weren't living there, just coming in, using the hotels and leaving."

"Like us."

"Yes, but—" Something, I could see, was troubling her. "You know that town we were in a couple of days ago?"

"Thorn?"

"Didn't that one look like you're walking through a van Gogh? On the road in—the light on the countryside. The whitewashed buildings and the little church with the angels. There was an angel inside the church and there was another angel as you were going in that watched over you and it was very pretty." Julie grew quiet and detached. She will do that sometimes; one minute she is with you, and the next, she is deep into thought and feeling. She returned to me now with, "That church meant the most to me. No one else was there, the angels were over us. I was thanking God that He let us come here and that we are healthy."

I remembered how Julie had lit a single candle in that little church, a reed-thin taper she'd placed in a row with many others, offering a silent prayer. I'd photographed her doing it, studying her face through my viewfinder, cheeks and brow glowing in the candlelight, eyes on the candles, her mind on God and her heart with Him. "What were you thinking then," I asked, "after you had placed your candle?"

"I was thinking that—I want to be better."

"Better?"

"Yes."

"How?"

"Better to you. Better to my family." We'd had a fight about something now long since forgotten, one of those quarrels couples have on the road, particularly before travel expectations have melded.

"We have to be good to each other," I said.

"Yes, we do," said Julie. "While we have time."

We each held to private thoughts for some minutes before Julie said, "The light here looks so different from light in North America. Maybe not in Canada where it's harder and more northern, but here every day the sky is gray, white, and pale blue—dramatic but still subtle. There aren't any grand views, no deserts or rugged mountains, but it's all so lovely. Look at that!"

Along the roadside were rows of trees with a low, blue mist hovering around their brown trunks. As every travel photographer knows, nature is at its ineffable best, its beauty most grand and surprising, just after dawn and just before sunset. "You live so long," said Julie, "for a few seconds of serenity."

That was the artist in her talking, and the woman who believed in God. It was all quite the same with Julie.

Chapter 14

"Okay," I confirmed with the road signs, "we're on the road to Amsterdam. Julie, you'll need to get into the left lane for Utrecht. Go right now. Okay, you're clear. Doing great."

"Damn," said Julie. "I can't be Europsycho driver anymore because the cars are slowing up behind me and stuck in front of me."

"All right, honey. We'll take a little longer to get there. We gave ourselves enough time."

The congestion cleared, and we were at speed again. "This is like driving a race car," said Julie. "Do you know how many of the signs on the road mean 'full stop'?"

"No."

"The square ones, I think. The other ones I think mean 'yield.'"

That brought to mind: "Do you suppose we should have been stopping now and then?"

"I almost figured it out, didn't I?"

"Good job." I reflected further. "Maybe we should have asked."

"We didn't hit anything."

"Nothing living, anyway." But I'd lost her attention again.

"I think of what's lacking here that makes everything so great," said Julie. "There are no shopping malls. You don't feel that push all the time to consume, consume, consume. There are no big billboard signs as you drive around the country. There aren't gas stations every ten minutes on the highway, just one half hidden by the road every now and then."

"Try to get ahead of the Amstel beer truck," I said. "That's it. Now watch it, those lanes are going to merge in front to the right as well. If you want to go behind these cars to the right—"

A roar sounded beside us, accompanied by a flash of black leather. Julie laughed. "It's a motorcycle! Europsycho on the move! I've never been in a country where you see so many people on bicycles. They go by in races, they go by exercising. A motorcycle? Wrong, wrong, wrong. Amsterdam! Here we go." The first sign naming our destination had appeared. A car sped past us. "I can see now how people like Porsches. Hit the accelerator and you're home."

But the traffic became thick again, thicker than it had been before. We stopped, we crept along. We stopped again. Cars ahead of us moved, but we were standing still. I glanced at Julie, discovered her asleep and nudged her awake. "I got bored," she said. We changed drivers.

At precisely nine-twelve we sighted the Rijksmuseum, found a lot, and parked. At nine twenty-eight, we entered Bodega Keyzer, a popular restaurant, for a final Dutch hot chocolate. At nine fifty-seven Julie took her place in the line forming outside the museum while I bought tickets. We crossed the threshold at ten-oh-four, and within minutes, waves of schoolchildren overwhelmed the cashier, ruining the chance of entry for anyone with an early-afternoon flight.

Thus did Julie get to enjoy the museum's row of Vermeers—the interiors with their incomparable window light and the sole exterior view, its low clouds and red brick exactly the same as we had seen along our journey. We discussed the composition and palette of *The Night Watch* until it was time to go.

The gas station before the airport was two pumps at a storefront. The attendant looked at our Opel with disdain. "I make regular visits to the States," he said in fine English. "When I go, I rent the Lincoln Town Car. It's better than that German junk you are driving. Better than the Japanese junk." He would willingly have run through the junk of the industrialized world for us, but we had a plane to catch.

At passport control at the airport, a thick-faced, uniformed man scowled officiously at me from his booth, asking me a question in Dutch. If you know English and German, you can sometimes comprehend Dutch, but I gave up and asked, "Do you speak English?"

"Don't you speak German?" he asked stiffly, staring at my German passport, then back at me, to see if the picture matched the face.

"A little," I said in German, leading him on.

"Only a little?" he answered, his German as gruff as his Dutch.

"I was born in the United States," I answered in German.

"Where do you live in Germany?" You could feel his excitement at uncloaking a man of espionage.

"I don't live in Germany, but in the United States."

This worthy sentinel at last let me pass, his suspicions still simmering. If there was yet a place in Europe for a border patrol, here stood a man determined to fill the ranks.

When I got home, I tried to write a travel article about the trip, but it wasn't working. Good travel writing isn't about places, it's about the experience of being in places. Nothing I wrote made sense to me. The rhythms were off. There were inexplicable gaps in the narrative, as if whole pieces of the story were being held in secret. I groped to the obvious conclusion: my experience had not been my encounter with the Netherlands; it had been my encounter with Julie's encounter with Netherlands. To deny that Julie was central to the story was to deny the essential truth of the experience and so to miss the point. The article, the first in my series *Travels with Julie,* was a surprising success. Far from being a burden on my craft, Julie was beginning to prove indispensable.

Chapter 15

August had nearly burned itself out when I earned another reprieve from the insurance company. In fairness to Julie, who had let me choose northern Europe last time out, we were now to fulfill her dearest travel wish with a plunge deep into the Italian boot. Because Julie understood that Italians value appearance, she brought twice as much clothing as she had to the Netherlands, yet her suitcase remained only partially full. I can't say how she achieved this second, more accomplished amendment to the laws of physics. Other aspects of my account of this trip must also lack for precision because portions of my notebook were defoliated by hair spray. I can say, however, that we had passed sufficiently down the romantic road as to take the same airplane this time, and we even sat together.

At Amsterdam's Schiphol Airport, I had made only a brief stop to change money, yet by the time I'd arrived at the baggage carousel, my suitcase was the last one left, carried like the solitary child on the merry-go-round at a rain-washed fair. At Rome's Fiumicino Airport, hordes bumped and shimmied to collect bags fallen over each other like Attic ruins. No matter. A few broken elevators and people movers later, and we were at the train platform. A heat wave was in progress, and the suitcases were like sacks of rice. I grew so dehydrated that Julie had to buy me mineral water.

It flowed cool and fresh, the bubbles tingling my throat. I remembered the hot bus of my student tour through Italy, the bare feet dangling over the armrests, the Tuscan heat wet, fragrant, and indomitable. I closed my eyes and, forcing that memory from my mind, I imagined the cool, green mountains of Switzerland—a reverie that would have unintended implications for our next trip.

A train, a taxi, and we arrived at the hotel then called the Pullman Boston. We checked in, and as we followed the bellman to our room, one of the desk clerks nodded toward Julie and softly said to the other, *"Bella."* Even more than in the Netherlands, we would thus attract attention throughout our stay. You can't help but admire a nation with good taste in women.

Julie opened the shutters of our room. We overlooked terra-cotta houses and the rich greens of the Villa Borghese, a public park. It was like a scene by Cezanne, filtered through the hot, iridescent light, except that the dome of St. Peter's improved the composition. That Mediterranean light: I'd forgotten how I'd missed it. No other light presents itself so seductively. We walked to the Spanish Steps, and while I was taking a photograph of the fountain, the tourists, the young men on scooters, and the pink stucco house where John Keats died, a Gypsy girl's hand slithered into my wallet pocket. I snagged the little mitt, its owner yelped, then she sauntered back to a corpulent woman who, from the comfort of a seat in the shade, was supervising an afternoon of robbery by several children, egging them on in Romany.

Julie and I had the distinction of being in Italy when its currency was at a record high against the dollar. Shortly after we left, its value would plummet, but because everything was comically, if temporarily, overpriced for Americans, few were in Rome. As best we could determine on our first day, there were exactly three others: a round-faced, good-natured doctor from Orange County, California, along with his wife and son. In a short walking tour of the city, we thrice crossed paths with them, the meetings moving progressively from surprise acquaintance to the hailings of neighbors.

Near Via Venato there was a small, famous restaurant called Piccolo Mondo. Almost no one was there that night. The waiter gave us a menu in English—always a danger sign. I'd have needed tweezers and a jeweler's loupe to find the meat in my spaghetti Bolognese, but the skimpiness of the portion assured that my ordeal was quickly over. The check arrived with a cover charge—a tax on body and patience levied by Italian restaurants. It came to ten dollars, and I had the impertinence to ask what exactly it was for. The table and the bread, said the waiter. Given the quality of the bread, there was enough left over in the charge to have paid for the table and its shipment home, so I protested. The waiter said to talk to the manager, and by the way, service is not included.

The manager was a heavyset man in late middle age, sitting at the bar, gossiping with a couple of regulars. We had a staredown. I said that no cover had been stated on the English-language menu. He said it was a customary add-on. Perhaps, I replied, but protein and flavor are customary as well. He pointed to the bill with a stubby finger as thick as a pickle and said he could do nothing. I smiled and said he would have to try harder. He took the bill from my hand, and in a grand gesture, tore it to pieces, his chin raised in self-satisfied defiance.

"Boy, that showed me," I said to Julie. I handed the waiter his fair share.

On the walk back, I said that nothing so far had disabused me of the belief that, for all its formality and refinement, there was something about Italy that warned you it could, at any minute, skid into grubbiness and petty thievery. There is a soft spot in the hearts of many for the charming, roguish Italian who is always polite, never quite honest, not overly hard-working, and somehow lives entirely well enough. Like the gifted schoolboy who waits until the last night to write his paper, which brims with intelligence but draws the grade of B due to haste, Italy stumbles along on compromise and mediocrity until, by the hand of some god or devil, it tosses off a Leonardo, a Verdi, a Marconi, or, to be fair to the lesser arts, a Ferrari or an Armani.

Germans, in contrast, can be aggravating, but for me, it is aggravation in wholly familiar ways. Going to Germany is like visiting my family: welcoming, spirited, and annoying. I like nearly all the people I meet in Germany, but when we have our tough moments, the Germans and I repeat patterns of bad behavior the origins of which are lost to us. It would be unimaginable for a German restaurateur to have destroyed the check; once inscribed with a price, the fairness of which had been calculated with excruciating care—like those notches at 0.2 liter on the beer glasses in Cologne—it would become an official document: inviolate, perfect, sacrosanct. It could no more be ignored than a traffic summons, the restaurateur no more capable of being talked out if it than a Frankfurt cop.

The worldly south, with its bravado, its grand and futile gestures, was known to me, yet it remained foreign. The north was masculine, hardworking, and obvious; the south was feminine, capricious, corrupt, free spirited yet circumspect. The south teased with beauty, broken promises, and lies. You could not make demands of the south; you had to seduce it. In earlier visits to Italy, I'd been cheated of a dollar or two in the course of a day and considered it the price of admission. At the prevailing exchange rate (one thousand lire to the dollar), I was now being cheated in multiples of ten—still not enough to matter, but I foamed with indignation fueled by an American sense of fair play. Add to that a Germanic righteousness of a kind that has frequently been calamitous for both Germans and their neighbors. Wouldn't it be fun, I asked Julie, to cheat the bastards back?

Julie's maternal family was Sicilian. She had come upon the idea independently. "So what's the plan?"

Chapter 16

On this, our second overseas trip, Julie and I were slowly accomplishing what all couples must accomplish if they are to remain couples: we were learning to compromise on points of difference that were new to us, to anticipate the other's needs about matters grown more familiar, and, ultimately, to fabricate a common approach by which uniformity of method and goal would transcend all differences. We devised an esoteric set of signals to help smooth over the rough patches. For example, if one of us should dawdle perhaps too long on a painting, double-scoop gelato, or shop-window purse, the other would take the role of an imaginary tour-group leader and call out, "The bus is leaving!" The laggard would be obliged to comply. Division of labor was also essential. I organized hotels and transportation; Julie orchestrated sight-seeing, earning her the venerable title of The Book. Given our experience in the Netherlands, I doubled as The Map. Harmony, of a kind, reigned—except about food.

Food became a leitmotif of this trip because it was Julie's belief that Italian cooking held supremacy over all other styles. We had Italian food when I was a boy. There was spaghetti in a red sauce, available either with or without meatballs. There were also macaroni and cheese, ravioli (option: beef or cheese), and pizza. The menus of Italian restaurants were short because, except for the odd chicken or fish, there was nothing else Italian to serve.

My as yet incomplete education forced Julie into the role of advocate. One night, over a plate of vermicelli in clam sauce, she said, "Hitler ate pasta for his last meal. I guess in the end he was coming to his senses." I replied that, as the other branch of her family carried such surnames as Hackett, McHatten, Musser, and Eschelmann, half her ancestors considered steak, potatoes, and beer a ripping good meal. That did nothing to ease Julie's suspicions that I was part of a German conspiracy to bring tasteless, fat-laden dishes to the unsuspecting size-four women of America. She would scrutinize three or more restaurants before agreeing where to dine. Disharmony was at the gates.

What a relief, therefore, that Julie approved Taverna Ripetta, a small restaurant near the Mausoleum of Augustus, without even checking competitors. There were maybe fifteen tables. The stereo played harmless Euro rock. The proprietress was Fatma U-Kordy, formerly of Egypt; she was a full-figured, zesty woman of no small charm. The Egyptian chef was back home on vacation, so she hoped we did not mind that she acted as his substitute. Her husband, Umberto Pizzi, a lanky Italian with black hair and a beard half gone to gray, likewise served as substitute waiter. After a perfect risotto appetizer, Julie elected the grilled *romba* (turbot). I note the original because I had studied Italian over the summer. Julie's Italian consisted of pointing to me in response to any question.

Fatma spoke English, but she was having trouble. "It is—how do you say? It is—aye! Wait, one minute, please." She disappeared into the kitchen and returned with a waiter's cart. On top of it, lying on a turkey plate like a patient on a hospital gurney, was an uncooked flatfish.

Fatma halted the cart in front of our table. "It's fine," said Julie.

"Fine?" asked Fatma.

"Yes, lovely."

"You want this?" Fatma's hand, poised above the fish, circumnavigated its perimeter.

"Yes."

"Okay, yes," she said obligingly and wheeled the patient into surgery. It turned out that Julie enjoyed her *romba* very much; she left not a scrap on her plate, although she couldn't help but notice the attention she was drawing from other diners.

One Italian word I had not learned is *ètto* (hectogram). It wasn't until the check arrived that we realized the price of seven thousand lire was for a single hundred-gram portion; Julie had eaten five hundred grams, or slightly more than a pound of marine life.

"Italian families—they eat fish on Friday and Tuesday nights," explained Fatma. "This fish is for a family, a little for all as one course."

"I ate enough for a family of five?"

"I suppose," said Fatma, adding, "People who order so much are heavy, but you—like this." She held up a single finger to illustrate, then brought desserts in honor of Julie's accomplishment—fresh figs with basil, a fruity and flavorful conclusion to the evening, generously donated by the management.

Chapter 17

M y favorite building in Rome, and one to which Julie and I kept returning, dates from the classical city. It is the Pantheon—a rotunda with a portico appended for both function and aesthetic balance and a grand dome with a hole left at its center through which a disc of sunlight trails across the walls and floors as the day progresses. It was built by the Romans in the second century and dedicated, democratically, to all the gods. In 609, it became the first temple in Rome to convert to Christianity.

The Pantheon survived decline and fall and worse. The barbarians who plundered Rome didn't dismantle it. Bernini, when he set about using ancient monuments as stone quarries for his architectural work, didn't scavenge it for parts.

I like to think that the gods have watched over their temple and do so still. The Jewish God is a manly brute, and it can be slow going for someone raised Jewish to see frail, bloodstained Jesus as the next best thing to God. Mary, however, is easy to understand. In its drive to reform the dependence that the ancient world had on iconography, Judaism tossed away the motif of the goddess. It was a terrible loss not to have the feminine add balance, grace, and, occasionally, womanly counterfire, to the masculine domain of Jehovah. Mary, uncommonly gentle even by the milder standards of the goddess—a title that she formally is not granted— is as much responsible for Christian humility as her son, and it is this humility that makes Christianity exceptional among the major faiths.

If the universe has any deistic intelligence, it is comforting to believe that the intelligence is not singular and solipsistic, but multiple and social, like humankind. The Roman building with the hole in its skull goes on strong because it is beautiful, but I like to believe (and this may be pure romanticism at work) that it also serves an unspoken function: it reminds us of pagan origins that modern faiths can only imperfectly mask. It answers the question "Is there a God?" with the welcome news that there are gods enough for all.

Chapter 18

Roman authorities contrived that every place we wished to see was closed or closing whenever we wished to see it. We were like sport fishermen who, having been assured that such and such was an ideal spot, spent great effort finding it, only to end the day eating hamburger. We became so frustrated that The Book would check *The Blue Guide* for closing times with the anxious diligence of a commuter pulling a train schedule from her briefcase.

The Palazzo Barberini, by obvious administrative error, opened as scheduled. This was deeply ironic for Julie, who had experienced similar problems with closing times on previous visits to Rome, with the result that she had never been inside the palace, despite laying siege to its doors on several occasions. Pungent with heat, the building was worn and dingy, its galleries poorly marked, its middle-aged guards slipping into torpor. Scattered patrons shot camera flashes into canvases by Caravaggio and Bronzino that boiled in the hot, wet air. No "Kein Blitz" warnings here; in a thousand years, the art of the palace may rot from mildew and fade under pulses of white light, but future generations will be compensated by still-extant images of the Krupp family at that comical mansion in Essen. Renovation work on the facade of the Palazzo Barberini promised a transition; for all I know, the museum is now as finely climate controlled, the displays as carefully organized, and the guards as assiduous in their duties as in any provincial Swiss museum that preserves the cow bells and milk buckets of generations past.

Indeed, at some point during the previous two decades, a conspiracy of architects and craftsmen had quietly begun the renovatation of Italy. The all-but-broken-down hotel, its carpet last changed during the Quattrocento, its keys dangling from handles fashioned from medieval church-bell clappers, was fast becoming extinct. Monuments that had formerly been sootily charming or rancid from pollution and organic grime were as scrubbed and polished as ships on parade. Julie remembered the Trevi Fountain as charcoal gray. It now glistened in white stone and gold lettering, its waters an inviting azure. The Galleria Borghese had recently reopened, its restored interior now worthy of its Bernini sculptures. All Rome looked like the Europe of one of those humorless mid-century comedy films, the kind in which the pretty American arrives and, one zany thing leading to another, marries money.

Air conditioning, however, was still relatively rare, and Roman interiors were no cooler than the streets. Nights were not much cooler than days, though night came on as peremptory blackness, quickly enveloping the view from our hotel window, save the dome of St. Peter's, which shimmered a dull, gauzelike gray through the humid air, day or night. By day, foreigners congregated on and around the Spanish Steps, some plopping barefoot into the fountain or drinking from it; at night, English-speaking buskers would try their luck, singing Beatles songs in a Bob Dylan accent, young Italians struggling to follow along.

On our fourth day, a Sunday, the heat broke like a spent fever. First came the heavy rain, announced with thunder and lightning that woke us at seven in the morning. Clouds carpeted the overhead sky, but clear spots to the south and west showed that the storm was moving rapidly to the north. The clouds poured cooling water onto the terra-cotta houses, onto the slender trees, and into the pool visible through the shutters shedding droplets to either side of our open window. When the rain stopped, the cool front for which it had been the advance guard liberated Rome. The next day dawned dry and forgiving; we boarded a train for Naples.

Outside Rome stretched many farms, some old and rustic, others so pristine they looked like settings for cereal commercials. The countryside beyond came in flat patches of kelly green and brown under orange roofs. We went slowly around a bend to the right, and a bay appeared below, a trawler bobbing sleepily, black birds floating on azure water reflecting geometric patterns, the sails of small boats unfolding in white. Then came more fields of green rhymed with muted brown; farther on, low, blue mountains strained to scrape the clouds. Then the fields grew parched and poor, the farmhouse roofs pleading for fresh tiles.

Before Naples appeared Centro Direzionale di Napoli, a new, commercial district in steel and glass, like one of those cold cityscapes of the

American South, cities where many may consent to work but few would think of living. I counted fourteen construction cranes.

Julie had been to Naples once before; on her good counsel, we were on full New York guard—eyes in the back of the head—the moment we stepped from the train. We knew enough to dodge the dubious cabbies lying in wait inside the station. There were many metered cabs outside, and judging by the customer base, some would wait all day before moving. One cabbie spoke English, and out of either righteousness or pique at the competitor at the head of the amassed cars, he explained to us the exact supplements for bags, lest we be overcharged.

Chapter 19

The Grand Albergo Vesuvio had electronically controlled riot doors that, should the chaos of Neapolitan street life dissolve into civil strife, would seal off the hotel like a fortress. Everything was clean and automatic, down to the electrically controlled shutters that could, in their raising, turn our darkened room into a vantage point over the sun-washed Bay of Naples and the Castel dell'Ovo, a twelfth-century fortification set on an island just off the shore. Each morning, fishermen would cross the bay in purring skiffs. Stout freighters, up from Salerno, would chug through the distance; thus would the day pass on the water until the sun set into the yellow bath it made for itself along the horizon, the windows of waterfront houses shining a farewell in amber.

The Castel dell'Ovo was accessible by a small causeway perpendicular to the bay road, Via Partenope. The castle harbored many pleasure boats, giving it the appearance of a medieval yacht club. By night, the causeway was a bazaar of aging fortune-tellers and their prey. A tall soothsayer, fair haired, younger, and more popular than his colleagues, sat at a cloth-topped table, his face footlit by an oil lamp. He spoke in a hushed, resonant voice as he unfolded tarot cards for credulous young women, their eyes fixed upon him as if he were the oracle of Apollo at Delphi. Women who had come to the causeway with men were spending a more provident time by kissing them.

On Via Partenope one morning, a thin, dark-haired young man crashed his Piaggio scooter into a parked Mercedes decked with white ribbon for a wedding. Man and bike flipped oven. Both crumpled to the street, but the man rose like the phoenix, seemingly unhurt. Then he saw his scooter, its front fork broken, and like a rider who knows he must put down his horse, he wheeled the victim away, sobbing. That evening, stinging smoke flowed across the causeway to the castle; there were sirens and lights. The next day, around the corner, a furniture showroom, its walls blackened, reeked of burned cloth and wood, the novel smells layering upon the exhaust-fume odor that was the city's workaday perfume.

Beyond the smoldering showroom were the famously compressed side streets of Naples. They were barely alleyways, each with clotheslines of fluttering laundry crisscrossing its narrow breadth like flying buttresses, the passageway musty and the walls soot stained. By three in the afternoon, the alleys were in deep shade, as an Alpine valley will fall into early darkness once the sun finds its nest behind bordering mountains.

The Neapolitan women, moving briskly through main roads, were often attractive, with fine, Roman features, dark hair and eyes; they were somewhat alluring, but clothed in a manner that Julie could only call sartorially uninformed: pastel dresses with cheap lace; oversized flower motifs, stubby black patent-leather shoes. "It's like everyone is dressed for parent's day at school," Julie said when we had briefly left the alleys behind. We came to a small shopping district. There were bullet holes in the window of a boutique featuring Celine accessories. "So much for good taste," said Julie.

This small act of violence was not under immediate investigation, but a squad of policemen marched impressively through the glass-roofed Galleria, moving with the purposeful dignity of a soldier chorus on an opera-house stage. "No pictures!" said one of the officers. Farther along, another officer did his best to give me directions, as down home in demeanor as the small-town cop who stands on the roof of his squad car to rescue a treed cat.

In a street market, a seafood vendor offered live eels from a plastic tub. A large woman three stalls down sold peaches and pears rolled into newspaper, the cups of her capacious brassiere serving as cash register: left for small bills, right for large. She wore a dress of indifferent pattern and had a jolly chuckle; she was the earth mother of traders, exchanging her harvest for banknotes, making change from her bosom.

A brawny man in makeup, earrings, soiled aquamarine tights, and clogs wearily clopped down the nave of the church of Santa Maria di Montesanto, crossed himself, prayed off the sins of the previous night, and departed, looking ever so slightly uplifted by his private supplication. Farther uphill, where the Corso Vittorio Emanuele cuts along the serpentine slope of Sant'Elmo, an artist sketched the vista. He was tall, courtly, middle aged, and of course he took a fancy to Julie. He explained his work in a voice much like his drawing—refined, exact, linear. The district dated from the fifteenth century, when it was the Spanish quarter, he said in Italian. I did my best to translate from a language I thinly understood; he was a kind man and, though he probably had the soul more of an academic than an artist, his drawing showed a fine hand.

How remote it all seemed from the other Italian cities I had visited, cities where fashionable clothes stood at attention in bright windows behind neatly lettered price lists, where the espresso machine was heard along with the tinkling of flatware and money at the *pasticcerìa*, and where the sudden whir of an engine or burst of animated conversation interrupted a street life superficially as orderly as that of France. There was also the Italy of the courtly greeting, of the gracious deferral to a lady, of small and suspicious eyes revealing little, promising intrigue. In Naples, it had all gotten out of control, like an unruly classroom from which the teacher had been absent too long. The frenetic part of Italian life had swollen into something twice life sized, pushing aside its refinement, its charm, even its intrigue. Naples was, however, a delightful place to be because it made no pretense of accessibility, because it ran by rules of its own improvisation, and because it cared not a jot if we were there or if we enjoyed ourselves.

Chapter 20

The National Archeological Museum had large rooms full of the paintings, sculpture, mosaics, and household objects scrounged from Pompeii and other ancient sites. Pompeii was a skeleton in stone; you could get from it a sense of the size of the organism that was a Roman city but gain little comprehension of its beauty. For that, you needed the museum. As we might have expected, the museum was about half restored, the old portion floored with terra-cotta tiles that rocked in place as we trod on them, the dark wooden doors deteriorating in situ, the rest pristine and rather posh. Watching over the place was a collective of bored, scruffy guards who took turns smoking under a VIETATO FUMARE sign. Four of them were needed to tear two tickets.

Italian museum tickets were lovely things, big and elegantly illustrated with the image of one of the better works contained within, the price as carefully articulated as the value stated on paper currency. Crudely stamped in tomato red across the face of each of these portable artworks was a new tariff exactly twice the old. Surely no one, in filing a petition in bankruptcy court, ever listed profligacy in museum admissions as a cause of his undoing, but the moral indignation of our first night in the country was yet unappeased. The plan I'd hinted to Julie about on that first night was now to be implemented. It was called Italy on the Half Price, and it worked like this: I would go up to the ticket counter, kicking against it to rouse the attendant from slumber or to distract her from conversation with a coworker. Julie, meanwhile, would smile invitingly at a male guard who, being Italian and male, would smile invitingly back. On entering, Julie would say that I'd be following with her ticket; she would say it in English, of course, but by now the guard had forgotten why he'd been hired. I'd follow Julie in, handing over the single ticket I'd bought. The purchase of one ticket, rather than none, added credibility should we be caught, but we never were. We were the Bonnie and Clyde of Italian museums, robbing the state of half its new double tariff.

The best view of Naples was from the end of a funicular ride up Sant'Elmo, from the parapets of the castle of the same name. The neighboring Carthusian monastery of San Martino contained a major museum. As we expected, it was partially renovated, haphazardly attended, and, oh, dear! those stamped-over admission tickets again.

"Italy on the Half Price?" asked Julie.

"You're on."

The young man on guard received feminine appreciation. I got the one ticket that served for two, and we were off to view an enormous carriage, a well-regarded collection of carved figures for nativity scenes of the kind that get plunked around a fir tree at the Metropolitan Museum each Christmas, and the sculpture that serves as the cover art for the standard-issue Neapolitan joke postcard: a nude, bending woman, her rump in the air. The work, *La Giumenta* by Guiseppe Renda, may not be a masterpiece, but there are those of us who like it.

Chapter 21

Hertz loaned us a Citroën for virtually the price of buying one new. The man at the counter was mildly contrite about it. He volunteered that the Citroën was garbage, but as his small office lost a car or two a week to theft, it could no longer afford to rent Lancias, Fiats, or Opels. Just the same, would we *please* garage the vehicle at night, and by the way, theft insurance is compulsory and you simply must accept collision-damage coverage. The insurance premiums cost the price of the car yet again, but it was better to be safe, he said. I explained that I thrived on danger and declined whatever the law allowed. I felt good about that; in World War I, pilots flew without parachutes as a point of honor.

Driving away was like taking the bumper-car ride. Vehicles passed each other in tunnels. They rode upon the raised trolley tracks, the speeding motorists daring public transportation to prove it had the mettle to flatten them. Lanes were created by need, not paint. Via Partenope was ruled for five traffic lanes; up to three more could be improvised if you had the nerve. On any crowded road, whenever a space appeared ahead, four cars would lunge for it, and whoever cared the most for his fenders hit the brakes first. Cars were generally small, and all were driven so fast that you might assume every wreck was a total, like the Piaggio that had met its end against the Mercedes; but the survivors of this catfight on wheels licked their wounds and stayed mobile. Doors may get dinged and bumpers twisted. Headlights and taillights may shed glass as a shaggy dog might shrug off fur in springtime, but you pressed onward. The air was lurid with fumes and exhaust, and gasoline pumps were more prevalent than at a Grand Prix. Stop signs commanded no respect. Traffic lights were advisory only. It was total freedom of the road, enjoyed by everyone except the numerous cops who, from a sense of duty or frustration, stayed in lanes, did not speed, and always used turn signals—until roused: at all hours, sirens punctuated the mayhem.

"You're from Manhattan," said Julie, as I power-shifted between two converging vehicles in rush-hour traffic. "You barely know how to drive."

"Look around you. Neither does anybody else." A Fiat sliced across our path at a forty-five-degree angle. "You thought I was just fine at this in the Netherlands."

"Who ever got rear-ended by a Dutchman? Wow! Will you watch it?" A truck had cut in front of us, nearly extracting the bumper. I swerved, downshifted, then floored it. The truck driver ate our dust. We were at the foot of Mount Vesuvius in minutes. The road ascended in hairpin turns past shabby restaurants empty except for the old women who worked them, sitting at outdoor tables, talking among themselves. Verdant hills followed the road skyward, yellow flowers perfuming the road even as it halted amid crags of red clay and gray slate. The sun was descending over the distant bay, a white beacon over anchored ships, and Naples lay there too, sunning itself with deceptive serenity. Brushfires burned below, sending up white, malodorous smoke that stifled the perfume of the flowers.

We respectfully bought two double-priced tickets and walked the long, rough path around the bulbous upper mountain. The path was made from sand, gravel, and tan volcanic detritus that coated my black shoes. A woman from Melbourne lost pace, huffing up the trail well behind her Italian cousin and a friend. A man bore a child on his shoulders, an old woman pushed herself along with an alpenstock. The inevitable Germans, holding guidebooks as if they were prayer books, walked with that characteristic Teutonic trudge that makes a trip to the corner grocery look like a daylong hike. All were strangely quiet; a volcano humbles you in a way that no ordinary mountain shorter than an Alp can imitate. Here was nature both serene yet menacing, a treat to be admired and, by its readiness to imperil, to be respected.

One minute below the top, an undisclosed tollbooth appeared. Two more double-priced tickets were required. "The nerve," said Julie, turning a frustrated eye at the expanse of inclined ground we had crossed since our last payment.

"Italy on the Half Price?" I asked.

Julie gave me the thumbs-up.

It's hard for a lone sentinel in a rickety box to guard a volcano from a determined trespasser intent on defrauding the Italian nation. Julie was in, and I followed, legal with ticket, morally appeased.

Gravel and sand—if that was indeed what we had been walking on— now gave way to vitreous lava that was first gray then burgundy red, then terra-cotta, and finally, near the crater at the top, a mixture of all. It crunched like cereal as we walked. Steam seeped from fissures in the crater's chiseled walls—nature's way of reminding us it would have the last word. The lowering sun caused the lava along the mountain slope to glisten, giving old Vesuvius the look of a dowager in sequins. Thoughtlessly strewn trash marred both spectacle and metaphor.

At the end of the path along the crater's perimeter, Julie came upon the last shop on earth. It was a shack where the man in attendance had only a radio for company. He sold postcards, silver jewelry, and black lava carved into reproductions of Michelangelo's *David* and Botticelli's *Birth of Venus*. He looked rather bored for a fellow who, if history ever repeated itself (as is wont to happen with volcanos), would do well to hold an Olympic medal for marathon running.

"So how do you get to work every morning?" Julie asked him.

"I keep an airplane in my pocket," he said. "Maybe you like a nice ring?"

Julie went shopping. I leaned into her ear and gave the signal: "The bus is leaving."

When we returned to the ticket booth, the mountain had been closed by a single rope across the entrance to the path. The man in the booth was calmly counting the take. Another day in the life of nature's grandeur, concluded.

Chapter 22

I offered to teach Julie how to drive the manual-shift Citroën, but the differences from the Netherlands being too obvious, she left the wheel to my care. Two more drives were attempted and, confounding the averages, safely concluded.

On one, I got us to Pompeii, where every parking lot by the entrance came equipped with a flack shouting, "This way for Pompeii." A woman directed us to a space next to the public toilet, which turned out to be her place of employment. The fare was three hundred lire per flush, but she added a single piece of paper towel to the bargain. Her desk was a white-clothed card table covered with devotional pictures of Jesus and saints. She said it was customary to give her two thousand lire as protection money—so that our car would come to no harm. I explained that the little Citroën was accustomed to these parts and had the fortitude to go it alone. Meanwhile, ten carabinieri surrounded Julie in the front office, ingratiating themselves.

We declined the invitations of a squadron of guides. Except for them and a few tired and hungry dogs, the disinterred city was all but empty of the living. I accidentally stepped on the paw of a sleeping, broken-down mongrel; he looked at me with abject eyes, as if to say he'd been expecting as much. I felt like the man who inadvertently tips over a beggar's cup.

Pompeii can, depending on how it strikes you, seem like a city or a grave, and it had a quality of the latter that morning. We made our way around, with Julie as The Book and me making contributions to navigation. A German couple bounded ahead of us, the woman in front carrying the biggest Baedeker in all creation, the man two paces behind with the map. They planned and executed perfect trajectories to all the important places; they turned out to be polite and helpful and directed us around the city as competently as if they, alone, lived there.

I had been to Pompeii on that student Grand Tour. One of our number, a reedy, anxious boy, had seen the city before, and he grew very animated when we arrived, bouncing like a hare, taking the boys to a hall in the House of the Vettii, where a scruffy man stood guard over a wooden box affixed to the wall. For a fee, the man opened the box, revealing the image of Priapus, weighing his torpedo of a penis against what looked like a sack of gold. The scale stood in perfect balance. "Is plenty," said the man with the prurient grin of a strip-show host as he pointed to the gold and to a basket of fruit attractively left on display for the god, "and plenty," he added, pointing to the organ of renown. Ladies were excluded from this educational detour, annoying the girls in our company. Reform now made far more licentious sights available to both sexes, the locks to them opened by guards who, we presumed, still barred access by the children and nuns among the scattered visitors that day.

Although we had steadied ourselves all trip long against the importuning of souvenir vendors, in Pompeii, I surrendered, buying a winged good-luck miniature penis in ersatz bronze and the paperback *Forbidden Pompeii*—a scholarly, illustrated look at the erections and copulations of classical antiquity. No greater evidence could present itself that I was advancing toward middle age.

Chapter 23

The Amalfi Peninsula juts from the western coast of Italy below Naples, pointing like an accusing finger toward the island of Capri. We intended to enter by the peninsula's northern elbow, but misnavigation now being a tradition, we stayed on the rambunctious autostrada, passing and being passed until we reached the southern anchor, Salerno. Even we could not mistake the fact we had blundered into a major port. On a great wharf, blue and red containers were stacked like checker pieces, the city climbing a hill beyond.

We doubled back, turned onto the peninsula, and were abruptly in Vietri sul Mare. Vietri sits in a bowl between mountains, the green-striped dome and tower of its signature church rising from an acropolis, the town radiating out to terraced hills and to the water's edge. The strong midday light reflecting highlights from every roof and cornice. Quietude at last prevailed. The village of Cetara, unveiling itself below rugged cliffs farther on, looked worn. On a small farm, an old, brown van substituted as a scarecrow. The seafront town of Maiori greeted us with Athens-style low rises of rude cement blocks, terraces stuck on their sides in a pointless effort to force charm onto them. The beach was a thin mud strip along the main road; the jetty was rock and concrete. Maybe Maiori had once been pretty, but pretty towns, like pretty women, become aware early on of their beauty and adorn themselves to make you aware of their desirability. Like pretty women, pretty towns become pampered, spoiled, and full of themselves. Maiori suffered from none of it, and from its lack of either beauty or pretension came a certain restful allure. In shop windows gourd-shaped cheese hung in nets. The cheese is called *caciocavallo* because you can throw the nets over the back of a horse (*cavallo*), the gourds rolling against the animal's flanks as it walks.

The corniche road that outlines the peninsula's perimeter cuts hairpin turns across the gray stone of its promontories, intersecting unexpectedly with the few mountain streets that penetrate its interior. Bare yards to our left at this point, the rock face dived into the turquoise sea. The air out here was fresh with salt and floral perfumes. There was no noise except the whir of our engine. Honking the horn or turning on the radio would have done an injustice, though the latter was impossible because there was no radio, Hertz having decided it would just get stolen.

We had moved into the prime tourist area, and soon we were among overstuffed buses that maneuvered the turns with difficulty. Each bus came with a businesslike young woman seated to the driver's right, chattering to her flock through a microphone. It was said that if a bus should stall, traffic would back up through nightfall. I could believe that.

In the town of Amalfi, on the southern shore, stands a handsome cathedral on a wide piazza. There are excellent ocean views. We could see why people would want to come here: it was pretty. We also got the sense, from the casual disdain of the townsfolk and from the brimming shops, that Amalfi had long ago been spoiled by its success. Here was a pretty woman of a town again, a few lovers' worth more experienced than most, her wardrobe fit to snag another. Like that woman, you would have to take the time to get to know her, to move beyond the prettiness that, by making her popular, made it so easy for her to behave superficially.

Small, white-washed Positano, farther west, retained much character and a sense of intimacy. It had charm and some sophistication, and you could overlook the fact that every shop, whatever its reputed specialty, sold the same garish sundress. Copies of the dress hung like laundry all around us—as colorful as candy and as plentiful and tasteless as weeds.

Sorrento, a seaside resort on the north coast, had good hotels and some expensive shops. Its narrow streets were lively with summer travelers from Europe, America, and Japan; commerce was indeed in the air, and a festive, middle-market complacency, of the kind you'd find in Key West, drove the numerous visitors from shop to shop. As in many European towns that became popular on charm, there were layers to Sorrento—the original layer of rustic simplicity, overlain with a veneer of imported sophistication, itself overlain with a layer of studied charm.

We stopped at a roadside bend where an old woman sat, a load of grapes beside her. She was plump and toothless, her bare feet black. The place and condition of this *fruttivendola* should give an impression of how hungry we were by then. Her fat husband, every pore on his face sprouting stubble, leaned into the car and motioned to bum a cigarette. My reserves of Italian were just adequate enough to report that we didn't smoke. His grunt and slight, futile wave of his palm was nonverbal assurance he'd been afraid we'd say that. Then he tried to sell Julie moonshine wine in a bottle that was clearly someone else's castaway. The woman overcharged us for the grapes, which we cleaned as best we could at the first opportunity, and we ate them with zeal.

It was night by the time we returned to Positano; we were tired and still hungry. Unwilling to dim her standards, Julie searched for a convivial restaurant and didn't find any until the few that had been open closed. We ended up buying yogurt, stale packaged bread, and some fruit in a convenience store. That wouldn't have been so bad had we not (a) missed breakfast and (b) skipped lunch.

"All these towns are run for tourists," said Julie as we got back on the road. "We're too late."

"By decades."

"At least. But would we have come here if we had to take a train to a horse cart?" she asked. "What if Sorrento was full of fishermen and basket weavers but the hotels had no running water?"

"Maybe there'd be someone willing to go out of his way to serve dinner." I'm at my worst when hungry.

"So what are you saying? I'm a dilettante because I take a shower every day?" Julie has international tastes, modulated by an American love of good plumbing.

"No, ma'am," I replied.

"What do we expect? It's like those people who say that if only we'd let the Cheyenne alone, they'd still weather Colorado winters in bison-hide tents—even if they were paid major reparations, which they should have been, and even with the lights of Denver up ahead. You can't blame people for wanting it comfortable and easy. The people here want to live nicely, and the tourists bring the money, right? The tourists want cappuccino on demand, and they get it. So the town isn't quaint anymore. Who wants to be quaint for someone else's amusement?"

One thing I was learning about Julie: she expressed herself with emphasis, even vehemence, and it was hard to argue against her. Once she had formed a position, contradicting her would be as complex as getting yourself undamaged through Neapolitan traffic. But she tended to be right.

A roadblock appeared, with a sign warning of fallen rocks. A detour would have taken an hour or more. We had seen the wire mesh used to keep the mountains from falling on passing cars. Somewhere ahead, a mountain had won. We waited, saw cars with Italian plates zip around the roadblock, then followed. It turned out that only a few small rocks had landed on the pavement. We weaved past them, were back in Naples soon enough.

Dark, empty streets stretched before us with such infinity of both quantity and distance that we could believe Naples was a treadmill of brooding slums. The bells that sound within an urbanite's head told each of us that we had lost our way. We said little to each other, silently hoping that downtown would appear beyond the next expanse of destitution. I did not want to alarm Julie with my private doubts that, once again, our navigation skills had come up wanting, but this was growing serious indeed.

We came at last upon a police roadblock. A dozen cops, deployed like United Nations peacekeepers, offered a welcome sign of collective authority. There was much light around them, from the squad cars, from streetlights and flashlights—or maybe memory exaggerates the light we saw as we emerged from the straight avenue we had taken through seemingly endless darkness.

We stopped. A policeman waved me past a truck that had stopped traffic in our lane. I lurched forward, bopping the bumper into a Fiat parked ahead and to the right. A policeman looked at us with a smug grin and checked the bumper of my unintended target. No damage. He waved me on. I got through the tangle of vehicles and officialdom and pulled over.

"Why are you stopping?" asked Julie.

"Because you have to ask directions."

She looked again at the chaos around us. "Why me?"

There followed the obvious answer: "Because you can't drive a stick shift if they, or we, want us out of here in a hurry."

Julie grabbed a map and walked the short distance rearward. She disappeared inside the firmament of authority and was gone an unusually long time, long enough, at least, for me to wonder if I should follow her. But when she did come running back, she looked as merry as a schoolgirl.

"Well?"

"He was gorgeous!"

"Who?"

"The cop! What a good-looking guy! He was saying, 'Oh, you American girl. I help.' Then all the other cops wanted to help. They were so nice."

"Julie, how do we get out of here?"

"Oh, I'm sorry. Turn around completely and make a left at the second light. You should have seen him: dark hair, dimples, and then his friend, the tall, light-haired one, came over . . ."

We returned to civilization in phases, by map and compass, adding an extra wrong turn or two for flavor until Naples surrendered the light it had so threateningly withheld from us, and a great, shiny piazza at last filled our windscreen. We reached the tunnel that led to Via Partenope and may or may not have been driving it at great speed in a lane reserved for oncoming traffic. It was late, this was Naples, and no one else on the road took offense.

Chapter 24

We learned a new word of Italian. We were in a taxi, headed for the Mergellina hydrofoil dock, when I realized the driver was taking us in the direction of the Mergellina train station. *"Scusi, no,"* I said.

"La Stazione Mergellina è sempre diritto," said the driver.

"No Stazione Mergellina. Invece Mergellina—" I was searching through my notebooks and papers. The hydrofoil schedule popped into view, and I found my solution. *"Mergellina per l'aliscafo!"*

"Si, si, l'aliscafo. Scusi!"

A sudden 180-degree midstreet turn confirmed I had been understood. I've forgotten most of my Italian, and Julie never learned much, but we are good for the word *aliscafo* (hydrofoil) for life.

The craft was scheduled to leave in seconds. I'd already had to prod the taxi driver into turning on his meter, and we now had a brief run-in about a supplemental charge of his invention, but Julie stepped in, handing him banknotes and demanding back ever more change until she was content.

We asked a porter if we could board in time. He said, *"Posso,"* and Julie ran ahead to get tickets. A horn sounded. The porter recanted: *"Non posso."* But a more optimistic colleague stepped in, scooping up our bags, sprinting with them on his cart, and shouting to the crew to hold that hydrofoil.

On this dock, for the first time on the trip, the general run of humanity was as chicly dressed as Julie. A troop of *Vogue* subscribers chased after us, using the same mad-porter technique as we. In minutes, we were all surfing toward Capri—a nauseating, forty-minute ride.

The Grande Marina was full of men in peaked caps sporting hotel names, but we had to scout for the van of ours, the Caesar Augustus. We found it off to the side, driverless. When at last the chauffeur appeared, we were his only passengers. He drove us up steep hills, past Capri town, toward the higher, more remote town of Anacapri. I note for those who believe in omens that the only sight our driver pointed out to us, and enthusiastically at that, was the good ship *Achille Lauro*, anchored in a bay. In October 1985, four Palestinian terrorists had commandeered the *Achille Lauro* off the coast of Egypt, shot to death an elderly, partially paralyzed New York City man named Leon Klinghoffer, and had his body thrown overboard—along with his wheelchair. Two months later, an official of the Palestine Liberation Organization offered an alternative theory for the Klinghoffer murder: he said that Mrs. Klinghoffer may have pushed her husband overboard to collect on his life insurance.

In December 1994, after catching fire in the Indian Ocean, the *Achille Lauro* would sink, killing several passengers. Reuters would report that hundreds of elderly passengers would be rescued from unsafe lifeboats with only the clothes on their backs—which for many was their bedclothes —that passengers would complain of cowardice among the crew and that about 148 neatly dressed Italian crew members would reach land while carrying their own luggage.

The Caesar Augustus Hotel surmounted a Capri promontory that plunged without diversion into the sea. We were greeted there by a little porter with a potbelly and a look of permafright. Another porter, called as reinforcement, was thinner and withdrawn. Both wore white shirts that were colorfully stained. There was no one at the desk when we arrived because the gray-haired manager was loudly abusing someone over a tele-phone in the back. We were able to check in only when he had finished his tirade, which was expansive and so took time to complete. We saw no other guests. "I'm not sure how I'm going to like this," said Julie quickly.

The tubby porter with the face of a frightened poodle escorted us through shabby halls to an ordinary but decent-looking room. It had a marvelous view of the sea, once you looked past the rusting white terraces and crumbling stucco of the Caesar Augustus. "I love the water," said Julie hopefully. It was turquoise at the cliff face and nearly purple where it deepened. A speedboat churned the purple into white.

"Fine. Then we stay," I said.

"I need a bath," said Julie. Barely two minutes passed before she was again behind me, arms crossed. "There is hair in the bathtub."

I looked. She was right. "Let's change rooms," I said. Back to the desk. "There is hair in the bathtub," I told the manager.

"It's not hair. The paint has cracked."

"You paint your bathtubs?"

"You want to see another room?"

"Please."

We were shown the one next door. Not a hair was out of place here, but it was smaller and not nearly as fresh. Back to the manager: "Okay, we'll take the original room—and some paper towels, please."

"You know that the original room costs more."

"A hundred and twenty thousand lire," I said.

"Hundred sixty," he replied.

"That wasn't the rate we were quoted."

He showed me the confirmation fax he had received from the Utell booking service. "This is the rate."

"That's not the rate on our confirmation," I said.

"A hundred and twenty thousand lire is a dream," announced the manager. "A dream!"

My favorite thing to do when arriving at a hotel is drop off my bags, pick up my cameras, and leave until nightfall, but Julie and I had advanced as a couple to the point that I could read in her expression that, mentally, she had already checked out of the Caesar Augustus. At her instigation, we packed for the beach and took a bus down to Capri town. Julie had been to the island once before, and by a sense of direction I had thought unavailable to her, found the Villa Krupp—the unassuming hotel where she had stayed when last on the island.

I waited on the sundeck while she inquired at reception. She dashed out like a woman possessed. "It's run by Germans. There is one room left, and while I'm asking about it, this guy from the U.S. comes in, and he's thinking about whether he wants the room, but the woman at the desk tells me she doesn't like Americans, and God knows what she thinks I am, but you— hurry!" I went in, greeted the woman in German, and with the aid of my German passport, booked the last room while the American dithered.

Back on the bus we went, past the *Achille Lauro*, grinning in the sunshine, up to the Caesar Augustus. I hasten to observe that we had yet to see the island, let alone go to the beach. We went to our 160,000-lire room, the one with the hair in the bathtub, collected our luggage, and walked to the desk. Tubby, looking more frightened than I had thought possible even for him, told us please to wait. He collected the manager, who arrived under full vituperative steam. I explained that we had reconsidered.

"Okay, leave if you want," he said. He began to write out an elaborate receipt.

"What's that for?" I asked.

"For the one-night stay," he said in a voice both brusque and smug.

"Let me repeat myself," I said with the gentility that is my trademark when forced to spend half a travel day in securing a hotel room. "We're not staying the night."

He looked up at me with censure and pain, but he was experienced enough at this game to see that he had lost; he moved for a consolation prize. "Then you will pay me for the fax I sent you!"

"Go ask Utell."

"Ask Utell?" he said with the shock of the unjustly accused, but he was addressing my back. We lugged our suitcases to the bus.

In my terse dispatch in the *Chicago Tribune*, I would later report: "If the Addams Family ran a resort hotel, this would be it." We liked the Villa Krupp quite well.

Chapter 25

Julie was sad that our hotel shuffle had burned the time she had allotted for a swim. We dressed for dinner and headed for the Marina Piccolo because, on Julie's part, it was at least on the water and because, on my part, Noël Coward had written a comic song about it. On the way, we noticed a woman coming up from a craggy path the entrance of which was posted as closed. It looked like a shortcut, one about which Julie had a vague memory. As every hiker knows, you should never take an unknown shortcut, but we started along a rutted, pitted, and downright dangerous trail as steep as a black-diamond ski slope. A stone rail was broken in crucial places, inviting an easy plunge to eternity. Julie stepped over rocks and fallen branches and kicked up dirt with her high-heeled sandals, the dust settling on her silk blouse, her Calvin Klein shirt and jacket.

In the distance we saw sunbathers, those to the far left being indistinctly but indisputably nude. Maybe the beach wasn't a place entirely without its curiosities, I said, and we pushed onward. We had to climb over great boulders before we were on the beach, which was isolated and stony. It was separated from the water by a low cliff of boulders against which a rough tide slammed at intervals. A thin, bearded man who may have been a hermit—or at least eccentric—had made a house for himself in a small cave, complete with bedroom, a covered patio, a cooking area, and a refuse dump. A spray-painted boulder announced:

RISERVATO

AL

NUDISTI

"You wanted a swim, right?" I asked Julie.

"Not that badly."

"It's still warm out. The sun hasn't set."

Julie was flushed with the embarrassment you feel when you are offered an enterprise that, though outside your range of comfort, lies just close enough that you can see yourself going that way on a dare. "There aren't any nude women here."

There had been one, but she now wore her bottom and was making to depart. A few naked men remained, two by two, presumably homosexual couples. I went to the water's edge and started removing my clothes. "You aren't really going to do that?" said Julie. I did, sliding in with the aid of a frayed orange nylon rope, thoughtfully affixed to one of the slippery boulders that would otherwise have made return to land a dicey affair. The water was cold but clear and indescribably welcome. Julie looked around, made the mental calculations required of a respectable woman in these situations, neatly folded all her fashionable clothing, and joined me in the water. The waves pushed us toward the rocks and the tide did its best to suck us out to sea. Green, living moss and gray, dead moss made the rock surfaces too slick to hold on to but left them treacherously hard and jagged should we be forced against them. The late breeze was salty and cool.

We had no towels. Dressed only in our underwear, we climbed past the troglodyte, who wouldn't answer my calls in English or Italian, though he burst into "O Sole Mio" when we were nearly past. "Anthem of the Italian hermit," explained Julie.

We were in street clothes and back at the top of the path when a Scotsman directed us to the Marina Piccolo; there we would find a bus back to town. We returned to the off-limits beach during our stay, and Julie went once on her own, causing a stir among a gaggle of American college men.

Chapter 26

The clock in the main piazza never stopped tolling during the night. It got so I could tell time by it: deep gongs were for the hours, lighter ones were for quarter hours. Three deep and two light meant 3:30 A.M. Four deep and one light meant 4:15 A.M. I had seen enough of Capri to be confident that few among us had pressing engagements at four-fifteen in the morning and that no one forced to listen was without the means to secure a wristwatch. I am from a land that flaunts its disregard for tradition, but the town clock is a custom ripe for consignment to history, at least after bedtime.

I tried to reach Peter and Susanne by phone at dinnertime one evening but could not get through. Gianni was home in Genoa, however. He reported that Enrico still slept with one of the bears I gave him; his name had since been altered to the simple but dignified Teddy Bear. Lorenza had the boys at the villa on the Adriatic coast, where we really must join them next time we were in Italy, he said. It had been some time since I last was in Italy, and I felt very far away from my friends. This was indeed Italy, but so different from rough and broken-down Genoa. This was an Italy of the imagination; it could not exist, and of course, it did not.

The color that season for women's shoes was gold, and for all the yellow shine given off by the footwear treading the main piazza, you'd have thought the gold said to be stashed under the Bahnhofstrasse in Zurich had been brought up for a breath of sea air. The Gucci outlet sold what Gucci will sell, at prices only 5 percent or so off what the branch in New York charged. For years I'd been buying neckties in Italy. If only because it seemed foolish not to, I bought one on sale at a boutique, then realized it was a Drake, made in England, which was foolish indeed.

With that memory still fresh in mind, we were sitting one afternoon in an outdoor café, gazing upon the rolling sea of chic that splashed to the shores of our table and cascaded over its banks whenever a Ferragamo handbag or Cartier-encircled arm should inadvertently crowd us. "Doesn't this place remind you of Positano?" asked Julie.

"More like Portofino," I said.

"No. It's Vail, but with surf," said Julie.

"The stupid Hamptons."

"I *like* the Hamptons."

"I meant some other Hamptons."

"Okay." Julie glanced around her, trying to pretend she wasn't doing that. "Looks like the Hamptons."

"Annoying, to come all this way—"

"Amazing how it all starts to look alike," said Julie. She deliberated on that the way she does sometimes: crossing her arms, her head bent, immune to all external stimuli. "I kind of miss Naples, don't you?"

I surprised myself by agreeing with her. Another revelation: Julie and I were thinking alike.

Chapter 27

Karl Marx got it wrong. The workers of the world represent no homogeneous class. To the extent that there are differences worth traveling to see, and ways of life so divergent from your own that to experience them for a short time is worth the journey, the working class and peasants provide that element so condescendingly called local color. During recent travels on my own, I had seen the thin and brooding men of the barren fields of Castile, soft caps seemingly molded to their heads, the stubble on their faces as coarse as the nearly nonarable bracken of their homesteads. I had seen the corpulent, muscular women of the Polish countryside, fleshy pink heads swaddled in their babushkas, working scythes ahead of oxcarts that, overloaded with hay, lumbered like elephants through the fields. Each scene had been distinct to, and characteristic of, its place. Here, in Capri, Julie and I had watched a fisherman repairing his net with artisan's hands—the delicate motions and the sudden, vigorous pulls with a knife, a scissor, a needle. I'd seen fishermen across Europe, but this small touch of refinement in a simple task was indisputably Italian.

It is the rich who are the true international class. The world over, whatever their nationality, race, or creed, they talk the same, dress the same, have the same values, loyalties, education, hobbies, and sex lives. They are masters of Capri, but only in season, and you can sit in the piazza and listen to conversations in Italian, English, German, Flemish, or Japanese, knowing with confidence that pretty much the same things are being said all around you.

We did find the middle class at play, after a fashion. Every couple of hours, a flock of day trippers would come to the main piazza under close escort by a saleswoman disguised as a tour guide. She would take her group to a sad cluster of flowering plants that she called the Gardens of Augustus. It was hardly worthy of a detour, let alone a sea voyage, and it had no more to do with Augustus Caesar than the Gucci store—or less, if you factor in the distinctly Roman profile of the gold sandals we had seen. The real objects of these tours were the two side-by-side perfume factories just beyond the gardens. I had strong doubts as to whether those factories really were factories—and why any Italian factory worthy of the name would have to post a sign that says FREE ENTRY in English.

Back among the gentry, all was not heaven either. In a shop for accessories, a noisy American woman in large costume jewelry and an expensive black-and-white outfit held forth a man's necktie as thick as a napkin. She said that the clerk who had sold it to her had assured her it was the widest tie in the shop, and right here, plain as day, on the counter, isn't that one wider? Wide is the style this year, isn't it? She had insisted on wide, and wide was what she was entitled to have. The woman behind the counter was mature, but with just enough youth remaining to give a hint of girlish beauty. She looked at her customer with imploring eyes and replied, "Please, what means *wide?*"

An African in splendid robes toured the Gardens of Augustus with his wife and three daughters or, perhaps more likely by the way the group was interacting, his senior wife, junior wife, and the children of the former. A young daughter was whining and squealing her spoiled heart out.

Back at our German villa, while taming windblown hair, Julie yanked out the hair-dryer plug, breaking the adapter plug, half of which remained in the wall. Bare prongs were thus left exposed. Realizing the error, Julie now grabbed both, closing the circuit and sending 220 volts into her body. I was out taking pictures and came back to find her sitting on the floor, caressing her numbed hand, grateful she had dried her wet palm before making a middle-school science project out of her stay at the Villa Krupp.

It was a cool night and we went for a walk. Our object was the Natural Arch, roughly twenty-five minutes from our hotel by foot. The center of town quickly fell behind us, and the real Capri started. There were small shops of no great distinction but some character, a furniture restorer and an honest greengrocer who, alone among his compatriots south of Rome, had charged us the same prices as those he quoted to his regulars. There were elderly people out shopping, trading gossip, looking robust and fit. The streets behind them were really paths, just wide enough for the three-wheeled open vehicles that were all the motorized transportation the Capri hinterland could accommodate. The paths were both serene and confining. Their stone walls seemed to push back the lush foliage of the villas that lined them, each house labeled by a number on ceramic tile embedded into a path wall. Lit shrines were locked into glass niches in the walls. The road forked at a small supermarket, the ruins of the Villa Jovis of Tiberius to the left, the Natural Arch to the right.

At least one villa had its own vineyard, the grapes, green and purple, as tempting as anything offered Adam. There were colorful gardens and men putting up white and colored lights for the Feast of St. Mary. A group of Germans was holding a lawn party. A boy with a foot swaddled in a piercingly white bandage was getting a ride home on the flat bed of a luggage cart, looking none too happy. The slight incline of the path we took and the increasing opulence of the houses lining it gave the impression of a journey into a temporal heaven, where thrift and avarice were equally rewarded and only a few had been granted admittance.

Just before the Natural Arch was an open-air restaurant named Trattoria Le Grottelle. What passed for its architecture was a cave, though all seating on this night was under a thatched awning, facing a long cliff-top framed by a jutting boulder—a view leading straight to the sea. The waiters were still setting up the tables. They told us that the Natural Arch was a must, so we pushed onward. It was a great, jagged slab with an arch cut through its center, giving it the look of a ruddy red, breaded onion ring. There was a serene quality to this quirk of nature, the way it brashly imposed itself onto the landscape, like a woman in a gaudy hat who thinks she is fashionable and, by the force of her will, makes herself so. We could hear the chirping of insects and the waves from the sea beyond, where an elegant, white ship stood at anchor, already lit. The moon came out, about half full. The breeze was cool and carried the scent of wild vegetation. It was as if nature were offering an answer to Chopin's nocturnes.

Back at the open-air trattoria, short, ever-smiling Aniello Farace, the maître d'hotel, said he was sorry, but the place was fully booked. Each table had a wooden block holding a slip of paper with the name of the reserving party. Most names were German. "We are always busy when the moon is out," said Mr. Farace, but he checked his watch, looked at Julie, looked around, looked at Julie again—and a table was hauled out from somewhere, set with linen and flatware, and we had the best meal since we had come to the island. The view from our improvised post was soon blocked by tall bodies from the Fatherland. When the bill came, we saw that Mr. Farace had reduced the cover charge that, back in Rome, had created an international incident.

We had done the beach, the shops, the cafés. We had seen the Villa Jovis, but a boisterous sea had made the Blue Grotto unnavigable. There was something about this trattoria, with its view of the rising moon, with its genteel service and fine food cooked in a cave, that convinced us Capri had offered its best and had no remaining mysteries. We had expected Capri to be the highlight, the prime destination that most short trips have and that, once reached, bring on that sense of triumph by which travel can become accomplishment. We both knew we had been wrong. We desperately missed rude and run-down Naples. In a backward way, you could illustrate the broad difference between Capri and Naples by the fact that, while the most famous guest at the Vesuvio had been Caruso, that honor at the Villa Krupp went to Lenin. We called the Grand Albergo Vesuvio, booked another room and prepared to leave the island.

The next morning, a porter cast three heavy, matching suitcases onto his three-wheeled cart, as if landing large but weakened fish. He roped them down and we climbed in back with them, giving me a final view of Capri, facing rearward on the cart, jolting at each turn from atop the suitcases. Up a path we went and around the perfume factories; through a tree-lined walkway; past the day trippers with their swaying bags of authentic Capri perfumes; past the coolly sumptuous Grand Hotel Quisisana, where I had successfully negotiated the use of the toilet; past Cartier and Ferragamo; past Gucci to the main square; past the milling and the seated regulars, their sunglasses permanently affixed on deeply tanned faces. They sat all but immobile, posing like artists' models, save for the slight motions needed for continually looking around, as if expecting something to come their way any minute, something that, we now understood, would never arrive. At the funicular that served the Grande Marina, Mr. Muscles graciously accepted the ransom required for his work, and we descended to our waiting *aliscafo*.

Chapter 28

The thermometers in Rome had come to their senses. Citizens had returned from their lengthy holidays, but the workaday spirit of September had not disrupted the calm of August; Rome had the feel of a hotel where guests slowly fill the breakfast room, eating rolls, drinking coffee, readying for a day of meetings, ignoring each other. We walked to the Colosseum and watched the moon rise over it, the curving, pock-marked facade glowing red in the liquid-blue light of impending night. The lion of the classical world, that monument to the barbarity of our civilization, offered its toothless grin for my color photographs.

I liked to reserve the last night of my trips for quietude, reflection, and packing. Julie liked to leave on a high note. She insisted on finding the perfect restaurant for our final meal. Whether out of pity for me over the day of virtual fasting on the Amalfi coast or out of a sense of fairness, after two weeks of fastidiousness about where to dine, and after rejecting several restaurants we had passed this evening, Julie at last let me choose. Relying upon a recommendation, I steered us to an outdoor restaurant where the menu promised no cover charge. My childhood training in Italian cooking now showed itself. "They have spaghetti," I said. "Good enough."

Long would be the days and hard would be the nights, end on end, in which Julie would remind me how she loathed the meal we were served that evening. Because the trilingual menu included German among its languages, she lit upon the unshakable notion that we were in a German restaurant—proof that culinary evil was afoot. I had no reason to complain; I had been hungry, and now I was eating.

The next day, we returned together to New York, each to his own apartment.

Chapter 29

We made it through Geneva and Neuchâtel with fewer than our usual run of mishaps, but we left Locarno without Julie's pants. They were white cotton, the bed linen was, of course, hotel white, and Julie had jumbled pants with linen and so missed them when we did the final room check. I had met few women who could turn themselves out so expertly as Julie, and fewer still who had the brains to match the beauty. The combination is enchanting, but while the brains are self-supporting, the beauty component requires maintenance. The decor can suffer for the effort: clothes on the floor, makeup streaks that turn a sink into a Jackson Pollock. It was perhaps inevitable that Julie's pants and the bed linen should have made company and so intertwined themselves as new and eager lovers.

It was May, and this was our first trip abroad since Italy, the previous September. The denouement of that excursion—unpacking in separate apartments—would not be repeated. Julie had finally moved in with me. The necessary but not unpleasant burden of unpacking back home, though now to be communally borne, was in danger of being prosecuted *sans-culotte.*

The hotel from which Julie exited Locarno pants-less was the Reber au Lac. Ever since my student tour, I always like to visit Switzerland after Italy; it calms the nerves. On that first hot day in Rome some eight months earlier, I had fantasized of Switzerland. Images of cool mountains and clean streets had imprinted upon me to the point of obsession and I had lobbied, as if on a holy mission, to make Switzerland our spring destination.

The German-born New Yorker in the room next to ours at the Reber felt much the same way. He exchanged greetings with us across our terraces. He said he came back to this undisturbed place every year, to this very hotel, in fact, to look at Lake Maggiore and to relax. There being little else really to do in Locarno, one can only imagine that he annually succeeded in his objective.

We took a walk along pleasant streets that looked Italian, though highly scrubbed. The mountains across the lake were blue in the afternoon mist. The towns dotting the mountains slowly gained light from within as the sun faded, and the boats swayed where they were moored, their white hulls rising and falling in the rolling blue of the lake. Julie said, "I really feel like I'm in Italy."

We had started in French Switzerland, and we were on our way to the German-speaking portion; the Italian canton of the Ticino was to be a way station. As with so much of our travel, and in our lives in general now, we were compromising in an esoteric fashion: Julie was in Italy, which she so dearly loved, and I was still in Switzerland. Though Geneva had been cool, it was already hot enough in Locarno to go for a swim, and our walk ended in a store that sold bathing suits. We got one on sale for Julie, but I had to explain in German to the incredulous salesgirl that the English logo THINK PINK on the trunks she showed me could have impolite connotations back home.

At the hotel each evening, dinner was served on the quick by young waiters, their efficiency rewarding them with the right to go home early. The largely elderly clientele were just as happy to retire shortly after an early dinner. A woman I took for one of the owners floated nightly through the dining room, greeting those regulars held in willing detention twice daily by the modest extra cost of the meal plan. More compromise: we had taken the plan, which solved the problem of where to eat in the evenings—the loaded question that had so often threatened to disable our tour of southern Italy. In this German/Swiss-owned place, the food was Italian enough to make Julie happy, and so peace and pasta reigned, united.

On my way down to dinner one evening, we met Regina, a Swiss German traveling solo. She said that her husband had problems that prevented him from joining her and that she had three daughters. One, living in Zurich, was a makeup artist for photographers, another was in sales, and—she indicated by putting a finger to the side of her head and turning it in brisk revolutions—the third was insane. Regina said she came here twice annually, in spring and fall, apparently to get a breather from her colorful family. She never came in summer, when the place was full of Germans, whom she dreaded. She said the shopping was best in Ascona. With touching modesty, she pointed to the skirt she was wearing and bought there. "Escada," said Julie when we were out of earshot—lately the uniform of the mature European fashion plate.

We ran into Regina again on the promenade by the Grand Hotel, and though she was off to an appointment elsewhere, she encouraged us to have a look. The century-old building was impressive, meticulously restored, and desolate. A pianist played for no one in a room that could hold hundreds. A single cadaverous old woman was the only sign of life— loosely speaking—in an enormous salon next door. The chandelier was an inverted ice cream cone in Murano glass, flowers of colored glass spreading above our heads. The manager said it was the largest of its kind in the world. The hotel was like many people we had seen in Locarno: old and prosperous and decently kept up, waiting for something to happen.

I had wanted to visit this shore of Lake Maggiore because Frederic Henry had rowed the pregnant Catherine Barkley here in their escape from Italy in *A Farewell to Arms*. It was like the time I went to Davos to be where Hans Castorp had come to terms with life and disease in *The Magic Mountain*. If you have a love for literature, don't waste your time visiting the places authors of prior generations have used as settings. The places have changed or worse, have obviously never been what they were let on to be. It reminds you that imaginative writing not only starts in the mind, but will often reach into verifiable fact only under cover of necessity.

As Regina had promised, we found in Ascona good shopping and a healthy number of what she had warned were new-money types. Ascona was a lakefront town with stucco houses painted in muted shades, with galleries, cafés, and those good shops. We arrived by boat in an intermittent rain that soaked the low, handsome buildings of Ascona, their finely painted walls gone dark and dull like the coat of a carefully groomed cat gone into the rain. Ascona was, therefore, quaint and prosperous, so prosperous that the quaintness had the preserved, studied quality so familiar from the French Riviera. "I used to adore these places," said Julie. "Capri, Positano, Ascona."

"Portofino, Mykonos," I said.

"Seen one, seen 'em all." It started to rain again. "The bus is leaving."

Chapter 30

"I won't eat a sausage, period," said Julie as we packed for Zurich, unknowingly shy one pair of white cotton pants. With our luggage tucked into nooks along our railroad car, the train rose into the Alps. Amid the shuttered, Italianesque houses, there soon appeared chalets with overhanging roofs, the wood aged chocolate brown. We slid into a tunnel at Airolo and emerged minutes later in Andermatt, where the architecture and station signs were German. We had arrived in Nordic Europe.

"This is what I always imagined Switzerland was like," said Julie, which was fortunate because the visit was nearly at an end, and few were the surprises yet in store for her. The Alps ascended in three shades of green to white blades cutting into royal blue sky. Mountain streams ran hard and fell from cliffs in lines of silver. Villages clustered around church steeples, the signs for station restaurants and hotels neatly lettered on stucco. Goats and cattle staggered along precipitous slopes. It was the Switzerland of the imagination, the Switzerland of Heidi and small-gauge model–railroad sets.

The German spirit showed itself again but without the edge, without the doomed sense of purpose. Swiss Germans get everything done as efficiently as the Germans; they just won't let it bother them. That had two effects on Julie: it relaxed her and it bored her.

It had been a long time since the Hotel Krone—that Zurich inn so small that I had frequently walked right past it while looking for it. Our venue now was the Baur au Lac, where a blonde sat in a Bentley in the driveway. A Japanese businessman was complaining to the concierge about a misaddressed gift, and the concierge, all smiles and sympathy, said, yes, sir, it will be sent to New York City for arrival Tuesday, of course by air courier.

I called our Locarno hotel and had the housekeeping service put out an all-points bulletin for the missing white pants. I suggested to Julie that we go look at some churches while our room in Locarno was being inverted and shaken. Inside one, the Peterskirche, or St. Peter's Church, musicians were setting up about fifty instruments of every description: piano, zither, gong, sitar, conch shell. That night, the three-man Faszinierende Klänge (fascinating sounds) would perform their "Gong & Klang" concert. Contemporary Swiss art is much about the pursuit of the sublime by the inexplicable.

"We were just saying it's a shame we don't have a photographer for the concert tonight," said André Desponds in German as he eyed my pair of Leicas. "Could you come back and take pictures of us?"

Julie and I had a dinner engagement with Ursula and Antonio Rossi, and the musicians had not even set up. But André was persistent. He calculated down to the minute how I could shoot a roll, get a cab to the bus stop, and make our connection for the Rossis' town.

"He wants to know what I charge," I said to Julie, who appointed herself my agent and publicist.

Even rich Switzerland has its struggling musicians, she figured. "Charge them for the film and a few francs extra for your trouble," she suggested, "so they don't think you're not good or anything."

We returned at the appointed time and worked quickly. "Let's try it more Californian this time," I said in German to the musicians, who had posed as stiffly as Victorian cotton merchants. "You on the right, please, chin down and relax. That's it—think California!" Tough going there, I thought; but I'd done my good deed for art.

André took out a wallet bulging with hundred-franc notes and handed me a couple. "Photographers are expensive," he said.

I then bought a pair of brown Bally shoes one half size too small. Why I would do this, when my live-in girlfriend could get them for me at home and at a discount, is one of those emblematic mysteries of travel. Even if you are not a souvenir hunter, a quality of possessiveness takes hold when you travel, and like the pain of an old injury, it can recur at any time.

On a Sunday afternoon during a visit to New York, while Gianni and Lorenza Bacchelli were walking down Madison Avenue, Gianni first saw, in a gallery window, the Miró lithograph I earlier mentioned as holding a place of honor in the Bacchelli apartment. Miró was a prodigious artist, and his editions are not unknown in Genoa, but something about being on vacation in New York City and walking by that gallery at that moment made possession of that lithograph essential. With great effort, the work was crated and hauled to Alitalia for the flight home. It became a proud but incidental part of everyday life. For me, it was one of the nice things they owned; for Gianni, it was the lion's head mounted on the trophy wall. I knew just how he felt as I now left the Bally Capital shop on the Bahnhofstrasse, only my shoes were too tight.

Chapter 31

I'd forgotten my speculation, given to Ursula Rossi on my last visit, that she might end up raising Katrina's son, Jürgen. He was five years old now, as was his cousin, Max, the son of Paula and her husband, Kurt. When I had last been to the Rossi house, Jürgen was weeks old, and Max was still in the making. Max now had a sister, two months old and asleep in the spare room. Antonio checked in, saw all was well, and gave her a little kiss. It was the grandparents' night to baby-sit for Max and his sister. Jürgen, as I had eerily prophesied, was entirely in their care, but for a reason I had not foretold: Katrina was dead.

I could speculate endlessly, as I am sure that all the Rossi family have done, about why Katrina would destroy herself, though she was beautiful, educated, and recently married, though she was comfortably provided for, though she was a proud mother. The government had made a famous and controversial attempt at helping addicts, down to giving them sterile hypodermics. It was probably a contaminated needle—of the kind that had caused the infection concealed by the bandage in Greece—that killed Katrina. The contagion this time was AIDS. It had happened short-lybefore Julie and I arrived, and Jürgen could still be heard asking after *Mutti*, as if she would come back and all would be put right in a way that he, so small, did not realize it never really had been.

I remembered how, after dinner one night on Mykonos all those years before, Ursula, Katrina, Katrina's lover, and the Greek German woman who slept in my hotel room went to the far side of the harbor and returned to a taverna where, through the doorway, we had seen Greek dancing the night before. It was brown walled, capacious, and disconcertingly empty. Fearing that Greek music was not the ticket on an island of discos, management had cranked up the volume to decibel levels unknown to me since fraternity parties. Waiters and a few guests, mostly locals, danced in the brisk, bopping Greek manner that requires of the amateur more gusto than precision. Katrina would not dance with us. When the music subsided for a moment, I overheard her tell her mother how *langweilig* (boring) it all was. It wasn't merely Katrina's choice of the word that struck me but the mixture of annoyance and world-weary apathy with which she said it. From the sidelines, she was looking out on the dancing as might an adolescent who awaits punishment from the principal of a school she has dared to expel her. I wanted to help Katrina that night, though I did not know what to help her with and would not, in any event, have known how. At exactly midnight, the Greek music stopped and Michael Jackson, the town crier of the island that year, once more wailed the chorus of "Beat It" into the hot Greek night. By acclamation, we all left as the taverna began to fill.

The Rossis were diligent with Jürgen, showing both parental concern ("Drink your juice") and grandparental forgiveness ("Don't worry about the spilled juice"). They were an illustration of the adage that, whatever happens, you have to keep on. I admired them for it. I knew their hearts were broken, but they had borne it well. I had to believe that Jürgen was twice a blessing: because he was a sweet grandson and because, by caring for him as parents, the Rossis would have less time to dwell on the loss of their daughter or the guilt that parents inevitably feel in these situations.

Jürgen was with Ursula when she waited for us the next afternoon at the bus stop near her golf club, on the outskirts of town. She and Antonio had just come in tenth in a couples tournament, which is a respectable enough showing for grandparents, I would think. You could see the course from the clubhouse restaurant, where we had a genial dinner. Antonio was now chief executive officer of his company, a fact Jürgen explained as, "Grandpa is boss at the office, and Grandma is boss at home."

You have these moments in life: not much is weighing on your mind, the food is good and the wine pours freely, and, most important, you are in the company of friends. We dined and talked until darkness fell, and then Antonio took us for a ride in his virtually antique, lovingly restored Volkswagen Käfer, or Beetle then long out of production in Europe— Jürgen on my lap in the backseat, the little car putting through the tame Saturday-night streets of Zurich, back to the Baur au Lac. We got out and Jürgen practiced his good-bye hugs on us—by getting a running start and jumping into our arms. Katrina's presence was still there, somehow, even as the world moved on and her presence would slowly fade, as the presence of each of us inevitably must.

Chapter 32

As I had promised Regina, I called her daughter in Zurich, the one who worked as a makeup artist; she was unable to join us because she was working in the morning on a photo shoot. It was a Sunday, but she was freelance, and I knew what that meant: you make your own hours, and spare time can become a moving target.

We left her to her job and took a train, arriving in Lucerne just before ten. There were relatively few tourists, allowing the town to look lived in and casual in a way that becomes almost impossible during high season, when tour buses are as plentiful as flowers in the boxes lining the Spreuerbrücke, one of the brace of covered wooden bridges over the Reuss. The other span, the Kapellbrücke (chapel bridge), was older and more distinguished until three months later, when a boat moored to one of its piers caught fire. The bridge, then aged 660 years, welcomed the blaze with alacrity. As 150 firefighters watched in frustration, the landmark was consumed, along with most of the 112 insubstantial—but sentimentally revered—triangular paintings ornamenting its rafters. Julie and I could not have been aware that we would be one of the last to see the original Kapellbrücke alive, nor would I have believed that an identical copy would be in place by the next tourist season, though it was.

A couple of years before, I'd gone through Korea, taking in pagodas that, though monuments of long renown, were actually copies replacing earlier copies torched or wrecked in war or other calamity. Is authenticity to be measured by carbon dating? Surely, as was suggested at the time, boards had been replaced in the Kapellbrücke since it had been built in 1333—perhaps all of them, several times over. Is Lucerne less authentically Swiss now that its main draw is a replica? What can be authentic in a country where any picturesque cluster of houses around a church might have its own tourist office?

A key reason for bringing Julie to Lucerne was to show her the place where I'd fallen in love with Switzerland and where, for a long time, I had dreamed of retiring. I even had this fantasy spot picked—on a hill, along the town wall. We climbed into its cone-topped towers and walked liked sentinels among them, along crenellated battlements. At the tallest tower, the Männliturm, I showed Julie the gentle town that cascaded down to its river. I admired with her the green hills that I've seen climb into low clouds.

I've noted the way, since my student trip, I enjoy Switzerland after a visit to Italy. On the student Grand Tour, in the full of the summer, our un-air-conditioned bus rumbled through the Italian peninsula: the endless procession of churches and monuments in need of a scrub brush; the gale-force traffic that held you within its grasp until you'd pay money to find a toilet; the execrable toilets demanding coins for entry;the national shortage of those coins, causing cashiers to give sticks of candy as change for banknotes. Then Switzerland. I awoke on my the first day in the country to bright sun and a cool breeze. We were in Lucerne. The Reuss flowed rapidly, and a produce market lined its banks. A little blond girl who looked like my image of Heidi selected five exquisite apples for me, helped me find the right bill to hand her, and then gave me correct change, her smile fresh and unselfish. As with so many images received in the white heat of adolescence this one has stayed with me, and it has helped transform me. I explained its power to Julie in the manner of a confession, then I asked her if she did not love the view we now shared.

"I've seen better," said Julie, then she added, "I'm tired." She could see my frustration and kissed me. "Come on, don't feel bad. We'll find a nice place to retire—sometime in the next thirty years."

We went to the local Picasso Museum, then we ate alfresco, Julie muttering how anyone could be foolhardy enough to dine on *rösti*. It was delicious. As we walked to the train station, a slight rain became a downpour, then a deluge. We were soaked and happy when we boarded for the hour ride back to Zurich.

Before we left the country, I called the Reber au Lac again. Success: they had found Julie's pants. I arranged for their safe conduct back to the United States. I had proved my utility. Julie said that the women who find men useful are the ones who marry. That sounds a tad cynical to me— none of the flowers, violins, breathless longing, and enchantments of women's fiction—but I will note that, not long after we returned home, Julie and I were engaged.

On Marriage

Chapter 1

No more fitting tribute to our engagement could have been had than
the fact that the announcement first ran not in a newspaper social
section but in a travel section—that of the *San Diego Union-Tribune*, when
it published my accounts of our Dutch and Italian travels back to back. No
more fitting tribute to me as a writer could have been had than the call I
received from a lady who said she represented the Italian Government
Travel Office, on behalf of which she wished, in the name of the Italian
nation, to register a protest regarding certain articles I had written. "You
said a good thing, then a bad thing, then a good thing," declared the
woman. "How could you do that? I love my country. It isn't right of you,
as a foreigner, to say such things." I told her I was only explaining what
had happened on our trip. There was nothing I could do to convince the
public-relations woman that Julie and I liked going to Italy; Julie and I
were summarily stricken from the Italian Government Travel Office's
party list. No more black-tie dinners with surprise appearances from
Connie Francis for us.

Others continued to invite us, the travel writers' party circuit in New
York being a particularly lively one. It soon became standard that, if I
should walk into a party filled with writers and editors (hosted, inevitably,

by public-relations people), I would be greeted with the phrase, "Where's Julie?" It would be superseded by, "There's Julie!" the moment she made her entrance, and all attention would, quite sensibly, fall upon her. It was making my job as a travel writer uncommonly easy. Where once I had to dig for my material, I now needed only to follow Julie with camera and microphone.

Peter and Susanne, who were also living together, were also now engaged. Peter had gone out on his own as a commercial photographer, specializing in fashion. This was not the life-insurance business. This was entrepreneurship of the most demanding kind. In a notoriously competitive and fickle business, Peter would be wholly dependent on his artistic talent, connections, and business acumen. Susanne was working for Kodak at retail, providing a steady income.

In March, we met them in London. Julie had never been to London before, which I found surprising, given the extent of her travels. We took a large room at the Milestone Hotel, facing Kensington Palace, where Princess Diana was then living, separate from (but still very equal to) the Prince of Wales. We'd flown into Heathrow Airport hours after it was struck by four improvised mortar rounds launched by the Irish Republican Army. Five more rockets landed the day after we arrived, and before we were to leave, another four would hit the airport. All thirteen were duds. I didn't know about any of it at the time, an unintended benefit of my habit of ignoring news while on vacation.

Peter had put on weight but had lost none of his boyish sweetness, and Susanne was the same quiet and prudent woman I had known for years. You can lead a happy life as a woman in Germany if you keep your thoughts to yourself, a happier one still if you hoard them for timed release. Susanne had mastered the German woman's trick of the measured response, the pinprick remonstration, by which German men are kept in line by those who love them.

In front of an improvised backdrop in our hotel room, Susanne took our engagement pictures. We all munched fruit from a bowl at a side table. The combination feast and photo shoot in our room got the London trip off to a good start; I remember the good feeling from that afternoon, though what we talked about is lost to me now—not that it should matter much among friends.

For me, London is a place of distant voices, of trains rumbling in unseen hiding places, of spurts of laughter and talk that come from the next street, only to vanish when you reach the corner. Footsteps echo on the pavement, buskers' guitars echo in the Underground stations as you descend an escalator echoing in its long slide past framed handbills. You can feel alone in a crowd in London—not the way you do in New York, because of activity, or as in Los Angeles, because of apathy, but because so much that is invisible remains an obstruction. To be called outgoing in America is to be given a compliment; to be outgoing in London requires not only bravery but also a prepared explanation for your behavior.

Make a pass at a woman in Paris and she'll accept it as proof of her irresistibility—and might take you up on it. Try it in London and she will look at you as if you have just brought on gastrointestinal pains. If London strikes you the right way, it can come across as a big city with civility and charm; if it hits you at a bad angle, you can leave it thinking you've spent your entire vacation inside a bank: waiting in line; trying to get attention; forking over money to cover petty annoyances; only getting the attention you deserve if you have connections; receiving respectful politeness just the same, but only enough to get the job done. My experience of this trip was the former, and Julie's was the latter.

We had not yet so differed in our opinion of a place. Julie had more free time, as I spent part of our stay at work with a lawyer from a British subsidiary of my company. "So, what do you think?" I asked her as we moved slowly through the European paintings of the National Gallery. I was, foolishly, expecting nothing more complex than, "Nice."

"The art is terrific, but this is a man's town," said Julie. "Rome, Paris—they're for women. They're all about fashionable things to see and to buy and really good and delicate food. The stores here are for men and everything is either very traditional or an exaggeration that is deliberately anti-traditional, which never works. It's like that kid with the blue, shellacked hair in a cone, like a dunce cap."

We had just seen the fellow on Charing Cross Road. "When he talked to us," she continued, "he was so polite. That's what happens when you make a show of fighting against strong tradition. It doesn't change you any; you just end up looking dumb."

At that moment, the actor, comedian, and travel writer Michael Palin walked by with a satchel over his shoulder. I nudged Julie and tried not to gawk. "Yeah, but the theater—" I said.

"It's fine, it's terrific, it's wet out, I have a head cold I can't shake, and—hey, is that *The Arnolfini Marriage?*" She disappeared into a Jan van Eyck reverie, and thus was her critique brought to an end. Years later, Julie would find that she really did like London. Three things had changed by then: she was healthy when visiting, the weather was good, and the city had grown more prosperous and fun. One more thing, perhaps: on this first trip, what bothered her was that I was taking her shopping. As a fashion stylist, her job was to assure that money (the customer's) and good taste (largely Julie's) stood united. Like a race-car driver stuck in rush-hour traffic, she sometimes brooded over the incompetence of amateurs. Peter and I would now test her patience.

Chapter 2

I had not yet learned that, in matters of style, my days of independence were over. The apartment was no longer looking its old, rugged self, though the neoclassical furniture and Elvan rug were indeed improvements. I had still retained, however, an atavistic, naive impression that, after nearly forty years of life, I knew how to dress myself. I have met dozens of men who had labored under similar delusions for the length of their own bachelorhoods, only to be disabused of them almost immediately upon marriage. The process had started for me even before engagement. My tailor-made clothes and got-it-on-sale fill-ins were already being supplemented by off-the-rack "designer" goods. Under Julie's influence, I was already the owner of one Giorgio Armani jacket—navy blue, modishly slouchy, double breasted—with more to follow as my stylistic independence constricted.

All of this is background to a West End matinee. Peter arrived for it dressed like an old Russian sofa. In the Feydeau play on stage, the costumes were farcically belle epoque, all stripes and bustles and raucous prints; in the audience, Peter was the sartorial hit in a scarlet floral waistcoat—what the British call a vest. Julie gave the obligatory respectful compliment to Peter about his vest, all the while staring at it as might a Southern Baptist preacher's wife at her son's copy of *Playboy*. Peter responded with an offer to take me to Favourbrook, the shop where he had bought his sleeveless masterpiece.

The young, articulate owner, Peter Vainer, had opened the shop five years before, after customers kept asking where he got the jaunty vests he wore while selling bespoke shirts. Favourbrook became an instant success, making vests for rock and sports stars, a symphony orchestra, and legions of bridegrooms weary of the British nuptial uniform of tailcoat and striped pants.

Peter, Susanne, Julie, and I entered the small Favourbrook store and congregated around Mr. Vainer. "Something with a slightly eccentric edge really is what we're trying to do here," he explained. "We have here in the shop about three and a half thousand fabrics," he added. "A lot of them are bits of antique Russian tapestry fabric that I get; bits from Poland, a lot of eastern European cloths." Most bolts were large enough to make only one to four vests.

The shop also had "weaved up" about two hundred original fabric designs, all in limited quantities. "Part of our attraction here is that you are getting something that is unique to yourself," Mr. Vainer continued, showing us a vest fronted by rows of feathers.

Peter eagerly thumbed fabrics. Into my ear, Julie whispered, "A style made in reaction to a style is no style at all."

"What are you talking about?" I asked softly.

"The mistake of antitraditionalism. Instead of following a new vision, it keeps looking back in anger. Doesn't work. Trust me."

Even as Cassandra spoke her warning, I was eyeing a vest in rich, olive-green moleskin (a cotton twill) hung on a peg over our heads. "So what do you think?" I asked Julie as Mr. Vainer slipped it on me.

"I don't know dear," she said. "If you want to, sure."

Translation: She hated it.

I turned to Herr Rüßmann. He gave me that knowing, confident smile that is nonverbal German for: "If you like it, as a point of male honor, you must buy it, regardless of price, and wear it constantly."

Susanne, of course, said nothing; she would step in only if Peter made an ass of himself.

"Okay, measure me up," I told Mr. Vainer. His tape enveloped my chest. "I'm a thirty-nine," I said.

"Indeed you are," he replied. The tape dropped to my belly.

"It's thirty-three."

"Oh, sorry, sir. Not anymore, I'm afraid." With that uniquely British ability to pacify with language, Mr. Vainer said he was measuring not my waist, but my "corpulence," a larger dimension.

Peter and Susanne left for the airport, and Julie and I walked across the street to the main storefront of my shirtmaker, Hilditch & Key. It's a woody shop, male to the marrow. If, along Jermyn Street, Favourbrook is like the honors student who pulls small pranks at a wedding, Hilditch is the worldly uncle who humors him. I examined samples of the strong, striped patterns in long-staple, two-ply broadcloth cotton that are an essential component to the British look. I started with a fine number in blue and red.

"The hot colors are white and taupe," Julie cautioned.

"For how long?"

"At least until the charge clears."

A few weeks later, it was with the joyful expectation of receiving a present from overseas that I collected my Favourbrook vest from the post office. It fit perfectly. I modeled it for Julie, who gave it a glance, then a feel, and then said, "Wear that to my office and you're dead."

Peter's words of male defiance were fresh in my mind. As German soldiers and British soccer fans know, you don't necessarily fight to win; sometimes you just fight for the honor of it. One morning, I put on my new Favourbrook vest, pairing it with a blue striped suit by the American designer Joseph Abboud—something Julie had talked me into buying. All Julie would say was, "You're ruining a beautiful suit."

That afternoon, I recalled that I lacked a few things for our next trip and made my way to the men's department of the store where Julie worked. A few paces in from the elevators, I greeted Asad, a salesman who specialized in Abboud clothing. "That's great what you did with the suit," he said, feeling Favourbrook moleskin critically with thumb and forefinger. "Where did you get this?"

I told him, then took him into my confidence: "Don't spread this around, Asad. Julie is very modest, but the vest was all her doing. She knew it was exactly the right thing to go with the suit. Did it all in her head from thousands of miles away."

"That's our Julie," said Asad.

Halfway into the department I ran into the manager. "I love that vest," he said. "The way it complements the suit. Where did you get it?"

Once again: "Keep it quiet, please. You know how modest Julie is. She picked it, put the whole thing together for me."

"She's amazing, isn't she?"

Within two days, of course, the entire store knew about Julie's fine eye for vests. And I like to think, though I have not a shred of proof, that I was partially responsible for the subsequent decision by the store's buyers to carry Favourbrook vests.

Even an amateur occasionally wins the tournament.

Chapter 3

I think now that, when I stared into the bathroom mirror as my train pulled into Luxembourg City predawn darkness seven years before, the tired face staring back at me was pleading for more than luxury. It ached to grow up; it was ready to take a wife.

I'd wanted to get married before I turned forty because there seemed to me something outré about a middle-aged man's second marriage, and to a beauty no less. Julie and I were to be married in late September, which meant I would miss my goal by five weeks. Julie inspected several potential venues before selecting the Stanhope Hotel, across from the Metropolitan Museum in Manhattan. We interviewed three Unitarian ministers, Julie rejecting one of them for the unkempt quality of his beard. None of the proposed wedding services would do, so she had me edit our own: a piece of the Old Testament, a piece of the New, a bit of Shakespeare. I thought the ceremony would last the afternoon but, spoken, it would prove to be of such brevity as to make the Gettysburg Address sound windy.

Peter and Susanne came over from Germany, Peter first sending me a list of lighting equipment I should rent, as he and Susanne were to be both wedding guests and photographers. On the morning of the wedding, therefore, I took a taxi to the hotel, carrying enough lights to illuminate a ballpark. I had to return home to get myself up as a respectable groom. Back to the hotel: Susanne acted as cheerleader, alternately encouraging and relaxing the sitters for the formal portraits, while Peter snapped. Yvonne, my companion on the Paris trip, served as stage manager, seating the guests, getting the string trio set up, cuing us when the curtain was about to rise.

We could not go on. The family and I were in a suite, waiting for Julie, who had disappeared into a bathroom to finish that last bit of makeup that never makes a difference to any man, but which every woman knows stands between triumph and ruin. Her father, in his blue, double-breasted suit, was smiling, looking uncommonly self-satisfied. "What's so funny, Burt?" I asked him.

"Three daughters," he said. "All in their thirties. None of them married. People were starting to avoid us."

Often that week I had heard the compliment about how relaxed I had looked for a man who was about to get married, though his first marriage had been a precocious failure and though he'd managed nearly to double his age before trying again. Even the receptionist at the hotel remarked how calm I looked. I felt great until I was standing in an anteroom with the minister, receiving final instructions, a string trio playing softly in the distance. I grew light headed, unable to follow what the man was saying. I felt as if I were surrounded by a wall of glass. Someone told me to move forward, and I was following the minister into a large room, where many people sat in chairs. I came face to face with my old friend Charles Whitelaw, and I stared at him wondering to myself, What is Charlie doing here?

Then I was standing next to Julie, and nothing in life could make me happier than to know we were there together, solemnizing hard-earned love. We gave each other a look that said, "We did it." As with other such signals that pass between a couple, no one else caught on.

Old Testament, New Testament, William Shakespeare, and out. No violent stomp on a glass (per Jewish custom); the vows were sealed tenderly, with a kiss. Everyone took elevators to the terrace. Open the champagne. Trade the string trio for a jazz combo, then, literally, it was all a piece of cake: getting married wasn't so difficult once you got a feel for it. And I'd done it once before, so I had the confidence of a veteran. We promised Peter and Susanne we would see them the following year in Germany for their wedding. We left the next morning for the Côte d'Azur.

Chapter 4

Our room at the Negresco was not ready because the king of Nepal and his entourage had not vacated the third floor, which they occupied in full. Michel Palmer, the general manager, came to greet us as the bellman brought in our luggage from the rental car. Dark haired and effusive, Mr. Palmer was one of those hotel managers who are everywhere in the building simultaneously and know all that is going on. He took us to the light-fare restaurant, La Rotonde, which looked like an art-nouveau carousel: horses above the booth seats; tin soldiers on the walls, breaking into motion now and then to play instruments in accompaniment of a carousel organ that was slowly driving the waiters to derangement.

With that adolescent showiness of cops everywhere, a police escort in crisp blue shirts and white kepis sped the Asian king away. We were taken to our room, number 312, called, by a plate on its exterior wall, the CHAMBRE DU ROY. It had a great, canopied bed, fleur de lis carpet, and a copy of a painting of Louis XIV that hung in the hotel lobby. Much use was made of gold, down to the sinks, toilet, tub, and bidet. We had a view of both sea and garden.

White walled and orange domed, like a frosted cake topped with meringue, the Negresco occupied only half its original building, the other half (facing away from the water) having been converted into apartments. The hotel and the apartments now shared the building like bad neighbors in a two-family house, a clear line demarcating where fresh hotel paint stopped and the dull, chipping exterior of the apartment house began. The former grand entrance of the hotel, now given over to the apartment complex, had gone both utilitarian and shabby. Life in this back end seemed to go on in a half light, as if the skies there had grayed, even as the Negresco enjoyed the Mediterranean sun.

Still, there was no doubt that the Negresco portion was a substantial upgrade from Mrs. Schwartzberg's Hôtel des Flandres of six years before. I told Julie how, since I was last in Nice, I had dreamed of returning with someone special and staying at this hotel. I told her about the doorman dressed like a circus ringmaster and the men's room in the motif of a Napoleonic officer's quarters. "We've all had those dreams," said Julie later on, as we were walking the cool, stony beach. "But it's so different when you come back to the place you've dreamed about."

Villefranche-sur-Mer, where, six years earlier, Isabelle, the French-woman I'd met on the train, had unburdened herself to me about her lover's death, and where American servicemen had gone on timorous breast patrol, was not the same either. To me, it felt both more businesslike and more assured that it would impress. It was fun, and it was pretty, but it was so in the way of a jocular, face-lifted divorcée at a South Beach bar, and not, as I had remembered it, as an ingenue sunbathing almost nude, pleased to be observed.

As Julie had intuited, the resort wasn't much different; I had changed.

Revisiting a place after a period of time is like rereading a book you first encountered when you were younger; the object has changed in relation to where you have gone in life. I'd now seen more of the world, had endured more of its teases and come-ons. My curiosity, like a wise parent, had guided me, and it had likewise let me draw, then redraw, my own conclusions.

Julie had a second theory: "A shrinking world means shrinking options."

"How so?" I asked. This time, we were in Villefranche-sur-Mer, following the servicemen's route along the walkway ringing the horseshoe beach.

"All the places you want to go to start looking alike. They're intended to look alike."

By the time we had finished walking the perimeter, we had jointly perfected the parlor game we had started to play on the Amalfi coast. It was now called Capri or Key West, and there were rules. What you had to do was guess in which direction of servitude to the travel business a town had gone since the days when it had acquired the charm or character that now drew the travelers. Had it gone fashionable and trendy, with the same boutiques found in the world's major cities and the same people found in the best neighborhoods in those cities? Or was it a permanent crafts fair, the butcher, baker, and candlestick maker having given way to numerous shops; galleries featuring boldly colored, hopelessly banal art; the stores selling, at slightly inflated prices, and for shipment anywhere in the world, selections of stained glass, table linen, cute animal figurines, one million varieties of T-shirt—and scented candlesticks? If it was the former, it was Capri. It could also be Portofino, Ascona, or St.-Moritz—except for whether you preferred to sunbathe or ski. If it was the latter, however, it was Key West. It could also be Positano, Sorrento, Newport, La Jolla, Santorini, or here, Villefranche-sur-Mer. I hadn't remembered the narrow streets in yellow, terra-cotta, and orange, or the listing, crooked archway. I had forgotten the Cocteau Chapel, at the waterfront, its interior painted by the artist in a style reminiscent of Picasso: one head facing upward, as in *Guernica*, except it had fish for eyes. Instead of a navy ship in the bay and rows of topless women, there were two cruise ships in the harbor, and the few women on the beach—with or without their tops—lacked the quality of chic that makes a nearly naked woman of ordinary proportions alluring, as opposed to merely diverting.

We had lunch at a waterfront café, where a diner one table over saw Julie's sweater fall into a puddle. She rescued it, letting it hang in the sun over a chair at her table, and it came out that she was from Zurich and worked for Antonio Rossi. She said there was a conference on in Monaco, but she didn't know where Antonio was staying. Julie and I assumed it must be the Hotel du Paris and we called, but Antonio and Ursula had already checked out. Then a pigeon scored a direct hit on me, which was disgusting.

Chapter 5

I was with my bride, this was my honeymoon, but I was anxious and so was she. So much had happened so quickly: the abbreviated marriage ceremony; the swirl of people at the reception, which had gone on for hours but had seemed to last ten minutes; the night in the Manhattan hotel suite, unwinding with the sitting room's bound issues of *The Strand Magazine* of A. Conan Doyle vintage; then the plane to Nice via Brussels. And here we were, married, on the French Riviera at the end of the season, the long stretch of pebbly beach gone oddly quiet on morning walks, our crunching footsteps the only noise between the sounds of sea and wind. It was hard for both of us to calm down, to lose the New York agitation that the stress of hosting families and friends had only exacerbated—to say nothing of the shock and incredulity surrounding the apparently accurate reports that we had indeed married each other.

One afternoon, we lingered over cappuccinos, considering the situation. There was no reason to leave the café, but we were both too agitated to stay. "Eze?" I suggested. Julie had also been there before, but quickly agreed. We parked the car at its base and walked up the inclined streets of the fortress village. Eze was romantic, this was a honeymoon—wasn't that supposed to be how you did it? No wonder so many good honeymoons take place in dull rooms not so very far from home, I thought, as I waited outside a tchotchke store while my wife (the thought of the word *wife* startled me) made some saleswoman unroll folksy tablecloth after folksy tablecloth I couldn't imagine Julie Behr (the new name was equally strange) ever buying. I was right. Julie bought nothing. We said little as we walked upward, past shops, galleries, and restaurants of irresistible charm, toward the garden at the village's pinnacle.

Julie halted in front of a store with candles or doorstops or paper-weights in the shape of cute pigs. With arms crossed, she said, "Capri or Key West?"

I shook my head in recognition. "Key West."

"'Fraid so."

"Let's get to the top," I said.

"Go ahead. I'll browse."

"You might as well come along."

In the company of middle-aged Americans and some younger Japanese, we paid the twelve-franc-per-head entry to the Jardin Exotic, got pricked by cacti, and had our picture taken for us by a winded young lady from Osaka, who earned an *arigatō* for her troubles.

Maybe Monaco would ignite that honeymoon feeling, we thought. Monaco was congested with apartment buildings, travel agencies, cars, and policemen; the cops let us stop traffic to ask directions, and they responded in good English, pointing the way to the Grande Corniche, this despite the fact that Julie very specifically asked for a Cornish. Julie stopped at a tourist office, where she had a young lady draw a map for her, which, of course, she ignored. The compass again confounded her. She told me to go left, on a hunch, I went right instead, and thus did we find our way to the Grande Corniche. We drove it by night, whipping around mountain curves, the headlights burning white upon stone walls that loomed ominously from all angles, Eze glowing like a candlelit shrine in the black void below.

Chapter 6

The law was laid down on a chalkboard for all to see:

> *pas de chèques,*
> *pas de cartes*
> *de crédit*
> *pas de téléphone*

Mr. Jean Giusti and his wife ran their small, single-aisle restaurant, Merenda, by the law, but they were not above invoking administrative prerogative. Madame brought the menu on a chalkboard, propping it upright on the table. When I dallied over the limited but interesting alternatives, she grabbed hold of my hand, fastened the board to it, and moved on to more profitable occupations.

"Your first time?" asked the man at the table next to ours.

"Yes."

"The menu almost never varies. You really should try the beef."

His English was too good for him to be anything but Dutch. He was a gynecologist and would not give me his name. He wore a white shirt and ascot, was gray haired and affable. He was dining with his wife, who was drunk and rather brusque. She said they had an apartment nearby and he said they did not. He had learned basic English from American soldiers after the liberation and had cleaned it up by instruction from an Oxford scholar.

"If you call and book lunch here for eight," he explained, "Madame Giusti will refuse because the place is too small. But if you ask for two tables for four, that's okay. It's part of the theater of the place, which they invent for themselves. Madame Giusti insists there is no phone, then how is it you are talking to her? It doesn't matter. There are no dinner reservations. You must always show up by seven, or there are no tables." He lit a Cuban cigar. Like many prosperous northern Europeans, the Dutchman had cool, distrusting blue eyes and an easy banter through which he counterfeited frankness. You could talk to such men for hours, held by gossip and obscure facts, learning nothing about them.

Monsieur Giusti was tall and thin and Madame was stocky. Both looked elderly but moved like adolescents; they were helped in the open kitchen to the rear by a much-harried young woman. Despite the comedy, both improvisational and rehearsed, these three clearly worked for their livelihood. There was a bottle of rosé and a bottle of red on every table, and that was the extent of the wine list except for the more expensive Vin des Merendas, which no one ordered. There was some fine art on the white walls, including a gouache on paper image of a woman signed MATISSE '52. "It's lovely," said Julie, whose favorite twentieth-century artist is Matisse.

"They should sell it and retire to the South of France," I suggested.

The beef was served in a red sauce with potato slivers and was quite good. I ate everything on my plate except a solitary slice of mushroom. Monsieur got wind of my recalcitrance. He loomed over me like a reincarnated Charles de Gaulle, inspecting the troops. *"Mangez le champignon!"* he commanded, and left the parade ground. Julie did the job for me.

The Dutchman was right that it was theatrical. We were dining in a theater of the absurd. The Giustis were clever enough to know that they were as much the reason for an evening at Merenda as the food. They were aware that they were being laughed at, and they appreciated the joke. They also knew that they were getting away with some pretty rude behavior—which, as jesters, they had leave to cultivate. Because they still had a restaurant to run, they simply incorporated the business into the act. They had, in short, reached that age when every free man and woman has the right to tell the rest of the world when and how to go to hell. They chose to do it with a laugh.

Chapter 7

The French Riviera, which, after all, specializes in this sort of thing, had not yet turned Julie and me into vacationing lovebirds. We, and it, kept trying.

There was the Coco-Beach, a restaurant with a room shaped like a ship's forward cabin, jutting from a cliff over the east end of the bay. We were joined by a hotelier who owned the Westminster (one of the belle-epoque landmarks of Nice) and who was a tennis buddy of a friend of mine in Paris; by a woman with an interest in a local art gallery; and by the wife of an investment banker who, like the wives of investment bankers worldwide, was pretty, intelligent, and made much of the fact that money and luxury were readily available, though hardly important to her. The convivial restaurateur, Henri Cauvin, served us all his signature "sandwich of the poor," now a local delicacy that is rather like a *salade Niçoise* on a sandwich. Thickly sliced bread was wetted with vinegar and oil from olives grown on Mr. Cauvin's own trees. Within the bread were sliced tomatoes; tuna fish; the characteristic, small olives of Nice; fresh basil and scallions. The hotelier made sure to greet the mayor, seated at a nearby table. It was the first Indian summer's day following some rather cool ones; bathers appeared as if from the ether, filling lounge chairs on the strand, and we joined them after lunch, cocktails in hand.

There was the day given over to art, at the Matisse Museum and then the hilltop Hotel Regina, where the artist had kept his atelier. The Regina was crumbling, chipping, rusting, and had holes in its glass; the great terrace had gone barren, the lobby nearly so. Its rooms had been converted into offices and, apparently, living quarters. Arab faces emerged above to drape laundry along rusting balconies. We'd seen old buildings like this that seemed to speak of better days. At the Regina, you could almost hear the voices of the belle-epoque elite, up here on the hills during their long winter holidays, safe from the imagined perils of Côte d'Azur water, gossiping, anticipating dessert and a good brandy. There was just enough life left in the place to allow the voices to speak, and just enough death in it to make us feel as if we were violating a tomb.

On the third night came the wood-paneled Chantecler—considered the best restaurant in the area (two Michelin stars) and fortuitously located in our hotel. The furnishings were Regency, the floral tapestry to our side was Aubusson. Crêpes both flavorful and fastidiously moist were followed by a wine-scented brown sauce bathing meat with spices, then by desserts of creams, fruit, and sorbet, then by cheeses correctly arrayed in ascending order of strength. How lovely it was to dine well with my bride, to savor each announced selection, the conversations around us whispered rather than shouted (as they would have been in New York), the waiters maintaining a watchful silence from a respectful distance.

The hushed formality was all too much for a couple from Orlando. They studied their menus a long time looking eager and then uncomfortable. Their defense was to fall back on an American familiarity of a kind more acceptable in the Magic Kingdom than southern France. They tried striking up a chat with their dour waiter. He was clearly uncomfortable with this invitation to fraternize. When small talk didn't get the couple very far, they tried the comedian's icebreaker: "So," said the husband, "where are you from?" The waiter replied that he was French.

Then something wonderful happened. That is, nothing happened any more than that the waiters were serving, we were dining on good food and drinking a half bottle of Château de Bellet, but something changed for the better. It was as if all the reserves of nervous energy rationed for the preparation and execution of a wedding had at last been expended, leaving room for richer things.

"We did it," said Julie as the dessert arrived.

Intuitively, I knew what she meant. I took her hand. "Let's really enjoy this," I said.

"Okay. Let's."

The entire character of the honeymoon changed on the spot. We were no longer chasing after an expectation of romance, no longer importuning happiness, merely inviting it. Happiness only comes where it is welcome; almost never does it appear where its presence is demanded. We let go our expectations and let the quirky, irrational joys of travel pull up chairs at our table, laughing with us, laughing at us. The remarkable thing is, we did it independently, almost simultaneously, and somehow, inexplicably, in unison. We were not only married, we were finally beginning to act like it.

In the morning, as Julie packed, I walked inland to the Hôtel des Flandres. I asked if Madame Schwartzberg and their family were still in charge, but the woman at the desk looked at me as if I had asked after Martha Washington. "Five years gone," she said. "Sold hotel and moved away." She had no idea where.

Chapter 8

Another drive along a coast road. I like coast roads. They are pretty, often entertaining, and as long as you can see water, you can be passably confident you haven't lost your way.

Stretches outside Nice were not dissimilar to Highway A1A in south Florida: the drab, new construction, the necessary terraces by which a building of no architectural interest might yet prove enticing to apartment hunters. There were pyramid-shaped buildings, which were amusing, then intermittent tracts of idyllic shoreline and scenery.

We stopped in Antibes, which was unexpectedly large and commercial. It was loaded with pastry shops, an indicator to me, as bookstores might be to others, that a town is home to a noble and cultivated population. Behind the fortified walls of a château is a museum devoted largely to Picasso's painted, sculpted, drawn, and kilned art of about 1946. As in the Picasso Museum in Lucerne, we enjoyed plenty of works that read like sophisticated doodles, but it was entertaining enough for an hour.

Cap d'Antibes smelled of salt and money—great villas on or near the sea were all we saw of the place, but we got the idea. The same held true for Jean Les Pins and then we were in Cannes, which is a French version of Miami Beach, with great hotels separated from the waterfront by the broad Boulevard de la Croisette. That's not intended as an insult. I like Miami Beach. I like movies, too, but I seldom go to Miami or to the movies, because they are both predictable. I found the public-relations director for the art-deco Hôtel Martinez and had her show us the kind of suite a movie star would occupy during the Cannes Film Festival. It was relatively capacious, with bedrooms on either side of the living room and expansive views of the Mediterranean.

On the promenade, a woman sashayed past. She was wearing an all-black pantsuit and high lace-up boots. CHANEL was clearly marked on her belt. "A fake," said Julie. I reflected to myself on the equally bogus interlocking Chanel Cs across the front of Virág's black shirt, back in Budapest. I'd long lost contact with her.

We had only to drive a couple of blocks inland from the water to see Cannes return to middle-class complacency, the shops and apartments gone utilitarian and commonplace. Most resorts are Potemkin villages.

The day was overcast, and as we drove, dusk came on by stealth, the darkened sky darkening further, imperceptibly at first, then perniciously, toward night. It was already steel gray, with an undertone of blue, when we came to the Corniche de l'Esterel. Our rolling two-lane road bent into hairpins, diving and climbing beside jagged rock formations that rose grandly in shades of burgundy, then broke open to reveal the brisk, blue-green sea. An abandoned house stood tall and isolated on a promontory. The roof of orange tile was the sole point of bright color on the changing canvas of our windscreen. The front gate had been torn from its post. Julie said she would like to own the property.

The countryside was uncultivated. There were no harbors or beaches, just occasional sets of stone stairs that led from the road to the red-rock shore. After a long run, we were through St.-Raphael and, by dinnertime, we had reached St.-Tropez, where the scene changed as if by jump cut.

"Capri or Key West?" I asked as we drove into town.

"Capri."

"Capri."

"Here we go again."

"It's what we're good at."

Chapter 9

Capri or Key West. State your preference, book your room, and move on. My nightmare of travel is that, one day soon, the earth will become a theme park—that, at some unmarked Amazon trading post, the last ratty bodega will shut down, to be replaced by a boutique decorated to simulate a ratty bodega. On that day, most of the world will travel to places like Eze; the rest will end up somewhere like St.-Tropez. Once a fishing village (and still the home of fishermen), reported at various times during the twentieth century to have been "discovered" by various known and unknown cognoscenti (including the actress Brigitte Bardot), it remains the quintessential Capri, with more high fashion and low comedy per square centimeter than leading competitors worldwide.

St.-Tropez retains the architecture of a village: narrow streets and faintly rustic houses line the harbor and crawl up outlying hills. At rare intervals, a perfectly sensible-looking, modestly dressed person, not of independent means, will cross the street, greet friends, and buy groceries—a sign that, somewhere behind the walls of this French Capri, remains a pleasant little town waiting for us all to go away.

It was low season when we arrived, and the rains came intermittently, heavy at times. On our first full day, the order was moderate rain, light rain, a few moments without rain, and a deluge that ran in crescent-shaped wavelets down the cobbled, inclined rue de la Citadel and emptied more substantial streets of visitors.

Just as Atlantic City's season had been made to creep into September with the Miss America Pageant, St.-Tropez had an annual regatta, the Nioulargue. We had inadvertently arrived as it was about to begin. Slowly, then massively, the off-season town restocked its depleted coffers of sybarites. Shuttered harborside bars reopened. Our hotel, the Byblos, accepted a stream of men in or near midlife, each in the company of a young beauty. Our suite had a view of the pool, on an island in which lay a lovely young woman, her voluminous breasts nonchalantly on display. On the television in our suite, a woman industriously fellated an exemplary penis.

One by one, the empty berths in the harbor filled with tall, swaggering sailing ships, their masts reflecting searchlights by night until the entire harbor seemed as if crowned by glowing latticework. Tall, swaggering, Anglo-Saxon men in yellow slickers disembarked. Maybe the wealthy ones found women, but I doubted the success of others, whatever their looks, for here was another place where money and beauty held court as king and queen.

It began to appear commonplace that a typical couple should be a Parisian in his forties and an alluring woman, aged south of thirty, dressed in the exaggerated French manner that, if it works, is sexy beyond imagination but that, if it misses in key detail, is vulgar beyond description. Julie, on her morning run, was passed by joggers in full makeup, their earrings and necklaces jangling. We became inured to the sight of spike heels, tights clearly defining the cleft of the buttocks, and nipples sprouting against thin cotton—on women in their fifties. You could tell the young and pretty ones from behind, however, by a sartorial shibboleth: big, black shoes, with heels thicker than table legs, that made the unpracticed wobble as they walked. You knew when you followed a wobbler that she had to be good looking because only a beauty could wear them and remain desirable.

Our hotel was full. Its discotheque reopened. A woman in a slinky dress strode through it, snapping pictures for money while a paparazzo stood watch outside. There were other women striding as well. They looked like whores, but so many other women did to us New York bumpkins, it was hard to say whether or not any of these had turned professional.

The overcast remained even when the rains failed, and few visitors braved the beach. One morning, we walked a strand just outside town, where an African sold leather jackets of dubious authenticity. Two middle-aged couples showed up and, amid much laughter, spread a tablecloth on the sand and set a fine picnic, complete with wine bottles and bud vase, threw off every stitch of clothing, and ate lunch. In the distance, white sails blossomed from the three masts of a ship heading south, the ship and the sails bringing majesty to the dull, gray sea. We were on our way to a Vietnamese restaurant at the request of Julie, but blundered instead onto Le Club 55, parking beyond a Bentley and a gaggle of German hood ornaments.

With its many open-air tables, the beachfront restaurant was the work of Patrice de Colmont: originator—indeed, the patron saint—of the Nioulargue. His hair was dark and shaggy and his smile effusive. He gave Julie one look and said he did indeed have a table for us. Soon every outdoor table was filled with families and couples, a display of alfresco chic unmatched by any other Capri yet seen by Julie and me. Château de Pampelonne and other regional wines rose under glasses rimmed crimson with lipstick. Air kisses smacked over tables scented with the perfumes of the moment and the far more inviting aroma of *coeur de rumsteak grille*. A cat flitted across the roof of the bar.

Weaving through it all, greeting seasonal regulars, was Mr. de Colmont, giving quiet orders to his staff and clearing tables himself when the need arose. His grace under culinary and social pressure reminded all who cared to witness that a restaurateur, like a symphony conductor, leads by inspiration and, whatever the talents of those around him, it is the man in charge of the tables who most influences ambience. On the beach just beyond, everything was shut; seaweed and driftwood lounged on the sand, fouling the gray air. You could count yourself lucky to sit here, paces away, as the guest of Patrice de Colmont.

We saw a young German couple who, similarly arriving without a reservation, were turned away, disappointed. We finished dessert, thanked our host, and left.

Chapter 10

By day, the sailing ships would race below the citadel in trials started by flares that lifted from a round tower and ignited with blasts that caused children to press their hands to their ears. The Parisians and the townies would crowd along the quay or sit on boulders to watch.

In the evenings, cityfolk would try their hand at boules on the town square. At the harborside bar Papagayo, a burly, blond American guitarist named Steve led his band through the same tunes nightly, selling, whenever he could, copies of their recordings. Julie and I would go there for the music, drinking Perrier priced like wine. "I'll bet I know what you're thinking," Julie said to me on our last evening at the bar. "You're thinking that all those babes are out there, and you're caught."

"I wasn't thinking that," I said honestly. Now I had to wonder if she was entertaining similar thoughts concerning certain tall, swaggering young men. "Were you meditating on marriage just now?" I was trying to be oblique.

"I was thinking: one of the nice things about being married for both of us is that, even though there are other candidates, the positions are filled."

She was right. The other candidates were strutting the harbor in clunky shoes, led by gaping cleavage. They cocooned themselves in yellow and set their sails for glory. They photographed or copulated for money, drank fine wines, and jogged in diamonds to keep themselves trim. They were out there, all right. Let them enjoy it.

Finally, on Sunday morning, the harbor was silent and tranquil. The middle-aged Parisians were asleep with their young women; the tall, swaggering yachtsmen slumbered belowdecks. Slowly, singly at first, the people of St.-Tropez crept back into their town, into the bakeries, the grocery stores, and the small fish market under the old arch behind the tourist office. They went to church, where the priest led them in song, laughing at himself when he missed a beat. They mingled below the bell tower after mass, then, like a protest march at the cry of "Police!" they scattered when the visitors poured from their hotels in search of coffee and aspirin.

But the townies would have their way. October had come. By the end of the week, the yachts would clear the harbor, to be replaced by the fishing fleet. The Byblos and its disco would shut, cafés would follow, the final pair of clunky heels would catch the last Porsche out of town, and St.-Tropez would return to its collective senses for the winter. We were on our way to the heart of Provence, where autumn was already in progress.

Chapter 11

Everything was packed except our pineapple. "So what are we doing with this?" asked Julie, holding the fruit like a queen with her orb. The pineapple was all that remained of a honeymoon fruit basket donated by the Byblos on our arrival.

"We'll take it with us," I said, "as a snack."

The queen lowered her orb. "After the dinners we've been having?"

In the manner proven so successful in the past, I drove and Julie navigated. Every second mile, it seemed, a traffic circle appeared. Little cars, aimed like cruise missiles, whirred across lane markers, cutting in front of us. "Don't get us smushed," said Julie.

"Which way is north?" I asked, doing a complete 360 amid vehicular chaos.

Julie stared at the compass as if it were an Incan artifact. "How do you make it point north?"

"Forget the compass. Check the map."

"How's that supposed to help?"

"Unless an arrow signifies otherwise, north is the top."

"Really?" She studied the map with renewed respect and we arrived in Aix-en-Provence by act of providence.

The main street, the broad cours Mirabeau, is shaded by aged trees. The café we chose, Les Deux Garcons, has a finely preserved neoclassical interior. We ordered coffee and it didn't take Julie more than three minutes to conclude that people here looked *normal*, to use her word. Gone were the playboys in Ferraris and their slick women in peril of bursting from Dolce & Gabbana bodices. A crafts market was in bloom along the cours Mirabeau. Women stuffed their purchases into the diaper pockets of baby carriages and quibbled over the price of second-rate table linen.

We arrived in Arles after dark and checked into the Jules Cesar, a hotel converted from a Carmelite convent. We changed and drove off for the best meal of our lives. Coming from a country where fine dining is nearly exclusive to major cities, we had not yet adjusted to the European phenomenon of the country venue, that temple of a restaurant, in the middle of nowhere, that becomes the object of a pilgrimage, a culinary Lourdes. For this evening, we would arrive in pilgrim's robes—I believe Julie's were by Ralph Lauren—at the Oustau de Baumanière.

The Oustau de Baumanière sits beside the ancient fortress town of Les Baux, the cliffs rising above it pockmarked from hackings for bauxite. Sergio Meloni, the courtly headwaiter, walked us past the Romanesque-style vaulted dining room to a back lounge, where we were to wait for the ceremony to start in this temple consecrated to the senses. We were given enormous blue menus, an encyclopedic wine list, and three kinds of hors d'oeuvres. Anticipation built. Suddenly, we were summoned for an audience in the dining room, and the ceremony began.

We started with *ravioli de truffes aux poireaux* (truffle ravioli with leeks), had a pan-cooked fish course *(filets de rougets poêlés)* that, based on robust mullet characteristic of the richly saline Mediterranean, was so remarkable that I forgot I usually bypass seafood. The main event was the house specialty, *gigot d'agneau en croûte.* The waiter brought over what looked like a football. With the dexterity of a surgeon, he pried into it, removing a leg of lamb from what was revealed to have been a cocoon of bread. The dish was dressed at the table, and the bread, which had prevented the juices from escaping, was left behind, as spent and forgotten as Christmas wrapping paper.

On my fortieth birthday, I had doled out the last of my Mouton-Rothschild '83. Had I known a bottle was going for two hundred dollars at a restaurant in France, I'd have saved it for my eightieth. We economized with Château Romanin, bottled at a relatively new, local vineyard in which the chef had an interest.

An American doctor was talking across tables, giving an earful about socialized medicine to a German dentist who listened with respectful patience. The doctor and his wife paid and decamped, and when the companion of the dentist left for a moment, she began talking to me. She took my picture with Julie's camera and said it would be special because it was my honeymoon. Her name was Lisbeth Hentsch, and when her companion returned, he introduced himself as Wolfgang Schneider, a businessman from Hamburg. When he heard it was our honeymoon, he kindly offered us a bottle of wine, which we declined, since we were already swimming in Château Romanin. The Germans said they like to visit France whenever they could, and that this restaurant was a favorite. They were staying at the Auberge de Noves and were glad to hear that we would be going there next. They had a bottle of Dom Perignon on their table, had enjoyed every course, but had declined dessert. "I've seen what sugar does to people's teeth," said Lisbeth. "I never have any."

Julie and I were at that moment enjoying *crêpes baumanière*, which were delightful; Julie said they were filled with meringue, but I was too filled with wine to know or care.

Wolfgang was well traveled. He said he had been to New York enough times to hate it. His real passion was collecting art.

"What kind?" I asked.

"Dutch and Flemish masters."

"Marvelous. Whose work do you collect?"

"I have a Brueghel and a van Goyen. I have a Ruisdael."

"Jacob or Salomon?"

Wolfgang beamed. "You know Dutch art?"

"Only the old kind."

"Then you must come to visit us in Hamburg."

"As a matter of fact, we're invited to a wedding there next year."

Just as the invitation was made and accepted, the waiter brought the second dessert Julie and I had ordered: *soufflé aux pistaches et au lait d'amandes* (pistachio soufflé with almond milk). Lisbeth stared at us, dumbfounded.

If there is an art to Provençal cooking, that evening, the Oustau de Baumanière was its atelier. While the coffee was sobering us up for the drive back to Arles, Mr. Meloni came by to ask how we were doing.

"I'm glowing from your wine, the food, and the sight of my beautiful wife looking so happy," I said.

"Ah," said Mr. Meloni knowingly. "That is gastronomy."

When we were alone again, Julie mentally added calories. "Do you really think we're going to touch that pineapple?"

"Yeah, why not?"

Something else, however, was troubling her more: "'Jacob or Salomon?' How did you know that?"

Chapter 12

The air of Provence was perfumed with lavender and the scent of burning wood, a fresh smell that seemed never to leave us, even indoors. The sun opened each clear day in a golden fire, settled into a midday shimmer through kelly-green leaves, turned the late afternoon into a vista of yellow, then folded into a lingering and gentle blue-velvet dusk. Roads were shaded on both sides by parallel colonnades of trees that met overhead to form an arcade, the columns in brown, the vaulting in green, dappled with flecks of sky. The orange-roofed buildings, listing with age, cut jagged patterns into fields and hillsides. Cézanne, van Gogh—the art associated with the region was, for all its advertised daring, really quite literal.

One of the arboreal colonnades contained an impromptu shrine. A single tree was generously ringed by flowers strewn around its trunk. There were bouquets with ribbons, one of which said, TO MY COUSIN. Shards of metal and glass were strewn among the blossoms—fragments of the car that had struck the tree and carried the cousin to his end. Some of the fragments were scorched, attesting to fire as well as impact. By remaining undamaged and rather beautiful, the tree mocked the man and machine it had bested. Traffic continued to ram through the blind turns at speeds guaranteed to keep local florists in clover. The flowers rustled in the slipstream of each speeding vehicle.

Arles has a first-century Roman amphitheater, still used for bullfights. Julie was disappointed that none was imminent. "It's something worth seeing even if you shut your eyes," she attempted to explain. There was also a fascinating church, the St.-Trophime. "I love the Romanesque style," said Julie as we faced the altar.

"Actually, the chancel is Gothic," I said. "You can tell by the pointed arches. The transept is Romanesque."

"A bit full of ourselves, aren't we, since 'Jacob or Salomon'?" But Julie, as The Book, verified my report with the *Michelin Provence* guidebook. There was no point asking for another opinion, since everyone carried the same book. The long, slender volume jutted from palms of all nations, a tourist's Rosetta stone in French, English, German, and Japanese. As we walked through the aisle of Roman and medieval sarcophagi in the bleak Alyscamps burial grounds, Julie paused in reading aloud to me, only to hear another American voice behind her, orating the same passage.

Then the mistral came. It happened gradually: a chill, a puff of wind, then gusts that could blow out the fires of hell. Here was the reason so many trees were permanently bent toward the south. Their leaves fluttered wildly, like tethered birds desperate to fly.

We arrived one windy evening at the Auberge La Regalido, chilled from the short walk from our parked car. Lucien Clerque, the Arles-based French photographer whose work I collect, was then in Los Angeles but, a true Provençal, he had written to suggest the restaurant, which was on the main road in the village of Fontvieille.

"Is the mistral always like this?" I asked the owner, Jean-Pierre Michel.

"Yes," he said, smiling with the kind of local pride that a Floridian reserves for selected hurricanes. "Much worse sometimes."

The receptionist wondered why we had parked our car on the street. She pointed to a video monitor showing a single auto on otherwise barren asphalt. "You can move it to our lot," she said. "For security."

The mistral was ripping down empty village streets. I pictured myself outdoors, bending into the wind to save our rental car from the youth gangs of Fontvieille. "Thanks," I said. "We'll chance it." The vaulted, stone-walled dining room betrayed a singular acoustical property: we could hear every word spoken by an elderly American woman sitting five tables removed, the sound clear and the syllables distinct, as if amplified. Mrs. MacCarthy's battle with jet lag and the difficulty her daughter faced in getting some kind of a zoning variance notwithstanding, we enjoyed the exotic but restrained *médaillons de veau, sauce crème et curry* (medallions of veal in a curry cream sauce) with the disquieting sense of dining through a ventriloquist's act.

Before setting out in the morning, I pointed on the map to the Pont du Gard, the enormous Roman aqueduct bridge that is a marvel of classical engineering. Julie's navigational skills were thwarted by persistent roundabouts and her habit of tossing the map into the backseat, where it disappeared under jackets and our still-intact pineapple.

"Oh, oh. I think we're in Nîmes," she said, studying the Michelin guide-book and signposts. "We might as well stop for the Roman amphitheater."

"We're going to the Pont du Gard," I said. "I'm not wasting time looking for an amphitheater."

And of course, at that moment, the thing loomed into view on our left—better preserved and more impressive than its cousin in Arles. We stopped, strolled, dined, and only made it to the Pont du Gard by late afternoon. It is a Roman aqueduct of enormous size and height and, whatever its impression as a work of engineering, not without a lingering beauty. We walked through the disused water channel carried high by three tiers of arches, bridging the formidable gorge of the River Gardon. The bravest among those in the water channel would climb atop its roof, moving with the dexterity of tightrope walkers, the mistral threatening to send them hurdling into the gorge. Julie and I merely popped our heads through openings between the roof stones—gopher tourists in search of a view.

Chapter 13

We arrived midmorning at the Auberge de Noves, just outside the village of Noves, before our room was ready. Wolfgang and Lisbeth had just left, unfortunately. The inn sat in refined isolation, distant even from the unassuming village for which it was named, and I hardly need mention that Julie and I got lost trying to find it. The *chef de cuisine* was the young, lanky Robert Lalleman, whose cooking was accomplished and elegant—as you would expect from a man whose every dish was tested first by the proprietor, who happened to be his father, Henri Robert Lalleman. Ambience expressed itself in the details, such as the table for two set for breakfast with the chairs facing the sun-dappled foliage and, in the evening, with chairs repositioned so that we could enjoy a view of the fireplace.

We deposited our bags and drove to the mistral-swept plateau of Les Baux, which contained what The Book reported was a Living Town, still in use, and a Dead Town, once the fortified home to six thousand but long since abandoned. We were well inside the Dead Town—deprived of houses and population, filled with almost nothing but souvenir and knickknack shops, tourist restaurants and bad exhibitions, when I made a terrible deduction: "Hey, wait. I think this is the *Living* Town." I was right. The Dead Town stood higher up the rock spur. It was a medieval ruin, an architectural Alyscamps.

Julie browsed one or two of the shops. "Capri or Key West?" she asked.

"Key West with a windchill."

"Let's go."

Our room was ready at the inn. "I'm taking a warm bath," said my bride, her hands still frozen from what we had now been assured was a low-grade mistral. I snapped some pictures of the grounds, and when I found the room, I came upon a singularly remarkable sight: my wife floating in the largest hot tub east of Los Angeles.

One morning, Robert Lalleman took us into the kitchen. He had lit out at seventeen to learn the craft of haute cuisine, returning to the homestead as a master chef. Eleven people were working in his kitchen with the quiet, intense discipline of Swiss watchmakers—cooking for maybe twenty guests expected hours later. If you want to know why food in France is both brilliant and costly, ask to see the kitchen. Food is to the French what mechanical craftsmanship is to the Germans, what tailoring is to the British and Italians, and what cabinetmaking used to be to Americans: an honorable craft, hard to master, that carries such respect, its practitioner is placed above what might otherwise be a ground-hovering rung on the social ladder. You don't need a college degree, just dedication, training, and a willingness to excel.

Henri Robert Lalleman, heavyset, mustached, and refined, inherited the inn from his parents, who are buried in the garden. His jackets closed with a belt of matching cloth, and it was rumored in gastronomic circles that the belts were periodically lengthened. He would gently call my wife Madame Behr, which pleased her far more than Mrs. Behr had in the short time she had had the chance to try it on. It can only be imagined what she thought of Frau Behr. She was keeping the last name Hackett, she informed me. It was fine by me, since I'd lived long enough with my family name to appreciate its cornball character. A Madame Behr thrown in now and then was giving a helpful boost.

Chapter 14

The city of Avignon was the residence of popes and antipopes from 1309 to the conclusion of the church's Great Schism in 1417. The former palace of the popes—more properly a fortress—was a museum containing what Julie called the gift shop of the popes.

The Jews of Avignon (known as the Jews of the popes) lived in a ghetto across the square and, according to The Book, survived such lapses in the city's famed prerevolutionary tolerance as regulations that forced them to wear ludicrous yellow hats and that had them locked into the ghetto at night. "Tolerance?" said Julie. "It's like Cracow in *Schindler's List*," the book she had brought for her travel reading.

We found the synagogue five minutes away, a handsome, eighteenth-century neoclassical building with a round interior. Standing outside was a man—apparently a guard—in a blue uniform and a security badge. "Do you work here?" I asked.

"I'm the rabbi," he said, introducing himself as Moche Amar. Born in Morocco, he had moved to Avignon and now served as a chaplain in the French air force, hence the uniform.

Julie was mastering Provence. "All right," she said as we entered Notre-Dame-des-Doms, the cathedral of the popes. "The pope's tomb is Gothic, the dome is Romanesque, and the galleries are later additions, Baroque, I'd say." The guidebook confirmed a perfect score.

Back in the car, Julie handled map and compass like a navigator in a cross-country rally. "Take a right onto the D571, head south four kilometers, then left at the D28." We'd come a long way from the days when we would miss our destination by an entire country.

Our dawn flight home was from the Marseilles-Provence airport; for the last night, we moved closer, to the Abbaye de Sainte-Croix, an inn meticulously restored from a twelfth-century hilltop monastery just outside Salon. We had our final dinner in the inn's restaurant. *Aiguillettes de boeuf sautées* (thin slices of sautéed beef), a little wine, then that ceremonial final scrape of the last of the dessert sauce. What better way to end a honeymoon? "We're all packed," said Julie, "except for that pineapple."

We had just finished our sixth gourmet meal in as many nights. Photographs of us would later show that, while we had started our honeymoon looking somewhat gaunt, we had both puffed out remarkably.

Even so, "Shame to let a whole pineapple go to waste," I said.

At 4 A.M. we began what Julie called the escape from the abbey. Down stone spiral stairs we carried our bags, through the darkened back rooms and under groined vaulting, past the empty reception desk and into the night. We punched a security code into a panel that buzzed open an appropriately creaky wooden door with wrought-iron hardware. At the car, Julie couldn't find our dirty laundry.

I buzzed myself back and found the bag in the lobby. We drove from the abbey, tore down the expressway at one hundred miles per hour, missing the airport. It was Julie who, by the road signs and the map, caught the mistake.

I pulled over. Julie charged from the car, and a group of truck drivers saw something you don't usually expect at 5:30 A.M. at a roadside diner in Marseilles: an American woman in head-to-toe Donna Karan, holding a Michelin guide and trailing unfolded maps, bursting in and shouting in English, "Where's the international airport?"

We made it to the terminal by six. "It's over," said my bride. "You have to give up the pineapple." I left her with a loaded baggage cart and pushed the car toward the rental lot, the prickly fruit rolling in the back-seat.

I returned to Julie just as she was checking in. "How'd it go?" she asked.

"Fine," I said. "And you know, the woman at Avis was quite touched by our gift."

Chapter 15

Marriage is about nothing if not responsibilities. To expect to provide well for a family on the remnants of a childhood trust fund and on an insurance salary was not realistic. It was time, at long last, to leave "Mother"—as the company was known to its employees—to free myself from the ample bosom and apron, to kiss her good-bye and to set off into the world of commerce, where I could start making real money. I accepted the position as first in-house lawyer at a computer-game publisher. As I stood in the insurance company mailroom, signing the employment agreement for my new job, I knew it was a rite of passage. A bicycle messenger took the contract away for countersignature. I watched him leave the building, helmet bobbing as he walked, and I stood alone, unable at first to return to my office, knowing an era was over.

I had been wondering what to do with all the skills I had honed in my bachelorhood. After years of practice, would I let atrophy my ability to cajole, flatter, promise the moon and stars, dodge committing myself, demand too much, give too little, win? Not at all. I was ready for the entertainment business.

I was still the only lawyer at the computer-game company, working doubletime, when Germany called me back, in the summer following our honeymoon. Peter and Susanne were at last to be married.

We arrived in Berlin in a heat wave. The room of our reputedly fashionable hotel was not air-conditioned. We walked together onto the Kurfürstendamm, the air thick with humidity and exhaust fumes, the traffic rushing past indifferent modern architecture and the bombed-out Kaiser Wilhelm Gedächtniskirche (memorial church), its imposing, unpleasant bell tower left standing as a reminder of the cruelties of war. Julie knew how important Germany was for me, it being my other country, after all. She tried her best, then burst into tears right there on the Ku'damm. It was no use trying to put a good face on it; she'd wanted a relaxing getaway, ideally to the countryside, and this wasn't even close. Although we had added Berlin to the itinerary so that she could enjoy the museums, the brutal heat (equal to that of Italy three years before), the prosaic architecture of Berlin (with the 1990s construction boom only just beginning to alter the skyline), and a whole lot of what she considered just plain ugly had combined to overwhelm her.

I took her to a café with outdoor seating on the lower level of the Europa Center, one of those stone-cold city-planning projects of the 1960s: office building, casino, urban mall. The complex was full of shoppers, kids, and creeps; it was not clean, but a fountain ran near our café table. Our waiter had an angular face with grooves up either side of his mouth, a thin, small mustache, dark hair, and earrings in both ears. He occupied most of his time by chatting sweetly with a pair of romantically linked young men at the next table. On the other side was a portly, middle-aged foursome; all of them were deaf. By tapping on a picture menu, they managed to show the waiter he'd brought the wrong dish for a white-haired man in their number, but the white-haired man waved in that brusque German way that says, "I'll take it anyway" without needing to speak, and he downed the thing in a few gulps. A dog urinated near Julie's foot; we paid and left.

To save this trip from total breakdown, I now improvised, offering to get the rental car early and take us straightaway to a country inn. But the sight of a rhinoceros in the zoo, nuzzling his horn into mud, brought just that quality of absurdity and charm that could not help but cheer up Julie. I'm always fascinated how it can happen that way in travel, how the most trivial of events—the nabbing of a duck in a public square, a jog through a military cemetery—can define what the trip was about or even how well you will have enjoyed it. We walked through the Tiergarten, past a broad expanse of semiclothed and wholly naked sunbathers, and stopped for refreshment at a café so pastoral it could just as well have been in the country.

Nearly six years had passed since I had been in Berlin, and I had waited nearly the whole of that time to do one thing: walk through the Brandenburg Gate. We passed by a monument that includes two seemingly mummified Russian tanks, the same Second World War model that the Czechs, on a similar memorial, had painted pink. We sidestepped the sculpture of a man shouting over the now-nonexistent Berlin Wall and walked through the Brandenburg Gate. The context of his plight now lost, he looked to me like an entrant in a hog-calling competition. You could not see a trace of the absurd city wall of socialist Berlin; the part that had barricaded the gate had been especially thick, making it all the easier to climb upon that night of November 9, 1989, when the East German government surrendered to popular will and let its people go.

The arch of the Brandenburg Gate passed over our heads like a bridge over a riverboat. It was surprisingly low. I felt terrific. Street vendors at the foot of Unter den Linden, on the opposite side, gave the same capitalist workover to the same Marxist debris—Russian watches and nesting dolls, East German military hats, gas masks—that I'd seen five years earlier in Budapest. At the tourist office opposite, the clerk, still dressed in her Communist-issue too-tight skirt and too-loose cardigan, stared with abject stupefaction as Julie asked her if there was not a charming hotel nearby, perhaps a Relais & Châteaux with a garden-view suite . . .

Chapter 16

Now Julie had heard everything. "A beer garden? Are you serious?"

"Have you done it before?"

"No."

"There you go, neither have I."

"That's why I married you: I respect your taste."

But she went. It was called Biergarten Wirthaus Zum Löwen. The outdoor music that hour before midnight was loud. The L-shaped dancing area was fragrant with sweat. Single men formed a crescent by the entrance, communally gathering courage, like boys at a high-school dance, to approach the very few unattended women. The band had the hard faces and the earnestness of the Slavic countryside. They played Spanish music, they played "Yummy Yummy Yummy I've Got Love in My Tummy," they played "Doo Wah Ditty," they played the Beatles, and they played them all to a polka beat. Dancers held each other as if to waltz, but not the tall and thin blonde in black microshorts; she kicked up her heels with such vigor as to imperil the groin of her partner. Julie and I danced to this music as best we knew how. Julie started to enjoy herself, to take amusement in the sight of the fat woman grinding away in fluorescent green, loose shorts and black brassiere. Her beefy partner, his shirt fully open, imitated every American dance move from Fred Astaire to John Travolta. She was a sight second only to the corpulent woman in a green dress, her dirty, bare feet flying and growing dirtier by the minute. Fred Travolta tried to keep up, slowed, then halted, relinquishing his spot to another as she, wobbling but nearly airborne, missed not a step.

The next morning, at the food halls of the KaDeWe, the largest department store on the Continent, Julie fell into the soup. The first faux pas was mine. I had gone for tea, as the store had a good selection from Dallmayr. At the food halls of Harrods and at Mariage Frères, in Paris, you can sniff within the metal tubs in which the leaves are stored, but not at the KaDeWe. The young attendant gave me that purse-lipped stare, chin lowered, that is the German expression of diplomatic admonishment. She scooped out a first-flush Darjeeling and stuck the ladle under my nose until tea leaves sprouted inside my nostrils. She was fine with that; protocol had been followed.

Julie, anxious that I not be seen to display bad etiquette, was satisfied as well. She sipped a cup of coffee. "Want some?" she asked. "There's a coffee machine out on a table back there." She left for a refill, but no sooner had I paid for my tea when Julie came back quickly, very distressed. "I need you. There's this little old lady yelling at me in German about something. I don't know what's going on."

Julie led me to the table where the coffee machine stood. Guarding it as if from imminent theft was another customer. She was short and old and built like a fire hydrant. She wore a pink blouse and carried a purse the size of an overnight bag. Just another grandmother out for a morning's shopping, but as a German grandmother, it was her right—nay, her duty— to see that rules, anyone's rules, were obeyed. No sooner did she see Julie return than the old sentry gave her the lecture of her life. "This is not self-service!" she declared in German. "You cannot just come in here and help yourself as you please. You must wait here until the attendant returns. She has gone off, you must wait . . ."

"What's going on?" Julie pleaded with me. "I offered her money, but she won't stop."

Smiling, I said to the woman in something like the formal, archaic German in which my maternal grandmother had given me small instruction, "That was most informative, my dear lady. We didn't know the procedure, but now we do. Many thanks for teaching us."

The sixth-floor java monitor tried to repress a grin—determined that I should never know I had charmed her. She fired off another sentence or two, but with weakened vigor. We left the field of battle to her, and she stood by the machine, meditating on our incompetence.

"What did you say to her?" Julie asked as we found the escalator.

I explained.

"That was generous. I told her to get a life."

"I don't think that got across."

"I hate this place. Let's get out of here."

I bought a leather jacket and got her out of there.

Chapter 17

We rented the car and got lost on the Autobahn while looking for Potsdam. Curving, clean roads pointed to a hilly, green countryside that reminded Julie of the German-settled regions of her native Pennsylvania. Squat, brown houses mingled with trees and tailored yards. Eventually, we blundered into the Wannsee district, which was pleasantly suburban. Julie jury-rigged a picnic lunch, we got lost again, and, by asking directions a couple more times, came upon two small patches of beach bordered by woodland. We tossed rye bread to inquiring ducks, drank diet Pepsis, and ate roast chicken, Italian grapes, and peaches. Julie liked the fruit tarts I'd bought and accepted with surprising good humor the lack of salt, napkins, a blanket, cutlery—not to mention bathing suits and towels. There was a large public swimming area opposite, but this being Germany, perhaps bathing suits were optional. On that hunch, we drove over and paid our admission.

We were right. Some time had passed since that first skinny-dip in Capri, and Julie was, by now, too practical a traveler to stand on points of modesty among total strangers. It was hot, here was water. The nude beach was at the far end, but here another self-appointed guardian blocked our path. She was a bit younger than the KaDeWe coffee patrol-woman, but tall, fat, naked, and ugly. She demanded to know what I was doing with the cameras. Nothing, I said, showing that all lenses were capped; we just wanted to swim. She didn't believe that. Surely something foul was going on. So there were rules here as well, apparently unwritten and communal, if our rotund informant was to be believed. All who came here were enforcing the rules, she explained, pointing to people who did not exist, as the beach was not terribly crowded.

I could have argued the point or just ignored this centurion, but the first rule of travel photography is never to alarm the natives. Julie and I returned briefly to the "textile beach"—the main area, which, as a family beach, was merely topless. Somehow, we managed to cram into her travel purse two Leicas with four lenses, two Nikons, watches, banknotes. We walked past the guard again, this time unchallenged, and had our fresh-water swim. It was very nice.

The corollary to the self-appointed policewomen of Germany were the mystified waiters, united in their incredulity over Julie's insistence on light food and no oil or dressing of any kind on salads. At a restaurant up the road from the beach, I showed Julie how to handle it: give orders. If you say, "Could I have that without oil or dressing?" you are requiring the waiter to obtain direction from the kitchen. He will look at you with anxious curiosity, hoping you will change your mind, or—worst of possibilities—conclude that he con-stitutes authority and veto the request on the spot. If he asks permission on your behalf, chances are it will perfunctorily be refused, to his relief. But if you direct that the dish you want must be cooked so, and the salad must be prepared so, *you* have become the voice of authority, announcing the task for which duty calls. Our waiter, challenged by my precise instruction, said of course it would be done so, and so was it done here and at each stop during the trip.

Julie was starting to grow more comfortable with Germany, and it would have been a successful day overall in that regard except for one incident on the walk back from the picnic. We had come to a large, off-white villa that could have passed for the Relais & Châteaux inn Julie had been seeking, the one with the garden-view suite. It brought her up short because her prevailing theory was that beauty bred contentment and that pastoral beauty was the most relaxing of all. The house we were admiring, however, was the site of the Wannsee Conference, where, in 1942, the Nazis drew up their plans to exterminate the Jews of Europe.

"How could they do such a thing here?" Julie asked, unable to assimilate the multifarious evil to which the villa had played host. So many ugly Berlin buildings were harmless, but this handsome one was a monument to terror. The house was in restoration and its gates were shut. A caretaker in shorts sleepily pushed a loaded wheelbarrow.

You can't get lost in Berlin without coming upon some place of historical importance for cruelty, stupidity, courage, or nobility. Berlin is the capital of a nation of extremes, one that, by observing all the little rules that it invents for itself, tries to harness and so master the ambition and discontents that energize it. Germany, with its mutable borders, is the brilliant but troubled middle child of Europe. It feels most keenly the consequences of its failures and takes small solace from its triumphs. Germany is the embodiment of nearly all that is good about, and nearly all that has gone wrong with, Western civilization.

Chapter 18

Mrs. Adolf Hitler was born Eva Braun on February 6, 1912, in Munich. Her family was lower middle class, her schooling was Catholic. She was a salesgirl at the shop of Adolf Hitler's photographer, where Hitler, then a rising politician, first saw her. He was forty and she was seventeen. Fair-haired Eva was outgoing. Photographs reveal a round-faced girl, a touch overweight, passably attractive, the kind of girl who, as the belle of a provincial classroom not offering much competition, comes of age with a view of herself as prettier and more sophisticated than she really is. Indeed, Eva would later insist that she and the Duchess of Windsor had much in common.

Over the years, Hitler and Eva maintained the kind of discreet courtship—carefully staged liaisons, separate rooms—that now seems quaint but that was politically necessary by the public sexual mores of the time. Like many young women, Eva thought her lover did not spend enough time with her, Hitler being quite involved first in getting himself elected and then setting into place his policies. His typically male reason for not marrying was that a family would distract him from his duties. His typically male aside to another man was that, "I have a girl at my disposal in Munich."

Eva expressed her frustration by shooting herself in the neck (1932) and by overdosing on pills (1935), but she survived both attempts. Her father, however, was killed by a bomb intended for her lover.

In his leisure hours during the long denouement when his side was clearly losing, Hitler, a vegetarian who believed in clean living, would counsel his circle against the twin evils of alcohol and tobacco and regale impressionable women with his theories about Jews, Bolshevists, art, and destiny. In the concluding weeks of the Third Reich, as Soviet armies closed on Berlin, Hitler took the government underground, to a bunker below the damaged Chancellery building. His business hours were filled with pinning medals on armed schoolboys, in firing his generals, in moving around his situation maps key military units that existed almost entirely in his imagination.

By April 25, the Soviets had encircled Berlin and were dissecting its vitals with artillery. Berliners, now living in concrete "flak towers" or in basements, were running low on food and water. Sanitary conditions deteriorated. Nearly half a million Soviet troops were committed to the assault, which was fought house to house. Berliners who survived the battle quickly discovered that fears concerning the enemy's taste for plunder, rape, and murder were well founded. "Flying courts-martial" were also held in the streets, summarily hanging German deserters from lampposts. Before it was over, about 125,000 of the city's population died, including suicides. In the final three weeks of the war, about three hundred thousand Soviet troops were killed in and around Berlin.

Amid all this misery, Eva Braun had a bright spot: after nearly sixteen years of excuses and delay, Hitler finally married her, in an intimate civil ceremony. On the guest list were Dr. and Mrs. Joseph Goebbels, Mr. Martin Bormann, General Hans Krebs, and four others, including Hitler's cook. The bride wore a gown of black silk taffeta. It was the first marriage for both. Earlier that day, Eva's brother-in-law, Lieutenant General Hermann Fegelein, had been court-martialed for treason. One version of the story had Eva refusing to intervene. In another, she protested only until she learned that Fegelein had been ready to run off with the good-looking wife of a Hungarian diplomat and with some of Eva's own jewels. Fegelein was taken outdoors and shot.

Hitler didn't sleep at all on his wedding night. A day and a half later, after dining on spaghetti in a light sauce, he killed himself with cyanide and, at last putting his trusty Walther pistol to humanitarian use, with a bullet through the brain. Eva, now on her third attempt, succeeded as well, with cyanide. For her suicide, Mrs. Hitler wore a blue dress with white collar and cuffs. She first removed her shoes.

The newlyweds' bodies were burned in a shell crater, sending smoke into the bunker's air vents and filling the rooms with the stench of burning bacon. One of the wedding guests, Mrs. Joseph Goebbels (Magda), consented, in lieu of suicide, to have herself shot along with her husband. As her penultimate act, Magda made herself the Nazi Medea, poisoning to death her six children by Joseph. They were Helga, Holde, Hilde, Heide, Hedda, and Helmuth. Only Helga, the eldest, showed bruises from a struggle. Those conditioned to the later murders and suicides of American cultists—and a cult, on a grand scale, was what the Nazis were—will be familiar with the mentality. (In another version of the story, a doctor killed the children on instruction from their parents, who then killed themselves.)

Thus did Germany's twelve-year dance with evil conclude, here, in a city Adolf Hitler dreaded even visiting. Berlin was too cosmopolitan, too Jewish, not Aryan enough for his Wagnerian tastes. At the end, Hitler felt that the German people had let him down, that they had proven unworthy, that the Slavic people had shown themselves stronger.

Berlin's answer to Germany's break with Western civilization was to rebuild by ignoring the plans of Hitler and, wherever thought necessary, the plans of generations before him. The grandeur, pathos, cruelty and kitsch that had identified National Socialism from its inception to its demise were expunged from city life and architecture, some to be replaced with Soviet-inspired monstrosities. Berlin would again become a kind of European New York, where the avant garde would flourish; where eccentricities would first be tolerated, even rewarded; where so many things were new and seemingly becoming newer; and where everyone, secretly or not, knew he was superior to anyone in provinces everywhere. As Berlin would reconstruct, other wartime bunkers would be unearthed, including one discovered while positioning a tumbling–wall for a Pink Floyd concert.

Chapter 19

World War II was about the Western democracies instructing three initiates to the playground of power—the newly unified Germany and Italy and the newly awakened Japan—that world stature was no longer to be had by conquest but by economic skill. The Italians got Italy to themselves, which is not at all a bad way to lose; even though they invented and perpetuated Fascism, there was something just comical enough in its prosecution and endearing enough in the Italian character for the world to forgive the Italians, and quickly. The Germans lost territory and had the remainder split into shares; the real end of World War II came in 1990, when West Germany virtually bought East Germany from Russia, which was short on cash, its own empire, both external and internal, rupturing along lines of ethnicity and nationality.

The West Berlin of 1989 (my earlier visit) was vibrant but brittle—a capital without a country. Beyond the guard towers and the graffiti-stained "anti-Fascist protection wall," sterile and solemn East Berlin had seen the captiol of a nation drugged by fear and ineptitude. East Berlin had then been visible to me only from a bus traveling at the speed of moderate traffic. A walk with Julie through its streets now revealed city blocks filled with grimy buildings pockmarked with the shrapnel holes of 1945.

One of the happy benefits of German Communism was that, because it squandered scant resources on spies, weapons, and drugged-enhanced Olympic athletes, it could not rebuild in the slapdash postwar style that so defaced the West. The Soviet construction projects were even more sterile than their Western counterparts, but there had never been money for enough of them. In the same way that Julie and I preferred Naples to Capri, we preferred dingy, shot-up eastern Berlin to the prosperous western part. The Pergamon Museum had been wonderfully scrubbed since reunification, and there was a lively flea market near it. Within a few short years, it would all be plenty more scrubbed and vastly more built up. One of the great city squares of the world, the Potsdamer Platz, would be rebuilt, as would Unter den Linden, the once elegant boulevard about which my grandmother would literally sing. The Reichstag would get a new glass dome and Berlin would be a world capital again.

In the middle of the twentieth century, Jewish Germans transited from citizens to pariahs; they ended the century as the nation's best-known and most often apologized-to minority and, in numbers, among its least significant. The Germans have been fastidious in their documentation and preservation of places where Jewish citizens had lived and of the things they left behind or had stolen from them. Neatly cataloged and tastefully displayed, their menorahs and Hebrew prayer books populate German museums. In Leimersheim, my ancestral village, the site where the synagogue stood, until destroyed by arson on the pogrom known as Kristallnacht, was made into a park fronted by stone Ten Commandments.

The Moorish Neue Synagogue of Berlin stands in the eastern part of the city. The world's largest synagogue when completed in 1866, it had the bulky solemnity of large houses of worship, like the cathedrals of Cologne and Aachen. Einstein played his violin there. On the day Germany entered the First World War, the rabbi led the congregation in a Sabbath prayer for German victory. At least its front facade was still upright when Julie and I visited. There also remained the forward portion of the interior, which contained the expected exhibits of artifacts such as bits of stained glass—remnants of Kristallnacht (figuratively, the "night of broken glass"), in which the building succumbed to arson. Further dirty work was done by Allied bombing in 1943. The remaining building ends abruptly at an open field on which the impressive height of the former nave is simulated by a steel frame. The place within which the sacred scrolls were stored is marked by a semicircular wall. The eternal flame had been found in a concrete slab built over the basement during the war. The lamp, which burns continually in all synagogues, had been used as metal reinforcement for the slab when it was poured. It is the size and shape of a football and very much the worse for abuse; its flattened ends hold the chain from which it once hung.

Also on display when we visited was a volume from the registry that the Nazis had used to help them locate and round up Jews. Pictures of a recent bar mitzvah were meant to convey the idea that Judaism was alive in Germany. A huge photo of the men's gallery in the prewar synagogue showed rows of suits and hats; the faces poking through spaces between were alternately stern or quizzical, like rows of matched doll sets.

I thought the display was well done, but Julie said, "It's not enough. It can never be enough. There should be memorials all over the country—a sign where every Jewish person lived, saying who he was and when he was taken away and killed. Simple, nothing fancy, but everyone would see, every day, the extent of the crime."

All evil ends in archeology. The lessons that may be drawn from evil, however, need translation by less exacting disciplines. I prefer literature and philosophy, but if theology is the method of choice—as it is for Julie—I am in favor of it.

Leaving the synagogue, I thought that Berlin was like a cliff face showing the layered strata of geological time. Visible to us, often in successive blocks or even successive house numbers, were the ascendant Berlin of Bismarck, the cruel Berlin of Hitler, the dismal Berlin of the Communists, and the healing, melding Berlin of reunification. There is another Berlin now, one that Germany deserves: a capital befitting a well-run republic.

Chapter 20

The man at the Lufthansa lost-baggage desk was chatty with us in that instantly familiar American way, asking about New York and Berlin, until he asked where we were staying in Hamburg. We said the Atlantic. He grew hushed, businesslike, servile: "Yes, sir, we will see to that at once." Unintentionally, we had pulled social rank.

While I was booking our trip, I had told an advertising executive from Frankfurt that I was planning to return to the Hotel Vier Jahreszeiten. "No, the Atlantic Hotel is the best in Hamburg," he had counseled, adding with characteristic exactitude, "and you must stay in room 410."

Room 410, white walled and upholstered in muted violet, gave us a view of the Outer Alster, its deep blue water decorated with sailboats and sculls. We were assured that the room was air-conditioned, but no amount of effort on our part could produce anything resembling a blast of cool, dry air. The next day, the great heat we had first experienced in Berlin reappeared like an unshaken head cold. Gnats and mosquitoes in fighting trim rose from the Alster banks, flitting across the exterior windowpane in an uncountable mass.

We called down for someone to do something about that air conditioner. There arrived a small, stocky, dark-haired porter, shorter and even more hapless looking than Emil Jannings in *The Last Laugh,* a German silent film about a hotel doorman in decline. Unable to coax more power from the air conditioner, he hit upon an idea. He moved toward the handle that would open the window.

"*Nein!*" I yelled.

Too late. As in a nightmare where you watch the terror unfold in slow motion and yet are powerless to stop it, I saw the little man's hand release the window latch. Hundreds of insects, yearning to breathe free, flew into the room, dancing on the high, white ceiling. The little man looked at me, and I can recall no face ever appearing so abject. He quietly called downstairs for reinforcements.

The decision was made that we would abandon what became known as the *Möckenzimmer* (gnat room) for a different *Schlafzimmer* (sleeping room) while overnight extermination took place and the porter, contrite, was sent to bed without his supper. Room 410 was pristine again by morning. You don't rate a hotel by its accidents, but by how well it handles them.

Chapter 21

O nce again, I was in town as the von Gronaus were leaving for a vacation, so we would miss them. We had come, however, to see Peter marry Susanne, and the two of them joined us in our room for champagne, each buzzing about final wedding preparations.

It was only when the talk lit upon Peter's stag night in St. Pauli, three days before, that something of a rift opened. "They took me to another planet," explained Peter about the arrangements his male friends had made.

"He came in drunk at sunrise," said Susanne calmly, "and made love to the toilet bowl." Peter replied that he had fared better than an English friend who, on his stag night, had been abandoned in St. Pauli, creeping on all fours.

With that report to help build expectation, we left together for a couples raid on St. Pauli, trying out the bars and talking of old times. I had a request, for I had missed one final, special place in my previous visits to Hamburg: Herbertstraße, which is bordered by red barricades lettered in white warning women and children that they are barred from entry. It is not that women do not go onto Herbertstraße, it is that the women who go there are hardworking entrepreneurs who are zealous in protecting their market. I escorted Peter on a final stroll down bachelor's lane. Whores beckoned from behind plate-glass windows. They wore only undergarments and many were eerily lit in black-light, purpling enormous, hardened silicone breasts. When they sat still, they looked as if chiseled from violet marble. Most of these statues were in midcareer, but one, middle aged and corpulent, was clearly marketing to a limited clientele.

The prostitutes advertised by rapping on window glass or by calling boisterously to the timid and uncertain parcels of men shuffling past. Most of the would-be customers were lean, dark-skinned foreigners—probably sailors from the port that, after all, had made St. Pauli the orifice capital of Germany. In what would appear to have been a buyer's market, the vendors had the upper hand, their brazenness serving both to alleviate boredom and to assert collective control.

Peter and I could not find Julie or Susanne back on the perpendicular Davidstraße, but young street girls, dressed in shorts or jogging tights, were hard at work, patrolling in front of McDonald's and Burger King, literally grabbing men before they could make it to Herbertstraße. These were the lean and hungry types, the ones not yet risen in their careers so as to afford the commercial rents of Herbertstraße, the ones the professionals of Herbertstraße most meant to exclude when they had banned all women from their territory.

Julie was in view when a tussle-haired blonde in a red leather jacket snagged me by the sleeve. She looked like a secretary on her evening out. "Go with me?" she inquired in German.

"No thanks."

She responded with the best sales line of her trade: "Why not?"

"My wife is standing there." Only this excuse would do; she let go my arm.

Chapter 22

The concierge desk of the Atlantic armed Julie and me with a route map so complete and well drawn that, even we, despite all our previous experience in losing our way, were able to follow it without interruption.

Wolfgang and Lisbeth, the couple we had met the year before at the Oustau de Baumanière, had made good on their promise to invite us to their apartment, in a fashionable, tree-lined district on the Outer Alster.

We drank mimosas on the patio, then went inside for a beautifully set breakfast: caviar, Oustau de Baumanière honey, cold cuts, breads, fruit salad; Lisbeth, the dentist, was in firm control: the only sugar was in the preserves and in a small bowl, for our coffee. The art collection was worth a trip to Hamburg. "Is that the younger Brueghel?" I asked Wolfgang.

"Yes, quite," he said. His evident pride of ownership was surpassed only by my pride in having gotten it right and not making a fool of myself. A fine van Goyen hung behind Julie's seat in the dining room, and the Salomon van Ruisdael was no less a delight. Lisbeth was charming and elegant in a low-cut, billowing dress. Wolfgang was living the life I would have picked for myself, with the solitary exception that my ideal included Chumley, the valet, and Fifi, the errant maid who only aimed to please.

What made Wolfgang endearing was a pride greater than that shown for his paintings, a pride that set his face to glowing when he talked about his children and the grandchild whom Lisbeth gently made him own up to. He showed us a picture of his son, then aged thirteen, and he quickly revealed himself as a tender paterfamilias. I should be so lucky at his age.

Chapter 23

Only the state can legally marry you in Germany, and Peter and Susanne had a wedding at the town hall of Altona. They were, however, determined to abide by tradition, both secular and religious. At a midtown restaurant, they held to the custom of the *Polterabend* (noisy evening). While Jews break a glass at a wedding, on Polterabend, northern Germans smash the whole pantry. Julie and I arrived at the restaurant to find guests lined up to pitch their least valued dishes against an upright board. The nominal purpose is to ward off evil spirits, but a pendant explanation is that the cleanup is the first task for the couple to perform together: initially, at least, Susanne held the dustpan while Peter swept up debris and placed it into a trash bin.

After much drinking, someone tipped over the trash. Peter was recalled with his broom. Also by tradition, a group of men kidnapped the bride, and it was Peter's honor to follow her trail from bar to bar, picking up everyone's tab, until he found and rescued her. On his return, someone upended the trash, and there went Peter with his broom.

As we packed to leave for the countryside the next morning, there to enjoy the church ceremony and wedding reception for our friends, Julie had a revelation: "I used to think of you as mostly Jewish."

"Maybe that's because I am Jewish."

"Yeah, but you are *completely* German."

I told her I doubted that, but it showed Julie had made her peace with Germany. She realized she was among a people who, with their precision, eagerness to please, and exacting standards, both pleased and frustrated her just as I do. She had taken to showing affirmation with the *ja, ja* of local inflection. Although a staunch red-wine drinker, she had switched to Riesling for the duration. She had begun to keep appointments on time. If we stayed in the country long enough, she might even have considered letting me have my way on occasion.

Peter and Susanne's religious wedding took place in a small but venerable Lutheran church in the wooded Kirchwerder suburb. The heat had finally moderated and the air was relatively dry. I walked with Julie through the church cemetery. There was a new grave, the mound bulbous, covered with decaying flowers and banners. The gravestones stood so close to each other and were gifted with so many flowers that the cemetery was like a garden. Some of the graves had stepping-stones carefully placed before them to allow the traverse of tight corners without treading upon the dead. A wooden bell tower stood to our left, and the church entrance was around back. The inside was white, with Baroque touches. It was restrained and harmonious, with only a huge painting behind the altar to add a taste of Christian grandeur. Everyone was in his Sunday best, but there was no mistaking the groom: Peter was in a beige suit and a flame-yellow Favourbrook vest. No one betrayed a sign of sleep depravation or a hangover from Polterabend; in Germany, a tough constitution isn't merely expected, it is presumed. The guests filled the pews randomly, without division by family.

The marriage of photographers was recorded by a photographer, but I was conscripted to form a second unit to record the ceremony from a front pew. Bells pealed, the last of the guests came in, and a hush fell as we waited. No bride appeared. Murmurs began, then conversations. Finally, Peter announced that she was coming, and the ceremony began. With a flourish from the organ, Susanne arrived in a simple white dress, a garland in her hair. A rapid procession followed. The minister was a round-faced, round-bellied man with dark hair and glasses and a gentle disposition. He wore a white-ruffled Vandyke collar and black robe. I translated the service for Julie, who recognized the prayers, repeating them from memory in English, as you might sing a remembered song on hearing its first line. All the prayers were new to me.

There were two psalms posted on a board, and Julie wanted to sing. I followed the German text for each, getting the tune for the first stanza, then pointing and singing with her at this, my debut and undoubted finale as Christian sing-along parishioner. The minister used quotations from St. Paul about love. They too were unfamiliar to me, but again, once I began translating them, Julie continued from memory. The message was to ignore bothers in life—such as the bride being a trifle late—and to concentrate on the big questions. Chief of all these big things, said the minister, is the blessing of love.

It was all as it should be: the young couple exchanging nervous, happy glances, the old women in neat hats dampening tears of gladness with white handkerchiefs, the pretty flowers decorating the bride's auburn hair, the pretty flowers decomposing atop the well-kept graves outside, and all of us listening to a gentle minister speak comforting words about the enduring power of love.

God is man's belief in himself, a projection to the heavens of his faith in his own decency, because God's love is man's love of his own good nature. I don't believe in God, but I believe in the redeeming power of love. Julie believes deeply in both. We held hands as we sat together in that church, as I sang the unfamiliar psalms so familiar to Julie, watching the marriage of these two young people who had only just met when I came to Germany a long eight years before. I can't say I was particularly sentimental in that church. It was something different that I felt: a belief in the goodness of others and a faith in my own marriage.

And what is a marriage but a solemnized turn in life? I suppose that if you marry often and well, a wedding here and there shouldn't mean very much, but there was a seriousness about Julie that matched my own, and I was feeling confident that our marriage would fall into the category of "real," meaning that it was neither capricious, expedient, nor transitory.

For the recessional at Peter and Susanne's wedding, the assembly exited the church under an arch formed by golf clubs raised like cadets' swords. Many more things of grand and petty consequence, in many more places, would follow in all our lives.

Epilogue
September 18–19, 1997

I try reading a travel book, *Labels* by Evelyn Waugh, but concentration fails me. Because nearly all the chairs are full, I'm sitting on a wooden side table, outwardly as calm as a minister with a prayer book, but I mechanically take M&M candies two at a time from a bag in my jacket pocket. Members of Julie's family are here. My mother arrives soon after the surgery has begun. I rise and begin to pace, up and down the waiting room. The waiting room at the hospital is a commodious corner of an upstairs lobby, and there is the steady clatter of a hospital going about its business. Three Hasidic men walk past. One, so scrawny he is barely half the size of either of his friends, wears a frock coat of embroidered silk. When his bulbous wife arrives, he all but disappears behind her skirts. I can't hear what the couple is talking about, but you don't say much in situations like this. A conversation may start up; it rolls along, the power fails, talk coasts into phrases separated by silences, then halts.

Two weeks before, Julie and I had been at a gathering of friends in northern California. The uncle of our host was sending an empty chartered turboprop back to San Francisco and graciously offered it to Julie and me. We sat in the cabin, playing cards, watching the yellow sun settle through clouds like a Degas maiden readying for her evening bath, then gently lower itself into the Pacific. The city appeared as a garden of lights along the bay, and as we flew toward it, we felt invulnerable in the way that travel will sometimes make you feel, as if all the world lies open to you for an eternity, and no harm can ever touch you. We took the redeye back to New York. The diagnosis of serious illness came four days later.

Tall and modest, Dr. Winton Bennett at last appears in the waiting room. He is still in his green surgical scrubs and looks tired. We had interviewed eight surgeons before selecting the team working on Julie this afternoon. Dr. Bennett proved himself a man willing to listen; he and I were discussing what he was to do, and the available alternatives, discussing them even as his crew wheeled Julie into the operating room. Now he is smiling, and he shakes hands with all, saying it went well.

I collect the family and we leave for dinner. When we are back, after dark, the waiting room is nearly deserted. The desk woman is replaced by a hapless security man. A deranged woman in a wheelchair harangues the guard and the man pushing her chair and demands of my mother-in-law if she ever in her life heard of such a thing: she, a cripple, coming here all these years, and yet this is what they do, she says. We never learn what is bothering her.

It is the following afternoon. We are unable to get Julie a single room; she shares hers with a cranky, elderly British woman.

I have a full legal and business affairs department working for me now, and I can't let things go entirely, not even for this. I must go into the lounge, to take part in a conference call that hooks me with my office in New York and with lawyers in London and San Francisco. Someone is watching television, and a nearby toilet keeps flushing. I apologize for the noise and sketch the circumstances.

"It's your wife in hospital, is it?" asks the voice from London.

"Yes."

"Gee, I hope it's nothing serious," says the voice from California.

I don't intend to go into any of it; all I want to do is get done with this call. Mercifully, it is soon over, and I am back with Julie. She looks okay. She has eaten a little, though almost nothing of what the hospital tried to feed her. A nurse comes in and rigs her with a mobile stand for the intra-venous fluid; the nurse calls it Julie's dancing partner.

"It's good to move around," says Julie, rising.

"Once around the hall?" I ask.

"Okay."

There is always some kind of motion in hospitals, but it always seems to be happening in a distance. By the time we reach a place where a doctor or nurses are talking, they have vanished, like the two large hares that, stepping into our path in the Grunewald woods of Berlin, leapt away in fright at the cock of my camera shutter. "Where are we going next?" asks Julie.

"Home tomorrow, if the doctors give the all clear."

"No, I mean, where are we *going*?"

Now I understand. "How about the fjords?"

"It'll be too cold. And I hate when it gets dark early and you want to see things. It's like when you were a kid and were sent to bed after supper."

"France."

"We were just there."

"We always like France."

"Yeah, but—what about the Caribbean?"

"Hurricane season. A small window, then it's the holiday rush."

"How about Switzerland?"

Now she's talking. "Zurich?"

"I mean to ski, this winter."

"Ski? You'll be in treatment. Don't you think—"

"I want to ski."

Julie's hazel eyes are firm, but they melt into an imploring, earnest stare, as if to say, "I need this." I believe that she does.

We'll all be dead for an eternity, our remains covered, burned, dissected, or put on display until the last fleck of our dust is consumed. You can grind yourself against the wheel of time, seeking money, fame, and position. You can just go to work each day, come home, have a drink, turn on the television, and watch what you have coming to you until you sleep, get up, and do it all over again. You can pray to whatever god you believe in that a heaven somewhere is a better place to be while what is left of you on earth yet finds its way to dust. You can expect your children to remember you and probably your grandchildren, but beyond that, don't count on it, and if someone or something should efface your tombstone, there won't even be a name left behind—not that anyone, by the time the name is gone, will care a jot. You have all of eternity to be nothing more, to have never been anything to anyone yet living, and as I look into Julie's eyes, for the first time since I've known her, I see she understands that. It's why she needs to go.

Travel is about nothing if it is not about enjoying all the good that life can give you, because as long as you can get up, crawl up, or get picked up and carried over the next ridge, there is a chance you will get more out of your life than if you stay where you are. Travel, in the end, is about life, and all of life is a fleeting sneer at death.

"Switzerland?" I ask Julie again.

"Ski trip."

I nod. "I'll look into it."

"We're doing it," she says.

———————

And damn it, we did.